A WEREWOLF, A VAMPIRE, AND A FAE GO TO BUDAPEST

THE LAST WITCH, BOOK 2

KARPOV KINRADE
EVAN GAUSTAD

http://KarpovKinrade.com

~~~~~

Published by Daring Books

~~~~~

First Edition
ISBN: 978-1-939559-69-2

~~~~~

Book License Notes

Disclaimer

CHAPTER ONE

The candles are lit and we are all sitting around the ouija board.

Me and the three Sexies, of course. Plus AJ and Michael.

My ex-unicorn was a last-minute decision--one motivated by his particular brand of magic. He was just glad we didn't need his blood again.

My palms are sweating and I wipe them on my jeans as I wait for Rune to tell us how to start.

I glance over at Rain, who's in the corner in her travel crib, worry gripping me whenever I'm not holding her, but she's still sleeping peacefully.

While her mother sits in a pentagram trying not to look nervous.

It's not working. I look very nervous.

This is the first time I've ever tried talking to the dead--on purpose at least--and there's a lot at stake.

Rune insisted on carving the ouija board himself after AJ suggested we 'ring up Nanny or Gramps on the ol' ouija' to find out what the letter means, what we should do about my glow-in-the-dark powers, and what they know about my dad.

Kind of a lot to ask from someone trying to enjoy the afterlife.

Much discussion has been had about the mysterious letter I found from my grandfather, predicting his own death as a murder and directing me to Budapest to find my father who I thought was dead. None of us, not even my all-knowing Sexies, has a clue what to make of it. How much, if any, can be believed?

So when AJ suggested we use her old ouija board from high school, everyone agreed it could work, but not with that 'crude mimicry of true magic.' Rune's words, not mine.

And now here we are. In the basement of the pub, surrounded by cobwebs and boxes of storage, with dust coating everything, we are having a seance.

AJ squirms, then leans in to look at the board.

Again. "It's just wicked crazy," she says for the zillionth time. "I see something different in the wood depending on how I look at it."

Rune smiles, pleased by the compliment to his craftsmanship.

AJ glances up, squinting. "It's like those trippy paintings. The ones that have a shape when you squint."

"What is the matter with your eyes?" Rune asks. "Are you experiencing discomfort?"

AJ bursts out laughing and punches the fae in the shoulder. "You elves have no sense of humor."

Rune just blinks.

I clear my throat. "Okay, let's get going. How do we start?"

Darius pulls out a dagger. "We each need to give a drop of our blood to the board."

Michael groans. "You said you didn't need my blood this time."

"I said we weren't inviting you for your blood," Darius replies. "And that is still true. But as you accepted the invitation, we now need your blood--as well as everyone else's--to proceed. If you object, you may wait upstairs."

With that dismissal, Darius cuts into his palm

and holds it over the board, letting a drop hit the surface.

The blood sizzles and then is absorbed by the wood. I can almost hear a contented sigh coming from the board once the vampire blood is no longer visible.

Darius and Zev are flanking me, so the vampire hands me the knife next. My first thought is how unsanitary this is. "Shouldn't we, I don't know, sterilize this between each use?"

Darius rolls his eyes. "It is a blade forged with magic and dipped in the running waters of Valiace. Your methods are rudimentary in comparison."

"Right." I sigh and accept the dagger. With an intake of breath, I slice, flinching at the sharp shock of pain. I watch in fascination as my blood hits the board, sizzles like frying bacon, then is absorbed. Again I hear--or rather sense--that same sigh. This time it's louder.

I pass the blade to Zev, who conducts his part of the ritual, then hands it to Rune. AJ's next, and when it gets to Michael, we all wait to see if he will do it or leave.

I think Michael himself is the only one surprised by his choice to slice open his flesh, releasing the silvery magic that is his blood. This time, there's an audible sigh followed by a burp, then a giggle, as Michael's blood is taken in by the board.

I glance at Rune, who shrugs. "This board has been given life so that it may become a portal between worlds. It is the only way to get truly accurate results."

"Are you telling me we just used our blood to make a new life form? One that can open doors to the dead?" I ask, thinking about every Buffy the Vampire Slayer episode I've ever watched. Which is all of them. More than once.

Rune cocks his head, his expression confused. "Did you not want to open the veil so that you could communicate with your ancestors?"

"I mean, just my grandparents, but sure, I guess. I just didn't want to, you know, make a whole new life for it." I glance down at the board suspiciously. "It's creepy."

"Well, it's done," says AJ. "So let's call them!"

AJ is way too excited about all of this.

I just feel slightly nauseous.

But that could just be the bitter green wild salad Rune made me eat earlier.

Darius nods to me and I clear my throat. "Everyone, take hands."

I close my eyes and focus my energy, trying to

carefully recall the words Darius told me I must use. "By the powers of earth, air, fire, water, and spirit, I do call thee, oh ancestors of my blood. By the sacred and most holy. By the sun and the moon. By the light and the darkness, I call thee. Come to me now in my time of need. Nanny and Gramps, come to me."

I release a breath and open my eyes, and we all lean in to place a hand on the planchette--the name for which I learned from Rune and refers to the little heart-shaped thingamabob that the spirits allegedly move to spell shit. I can't stop thinking about how close the earth-made ouija boards are to this deftly made object created by an actual magical being.

"Are there any spirits with us tonight?" I ask, and though I'm not trying to modulate my voice into a spooky seer, it happens anyways, much to my embarrassment when AJ snickers.

Nothing happens immediately following my question, and just as I'm about to ask it again, the planchette jerks across the board and stops over the word YES.

I look around the circle, eyes wide, slightly out of breath. "Did one of you do that?"

They all shake their heads.

And I believe them. I mean, why would they try

to prank me on ghosts? I already know everything is real. I'm a glowing witch, sitting in a room with a werewolf, a vampire, a fae, a sea nymph and a unicorn.

A ghost is nothing.

Still, I haven't done this since I was a silly kid with AJ and we were trying to freak each other out. It was never this dramatic back then.

"Is this Ed--Gramps?"

It jerks to the NO.

I swallow, beads of sweat forming on my forehead.

"Tilly?" I ask, a painful swelling of hope causing my voice to shake.

The planchette circles around the NO, then lands back on it.

Shit.

"Can you reach Tilly or Ed? I need to speak to them."

Again, NO.

I lock eyes with Darius, and his voice floats into my mind like a caress. *Ask if it intends harm.*

I nod. "Do you intend anyone in this room harm?"

This time it lands in the middle of NO and YES.

"What does *that* mean?" I ask, frustrated.

It was rhetorical, mostly, but the spirit begins to answer, moving the planchette over the board with such force and speed that we all have to let go or get dragged around.

And now it's moving on its own from letter to letter.

N-E-U-T-R-A-L

"So you have no intention one way or another?" I ask.

It moves to YES.

Darius frowns. *See if it can tell you about your father.*

"My grandfather left me a letter before he died telling me to go to my father. Do you know anything about that?"

YES.

My heart flutters in my chest as I struggle to think of questions that can be answered with YES or NO or a simple word.

"Is my father still alive?"

It moves to the spot between YES and NO again.

"Maybe?"

Again it circles itself and settles back on the middle spot.

"How clarifying," I mumble.

"Should I go to Budapest to find my father?"

YES.

Ask if you will be safe, Darius insists.

"Will we be safe?"

Nothing moves for a long moment, then it begins to spell a word.

D-E-A-T-H F-O-L-L-O-W-S Y-O-U

"Death follows you," I say. "Like, follows me to Budapest?"

Though there are no windows down here, a gust of wind blows through the room, extinguishing the magically lit candles. The floor begins to shake, and everything in the room rattles. The planchette moves around the board wildly, settling on nothing particular, then Michael stiffens, his eyes widening and going white.

"I told him," he says, but it's not his voice coming through his mouth.

"Nanny?" I ask, reaching across the board.

Michael/Nanny takes my hand, and I swear I feel her paper-thin skin against mine. "It is, my dear. I only have a moment. They are... pulling me back."

"Tell me quickly," I say. "What's going on? Who's my father? Who killed Gramps? What's in Budapest."

"I told him," she says again. "I told him they'd come for him. But he didn't listen. He was a part of them once. Then they came for him. But they were all too late, weren't they?"

"Nanny, what are you talking about? I don't understand."

"Find your father," she says, eyes refocusing on me. "Find him and then you will know the truth."

Michael slumps forward, his eyes returning to normal. The wind around us calms, and even the candles re-light.

"Are you okay?" I ask Michael.

He nods. "That was... wild."

"Unicorns are particularly receptive to visitors from the other side," Rune says in his lecture voice that's starting to grow on me.

"Do you think the other spirit is still here?" I ask. When no one answers, I look to the board. "Are there any spirits present?"

When nothing happens, I ask one more time.

Still nothing.

"I guess that's all we get," I say, disappointment coloring my voice. I had hoped to answer this latest riddle with something other than just more riddles.

AJ yawns. "At least we can all go to bed now. I'm exhausted."

"This doesn't help us," I say as I stand, my joints creaking with the movement. Lord, when did I turn into a 95-year-old woman? "What she said doesn't clarify anything. Maybe she told my grandfather something that made him believe someone was trying to kill him. Maybe she mentioned my dad. But what does any of that mean? Why didn't someone save Ed?"

"And who was the rando party crasher?" AJ asks as she dusts off her jeans. Before anyone can answer the question, her mind shifts gears at a pace I can barely keep up with. "You know, this space is huge. You should really fix it up. You could do a lot with it."

"Ha. Right. With what money?" I ask as I pick up Rain.

Zev grabs her crib, collapsing it in one fluid movement like a damn pro. It feels weird that he's the sexiest when he's doing mundane tasks, but I can't help it. Any one of them could melt my panties off by doing the dishes, burping Rain, or sweeping. It's ridiculous.

AJ huffs and heads towards the stairs leading to the bar. "That's very limiting thinking that will not help you manifest a higher path."

"Oh Lord, AJ, are you reading self-help books again?"

She shrugs. "I figure if I want to tap into all my

sexy-ass power, I should do some research. Find my center. Become one with the universe. All that jazz."

I nod. "If you learn anything that could help me stop glowing, pass it on. I'm so over being a perpetual night light."

She chuckles. "It's pretty. But yeah, I will."

We all head upstairs, Rain staying asleep in my arms the whole time, which I count as a small blessing in a very strange night.

Once at the bar, Zev sets up the crib again and I lay Rain into it as Rune makes us all drinks.

We sit around a table and clink our glasses together as I say my favorite Irish toast. "May the best of our past be the worst of our future."

It always makes me think of my ancestors, and the stories Nanny used to tell that were passed down to her from her great great grandmother. Those stories seemed like fables at the time, legends of the old world, of fairies and magic and fanciful imaginings. But given what I know now, I wonder how many of those stories were closer to the truth than I realized.

"So I guess we're all going to Budapest," I say, my mind returning to our current reality. "Well, you don't have to go, Michael. Obviously."

He shrugs, his golden blond hair glinting under the dim pub lighting, his blue eyes twinkling with mischief. "My husband and daughter might not like me leaving, but if you get into a bind, you know you can call me, Bernie."

"Thanks, Michael. I appreciate it." Nothing like having a unicorn on call in case of emergencies.

"I won't be going either," AJ says, setting her glass down firmly and locking eyes with me.

"What do you mean? Of course you will."

"B, someone has to keep the bar open while you're gone. I won't let you lose this place. I know how to run it, so I'll stay and handle shit while you go figure out your destiny."

I've given thought to what would happen to the bar, but I figured we could close temporarily in hopes that Budapest wouldn't take too long.

As if reading my thoughts, she shakes her head. "You know you can't afford it. Let me do this." She leans over the table to grasp my hands, her expression earnest. "I won't let you down. Let me prove myself."

Tears sting my eyes. "Oh hon, you have nothing to prove. Of course I trust you with the bar. I'm just gonna really miss you."

She smiles through her own teary eyes. "We'll see each other soon enough."

Michael stands. "I think this is my cue to head home. But just so you know, I'm happy to help out in

KARPOV KINRADE & EVAN GAUSTAD

any way I can while you're gone. I just finished writing a book so I'm taking a break to research my next novel."

"What kind of research does a unicorn need to do to write fantasy?" AJ asks with a snicker.

I kick her under the table. "Be nice. He's offering to help."

She nods. "Sorry. Yeah. Thanks. I can see some serious uses for those abs of yours."

Michael turns a darker shade of pink as AJ laughs, then stands to join him. "I've got to get going too."

She links arms with Michael. "Care to give me a ride home?"

He nods and as they walk to the door, I stand. "Thank you. Both of you."

Once they are gone, Darius flashes over there to lock up, then flashes back before I can blink.

I think I'm actually getting used to it. Which freaks me out a little. It's astonishing how quickly we can adjust to the insane. But I guess it's how we've survived over the centuries.

I sink back into my chair and take another drink, studying the three Sexies sharing the table with me.

Darius keeps his face impassive, but his emotions are bubbly. At least that's the best word I have for it.

Why do you feel weird? I ask through our mental connection.

He raises an eyebrow, his dark eyes boring into me. *Weird? Whatever do you mean?* He shrugs and fusses with his pitch black hair, though it is as perfectly coiffed as always.

"You two care to share what you're discussing?" Zev asks, and his unique accent combined with the huskiness of his voice makes even such benign words sound seductive, sending a shiver up my spine. "Darius is bubbly," I say.

Zev nearly spits out his drink when he laughs. "Bubbly?"

Darius narrows his eyes. "I am not *bubbly.* Nor have I ever been *bubbly.*" His clipped British accent is even more striking when his feathers are ruffled, I notice.

"Fine, edgy," I say, choosing another adjective.

"I am concerned by the seance this evening. It did not go as planned."

Rune finishes the last of his drink and stands to collect everyone's glasses. "Spirits are always temperamental," he says. "The fae are very careful about contacting them. Once a soul passes into the next life, they are meant to move on. When we seek their spirits, we are tethering them to this reality."

I sigh. "Damnit Rune, why didn't you tell me that part before we did this? Now I have a sentient ouija board and an upset ghost to deal with and I still didn't get any answers."

Rune shrugs as he walks to the bar to begin cleaning up. "I assumed you knew."

Zev chuckles. "Rune always thinks everyone knows everything he does. It's his most annoying trait."

"At least I assume the best of others," the fae says from behind the bar as he washes the glasses. "You, on the other hand, think everyone is an idiot until proven otherwise."

Rune looks smug, his long silver-blond hair pulled back in a leather strap, his sky blue eyes twinkling with humor.

"And you both have the tedious tendency to pontificate on your own geniuses," Darius says with an exaggerated yawn. "It's exhausting."

"You're like squabbling siblings," I say with a chuckle.

Darius glances at the werewolf, whose forest green eyes look shadowed by thoughts of the past. Zev's jaw clenches, and he brushes a lock of brown hair from his eyes as he nods at the vampire. "We were once just as siblings, were we not?" he says softly.

Darius breaks eye contact, and stares into the distance. "We were. But that was many years ago."

"Not so long for those with no expiration date," I say, pulling my grandfather's letter out of my pocket and studying the words I've already memorized. My eyes get watery as I think of the time I lost with him while I was in New York. Time I'll never get back now. "You have more opportunities than most to make things right with those you love," I remind them.

Darius flinches and Zev looks away. Rune is the only one who holds eye contact with me, but freezes as a glass slips from his hands, shattering onto the floor. The fae straightens, staring at his empty hand. "Something is here," he whispers.

Just as he utters the words, a cold wind blows through the bar and the lights flicker on and off, then all the glasses begin flying off the shelves.

"Curses," Darius says as Zev growls and shifts into wolf form.

"What is it?" I ask, the hairs on my arms rising, magic crashing through me and lighting up my skin.

Just as I look down at my glowing fingers, I see the letter in my hand burst into flames. I scream and drop it to the table, then scream again when I realize my fingers are on fire. Pain flares in me, burning not my skin but my insides as my powers take control of me.

Before I can ask for help, more glass shards explode around us as chairs flip on end. "Looks like one of our ghost friends has decided to stay," Darius says grimly.

CHAPTER TWO

"Make it stop!"

I'm not sure if I'm talking about the flying dishes or the fire raging from my fingers, but as I say the words, my hands sizzle out, returning to their normal color and temperature. There's a small pile of ashes on the singed table--what's left of the letter to my grandfather, but no flames.

I shake from the surge of power I couldn't control. Time seems to stop as I look at the remains of the letter; the only evidence of my father, of what happened to Gramps, destroyed..

But when another glass shatters to the left of me, I'm brought back to the present. A ghost is haunting me. And ruining my bottom line. I'm honestly more concerned with replacing pint glasses than I am the haunting part. As scary as a specter flinging dishes would have been a week ago, my perception has changed drastically and now I find myself more annoyed by paranormal problems than frightened.

Glasses keep flying and crashing, followed by a few bottles of whiskey. Rune stands behind the bar, closest to the pesky spirit and tries to trace its movements. He stays deathly still, biding his time, while I watch my restocking fees soar.

I want to intervene, to do something, but fear paralyzes me. Fear that my fingers will light fire again and I won't be able to control it. So I wait, watching as Rune handles the ghost.

With his usual deftness, the fae unleashes a handful of dark orange powder into the air above the bar. It settles around a form, creating a vibrant outline of a man. It looks like a 3D graphic from a video game or something, but it's there, in real life, hovering above the countertop.

As soon as the dust touches the figure, it freezes. I can't tell if that's an effect of whatever Rune threw or if this ghost is just embarrassed he got caught throwing all my shit around.

"Be still, specter," Rune says, slowly advancing toward the ghost.

"Ask him who he is!" I yell, eager to finally get

some answers. "Where did you come from? Why the hell are you breaking my things?"

"Easy, Bernie," Zev says in his bassy, calming voice. "Unless I'm wrong, and I'm sure professor Rune will correct me if I am, a deceased spirit cannot communicate without the proper medium."

Rune nods. "That's true. We can only hope to send him--"

"I can hear you."

The voice emanates from the spirit, which causes Darius to instinctively grab my arm while Zev growls and Rune prepares to throw another ghost-thwarting powder.

"And you can hear me," the ghost continues.

"How?" Rune asks, barely above a whisper.

"You brought me into your realm," the spirit answers calmly. "You created a door, and now I walk between here and the afterlife."

Perfect. We've got an angry ghost that now lives at Morgan's Pub, breaking my shit and free to come and go as he pleases.

"What do you want?" I ask, exasperation clear in my voice. I don't have time for this.

"I want you to leave," the ghost responds, being a complete dick about everything.

"Yeah, well this is my freaking bar and I--"

"Because if you don't leave," he cuts me short, the volume and echo in his voice intensifying. "You, your baby, and all of your friends will die."

The spirit's words could be interpreted as threatening, but that's not the vibe I'm getting from him. More like he's trying to help.

Due to either the eerie tone of the ghost's voice or all the shattered glass, Rain wakens, crying softly for me. I rush to her, picking her up and tucking her against my chest, doing my best to protect her from… my life.

"Who's coming?" Darius asks, sharing my belief that the ghost isn't planning to do any killing.

We all wait with bated breath, standing in silence and hoping for an answer. Instead, the sparkling flakes thrown by Rune start to fall, dissolving the form of the ghost. The figure isn't moving to another spot in the room, just disappearing before our eyes.

As the last bits of colorful dust fall to the bar, we hear a final whisper from the invisible visitor.

"They all are."

And then he's gone, leaving a layer of powder on the copper bar.

I exhale a breath I've been holding in too long and my shoulders slump as I realize we're alone. For now.

Rain begins to cry again, and I think at first it's because I'm holding her too hard in my efforts to protect her. But when I look down, I see her blanket is singed, her tiny little arms have glowing red fingerprints on them... and my fingers are burning.

Darius is at my side in an instant, taking Rain from me before I drop her on the floor of the bar. And without a word I race outside, swallowing the sob that's rising in me.

I hurt my child. I burned her soft, perfect skin.

A light rain starts, and as the water hits my flesh, it sizzles.

I slump down against the wall and bury my head in my hands, sobbing.

It isn't long before I feel a wet nose pushing into my hands.

I flinch back, worried I'll burn him, but Zev shifts from wolf form to take my hands in his.

"You can't hurt me," he says softly. "I burn like you, hot and fierce." He puts a hand on my heart and takes mine to place on his naked chest.

His skin is hot to the touch, just like mine. And his heart is pounding in beat to my own, too fast, too loud.

"I hurt my baby," I say, the tears turning to steam on my cheeks.

"Rain is fine. Rune cooled her skin and says there's no injury to speak of."

"It could have been so much worse," I say with a sinking heart. "I can't hold her." The words ache as I say them, but I know this is how it must be for now. To protect her. "Not until I get my powers under control. I can't risk her."

Zev's eyes are sad but he nods. "We will make sure she has her every need met. And you will master this. I know it." His gaze bores into my soul as he speaks. "I know you."

I nod. "You're right. I will. I have no choice."

He kisses my lips lightly, then stands, lifting me up as he does. "Let's go deal with the ghost, shall we?"

THE SEXIES TRIED to talk me out of calling AJ, but they lost that fight before it even started. Either my friend is coming with us to Budapest, or she's moving to another state, but she's sure as shit not bartending at my haunted establishment. Morgan's can close, for all I care. There must be a "brought back a creep from the dead who won't leave and can't be killed" clause in my insurance policy, right?

Turns out there isn't. Also turns out AJ is exactly as stubborn as I could have guessed she would be.

"Not on your life, B," she says, staring up at me while sitting on my bed. "The ghost we brought out of retirement gave you a warning and now I can't help you? Bullshit, the bar stays open."

"AJ, he was throwing glasses--"

"Do you know how many of your pint glasses *I've* thrown?" she asks, knowing damn well I'm still mad about the number of times I got in trouble as a teen after a hammered AJ broke a bunch of glasses.

It's a standoff. My worry for AJ against her worry for me and Rain. Even if I tell her not to, she'll come back and open up the bar. Aside from caring about my future, she loves flirting and knowing she's in control. She's the happiest she's been... probably ever. Who am I to take that away from her?

"Fine," I say. "Stubborn bitch."

"Takes one to know one."

I'm proud of us for maturing so well as we've aged.

"Alright, since you're here and you've already shot down one request, can I ask you to help me pack?"

Her face falls and I move toward my closet, needing to get my bags filled while Rain's with the Sexies in the other room. If she didn't like being told not to tend bar, she really won't like hearing that we've decided to leave in the morning.

"Look, I think you're right," I say as I look for the duffle that hasn't been used since I moved back from New York. "The ghost came to warn us, not to haunt us. All signs point toward us leaving ASAP."

"But…" AJ trails off, knowing there's nothing she can say or do. Her eyes drift over to Rain's empty crib, and I realize that I might still be AJ's fave, but my baby is a close second.

"We're coming back, A."

This isn't the type of goodbye you can prepare for. I have every intention of returning home after I find out who or what my dad is, and figure out a way to control these ridiculous powers, and fend off a council of magical beings trying to steal my kid. But AJ and I both know I'm not making any promises.

I start throwing shit into my duffle, tossing every type of clothing for every type of season because I know nothing about Budapest. AJ just stands a few feet away watching me, not helping or speaking. If someone was just observing our body language through the window, they'd think this was an awkward breakup.

"I know you're coming back, but…"

AJ can't quite finish her thought before turning away to hide her tears. My girl's not much of a crier-- didn't shed a single tear in front of me when I moved to New York, even though she later confessed to sobbing her way through two full pints of mint chocolate chip later that night. I'm not surprised she's trying to keep up that tough exterior, but we're both scared shitless right now and this conversation is pretty emotionally overpowering.

"Look," I say, picking up where she left off. "I'm traveling with the most powerful dudes in the universe. And dudes who have pledged to protect *me*, not just my baby."

AJ nods, then gives me a questioning stare. "For the record, I'm not keeping this bar open so you have a job when you get home. I'm planning to take Morgan's over when you move away to be famous at piano or whatever. Because that's still what's going to happen."

I laugh, despite knowing she's totally serious.

"Fair enough," I say. "But that's all the more reason for me to go now. No concert hall's going to book a piano player who glows and needs a vampire to drain her neck every few hours. Speaking of..." I look down at my hands which are starting to crackle with electricity. Panic grips me for a moment, but I take a few breaths and try to center myself the way Rune taught me. I don't think I'm in danger of losing control, as long as this power is drained from me soon.

Oh, Darius?

I've taken to calling my vampire footman with my thoughts whenever I need a reduction in magical powers. Whether it's practice or a strengthened bond from Darius constantly sucking my blood, I've become far more adept at conversing with my mind.

Within seconds, he's standing in the doorway, mixed emotions on his face. He doesn't like being told what to do, but I know he loves my blood and he certainly doesn't seem to mind pressing his body against mine as he feeds from me.

You sparkle, he says, the teasing lilt of his voice clear even through mind speak.

Yes, ha ha. It's very funny. I raise an eyebrow. *Now come do something about it, please. It freaks me out.*

Though the vampire succeeded in lightening my mood, he can still sense the fear in me. He dashes across the room and is behind me in a flash. He runs his thumb over the pulsing vein in my neck as he presses his chest against my back.

I shiver in anticipation of what he's about to do.

"I'd tell you two to get a room," AJ says with a disgusted sigh as she heads to the door, "but I know this *is* your room, so I'll be on my way."

The moment she reaches the hallway, Darius flicks his wrist, closing the door firmly behind her, and with a small twist of his fingers, the door clicks locked.

He still has a hand on my neck, the coolness of his skin sending waves of heat through me in a striking juxtaposition of sensations. Our bodies are so close I can feel the hard flexing of his abs as he shifts, dropping his hand from my neck to my arm, letting his finger trail my sensitive flesh. I suck in a breath as my legs become less stable than I would like and the butterflies in my stomach begin to swarm.

He slides his other arm around my waist, pulling me closer to him. I feel his breath on my neck as his mouth hovers above my flesh.

My skin pulses--from pleasure or power it's hard to say--but I feel alive with a kind of energy I can't describe. And the electricity of his every touch feels heightened to an extreme that is becoming harder and harder to endure while keeping my clothes on.

You smell delicious, he says to my mind, his mental voice husky and layered with need.

I'm sure I'll taste even better, I say, trying to keep my voice cool and unaffected and failing miserably.

I feel the proof of his arousal against my back, and I lean into him, teasing his hardness with the friction.

It's his turn to suck in a breath, but before I can gloat about my small victory, his arm tightens around my waist and he plunges his teeth into my neck.

The pain is a dark thrill running down my spine and pooling at my feet, and I moan and drop my arm over his, intertwining my fingers with his as he drinks deeply from me.

My head spins, my knees buckle, but he doesn't let me fall. His grip is firm without being bruising, just enough support so that I can lose myself in him without fear.

He asked me once if I worried he would take too much. I told him no, and it's true. Each time he feeds from me the silver threads that dance between us grow stronger, forming a deeper bond than I knew was possible. It's impossible to feel fear of him hurting me, when we've already saved each other's lives.

I can feel the moment he approaches that invisible line by taking too much, like my soul is dancing on the edge of life and death, and once again he pulls back just before going too far.

When his lips pull away, when air hits the tiny bite marks on my neck, the distance between us feels immeasurable. I fight back tears once again at the absence of him and wonder if this is a normal vampire effect. It's a good predatory move, making the prey crave the hunter as much as the hunter craves the prey.

His tongue flicks at the small wounds, instantly healing them.

I look down at my hands and note they are no longer glowing or sparking like fireworks. Turning in the vampire's arms so I can face him, I'm about to offer my thanks for once again saving me--and distracting me--when he cuts off my words with his mouth on mine, crushing us together in an almost painful embrace.

His tongue brushes against mine as he deepens our kiss, exploring my mouth with his as his hands rub down my back and over my ass.

I arch into him, my breasts aching as they press into his hard chest, my fingers digging into his back, clutching at his clothes.

I want you. His mental voice is full of need and urgency.

His hands move to cup my ass as he lifts me up. I wrap my legs around his waist and he carries me to the bed. At this angle, I feel the hardness of his arousal pressing against my own desperately aching body, the clothing between us a hardship I can no longer bear.

He lowers me to the bed and with supernatural

ease he pulls off my pants and underwear.

I feel suddenly self-conscious about my postpartum body, and I try to move in a way that will maximize my sexiness and hide the mommy bits, but Darius places himself between my knees, spreading them as he runs his hands up my thighs.

"I don't need to read your thoughts to know what you're thinking," he whispers, his fingers lightly brushing up against the sensitive flesh between my legs.

My body quivers with pleasure and a growing need and impatience. "You're too dressed," I tell him, even as my mind is a bit in shock that this is really happening.

Am I actually about to have sexy time with a vampire prince? My life is wild.

"Very well," he says, and moves apart from me just enough to pull off his shirt and remove his pants. He does this much more slowly than I know he can… which means he wants me to enjoy the show.

So I do.

He moves with such fluid grace it's mesmerizing, pulling me into a trancelike state that I have no desire to fight. Once he is naked, he stands before me, every line of his hardened body a testament to nature's artistry, and I nearly choke on my own tongue as I finally get a really good look at all that awaits me.

Holy heaven help me.

He grins, clearly reading me like a splayed open and ready-to-be-devoured book. "Now it is you who wears too much," he says, crawling onto the bed and over me. He makes quick work of the rest of my clothing, reverting back to his vampire speed and impatience, which suits me just fine.

With nothing between us but flesh, he presses into me, our bodies conforming to each other's as he slides a hand under my head and gazes deeply into my eyes. The dark depths of his undo me, like a black star he uses gravity against me as I fall into him.

"I don't know if my kind have a soul," he says, as one hand caresses my head while the other dips between us to tease my body into greater need. "But if I do, you are its mate."

His words, the movement of his fingers, the feel of his mouth on mine again, claiming my lips... all of it brings my body to the very edge of a cliff. But before I can tip over that cliff and enjoy the explosive freedom of that bodily flight, he tenses and then disappears, the weight of him replaced by an awful emptiness and a chill in the air. I blink and he's fully dressed, hand on doorknob.

His face is a cold mask. "Get dressed and run!"

And then he is gone.

It takes me a moment to realize he's not coming back, and the throbbing of my body for his will be left unmet, even as I struggle to understand what the hell could have torn him from my bed and that moment with such haste.

I'm afraid of learning the answer to that question.

I follow his instructions, getting dressed quickly as I strain to sense anything amiss.

I nearly trip over my Budapest bag on the way out, and I kick it to the side. It has everything I need for international travel, but I keep unpacking and packing it, nervous in a way I can't explain.

I step out of the bedroom, my nerves on edge as I look around for Darius.

When I walk into the living room, I'm surprised to see no one. Darius only walked out of the room seconds before, so he should be here, and I can't imagine where the others would have gone. And AJ? Where's she?

I stand alone in silence, and that's when I notice it's not actually that silent. There are sounds coming from the bar.

And a smell.

Smoke.

I run out the back door and down the stairs, the crackling of fire getting louder with every step. I can also hear people struggling, and a baby crying.

I glance down at my hands, an irrational fear that I started this fire overtaking me, but no, that's not possible. This wasn't me. But if not me, then who?

Before I reach the back entrance, the door flings open and Rune sprints out, his beautiful silver hair singed by the flame. Right behind him is Zev, in wolf form, carrying--with his enormous, intimidating jaws--the knotted end of a blanket bundle that squirms and lets out little cooing sounds.

"Rain?"

"Run, Bernie," Rune says, taking me by the arm and turning me away. "You must run!"

The urgency of his voice makes me want to obey, but I can't blindly follow. "Darius?" I ask, resisting Rune's pull.

"We'll meet Darius in the woods," Rune says, giving me another tug. "If he survives."

CHAPTER THREE

I don't have time to react or respond before Zev the wolf ducks his head between my legs and hoists me onto his back. I clutch his fur, holding on for dear life as we bound into the woods.

"What about AJ?" I cry out, remembering that she was here before Darius and I had our alone time.

"She left before they arrived," Rune answers, annoyingly light on the details as we charge further and further from the bar. I can see smoke billowing out of the windows, but no visible flame.

"Who are *they*?" It's frustrating to have to ask this question, but I get that neither Rune nor Zev feels like talking right now.

"They're fae," Rune answers through pursed lips, clearly not happy with the acts of his kin.

As we near the woods' edge, I roll off of Zev, my fall broken by a patch of leaves and snow. The werewolf and the fae have to stop and turn back to me.

"Bernie, we must hurry," Rune pleads with me. "We're outnumbered and can't allow them near you or the child."

"And I can't survive more than half a day without Darius sucking my blood," I fire back. "So we're not going to just watch one of our own die before this stupid quest even starts."

It's weird saying one of our own, especially referring to this group that doesn't have two members of the same species. But here we are, bound by incomprehensible trials and near-death experiences, and about to go through a few more. If Darius isn't one of our own, who is?

Rune doesn't move right away, weighing my words. Zev, however, morphs from wolf to human, transitioning Rain from his jaws to his arms as he rises. It shouldn't be sexy, but so help me Jesus it is.

"She's right," Zev says, a few burn marks on his naked body. "We're out and we've regrouped. On top of that, we've got a secret weapon."

He looks me dead in the eye, and I understand what he's asking. The trouble is, I have no idea how to do it.

"What should I do? I don't have any control, I don't know--"

He raises a hand to my lips, stopping my panic from escalating any further.

"I've seen what magic can do when your heart's behind it," Zev says. "Darius needs you. Let's go."

He puts an arm around me and we turn back toward Morgan's, a knot forming in my stomach as I consider the task before me. I'm not ready for this. I can't face off against a magical being, let alone match any power that's too great for my three princes. This is too much. I'm about to turn back to Zev and Rune and tell them I need help, that I need Darius...

But that's just it.

I need Darius.

And if I'm being honest with myself, I don't just need him. I want him. I crave him. He may not know if he has a soul, but I know he does, and ours are inextricably bound. I will not leave him.

Darius.

The knot in my stomach doubles in size, but now it feels like a raging fire and not a fit of nerves.

An intense tingling spreads through my body, igniting every inch of my flesh and blood as it works toward my fingers. I have the same sensations I did the night I killed my mother--nothing makes sense, I know not what I do, but I'm acting on impulses that can't be denied.

I feel Zev fall away from me as trails of white-hot light shoot out of my fingertips. An ear-piercing cry erupts from my lungs and through my mouth, a sound so loud and shrill I can't believe it came from a human.

The light blasts into the bar, shaking the foundation and making me worry for a moment I've done more harm than good. I hold the scream and the magic outpouring as long as I can, until my head grows faint and my knees buckle beneath me. I hit the ground in a heap, spent from my unbridled outburst.

Zev and Rune are immediately beside me, each with a hand under my arms and helping me stand.

"Are you alright?" Rune asks.

I nod slowly, trying to control my breathing and settle my heart rate.

While the fae and the werewolf have their focus on me, my eyes catch some movement at the back door of the bar.

Through the smoke and ash, I see a sexy, disheveled, smoldering vampire walking my way.

Darius... I speak in my mind.

Thank you, he whispers back.

Zev catches my gaze and looks up. You'd have to be paying close attention to notice, but the slightest hint of a smile crosses his face.

"Look who's still immortal," the werewolf says.

Rune speaks a little less playfully. "The others?"

"Dead," Darius responds. "They can swap bar stories with the ghost now."

Rune breathes a sigh of relief. Whatever his feelings about Darius and his fellow fae, it's clear he has no trouble choosing a side in this fight.

I look past the vampire and see that, somehow, my bar is still standing. Smoke drifts out of the windows, but it's not billowing like before. Darius reads my face and addresses my obvious concern.

"Morgan's is fine," he says. "Your spell put out the fire... or rather, sent it after the fae. Once we clean out the bodies and replace a few floorboards, it will look just as it did."

It feels silly to care so much about a building when death seems to be nipping at our heels, but Morgan's is like a family member. It *is* a family member.

"Is it safe to stay here tonight?" I ask.

Darius shakes his head. "We need to leave immediately. There will be more attacks, and we've nowhere to hide in Rowley." He looks at me lovingly with his dark eyes. "It's not fair to ask you to save my life a third time."

Compliments from such a powerful man carry a little extra weight, and I want to bask in this one for as long as I can.

Unfortunately, he's right. We need to leave yesterday.

"Are we safe to go back inside?" I ask the group, thinking about all the baby gear I don't currently have with me.

"Every second is precious," Zev says, sniffing the passing breeze for signs of assassins. "But we can gather things before we set off."

Without so much as a glance at any of us, Rune starts walking toward the bar. "I'll clear the fallen," he says, his voice ice cold. We all watch him go; Darius might have been closest to death, but these events have been just as traumatic for Rune.

"Okay," I say, turning back to Zev, who's holding Rain. I inch closer, peering at her small face, making sure she's unharmed. Making sure not to touch her. "I need to grab my phone to text AJ and throw some stuff for Rain in her diaper bag, then we'll head to the airport."

. . .

WE HEAD out about 10 PM and the roads between Rowley and Boston are mostly empty. We're in the airport parking lot in less than half an hour, giving us just enough time in the car for everyone to agree that the fae went after Darius first, and he'd be dead if not for my newfound powers.

After texting AJ a long, final plea to stay the hell away from Morgan's, I get a chance to reflect on what happened. These magical bursts are still new to me; I've only focused on how to keep my powers from consuming me, not about what they can actually do. Tonight, for the first time, someone told me to use my magic... and I did.

It's thrilling. And a little scary. Given I nearly ignited my daughter with those same powers.

As I get out of the car and grab the diaper bag, I look up and catch Darius' eye. There's a hard look to his gaze that softens when it lands on me, and I shiver with delight at the effect I have on the vampire, and the effect he has on me. It's intoxicating.

"Bernie," Rune says, breaking me out of my trance as he carries Rain in her car seat. "You'll have to take the lead on this. I have no experience with your aero ports."

Rune's pronunciation of airports reminds me that while these guys might pass for normal humans, they actually hail from entirely different worlds. I'll need to remember that as we embrace the exciting adventure of international travel together.

"Right. It's easy, you just follow me and... " I stop explaining when it dawns on me I haven't thought any of this through. "Who here has money?"

Rune pulls a small bag of coins from his cloak. Zev just shrugs. Darius takes a long gold chain from his pocket, something I keep expecting to have a watch on the other end, but it doesn't.

"Okay, put your non-money away," I say, confident we won't be able to pay for tickets in pure gold. "I'm going to use credit cards, probably five or six of them, so just don't try to help."

We cross the bridge from the parking structure to the terminals and walk through the sliding glass doors.

Heading toward the ticketing counter, I realize how little Earth stuff I've done with these three. I smile to myself, thinking there's no place like an airport--or should I say *aero port*-- to show some paranormals a good time.

"Hi there, where are we going today?" a friendly young clerk asks as we approach.

"Um, Budapest. One way." I almost laugh when I say the words, the absurdity of everything hitting me hard now that I'm out of my magical bar and in the real world. Just buying four one-way tickets to Budapest on a whim. No biggie.

"Alright," the attendant says as he starts typing away. I steal a glance behind me, enjoying the sight of the Sexies trying to act normal and failing miserably. No one can look this good and hope to blend in.

"We've actually got seats on a flight leaving in just under an hour," the clerk says. "Will that work or do you need more ti--"

"We'll leave now," Darius cuts in, unable to control his take-charge instincts.

No talking from you, I scold him in my thoughts.

"The soonest flight would be wonderful," I say to the clerk with a smile.

Why is this taking so long? Darius asks my mind.

It's been ten seconds, I think back.

Exactly.

God give me the patience to endure a twelve-hour flight with these men.

With our boarding passes in hand, we head from the ticketing area to the security checkpoint, and I'm overrun with fear about the photo ID situation. Do fae have driver's licenses? I'm pretty sure werewolves don't. Is Darius going to show a centuries-old birth certificate? Why the hell did I think we'd be able to board a flight?

Naturally, my worries subside as soon as we get to the front of the line and I hear Darius speak to the TSA agent.

"We are allowed to pass without showing you documentation. It's of no concern to you and you'll go about your business."

With a blank look on her face, the middle-aged woman at her tiny kiosk just waves us through. TSA Pre-Check has nothing on vampire mind control.

Passing through security takes a little more finesse. I have to tell the Sexies to take their shoes off four times before they acquiesce, and Rune gets some very suspicious looks when he loudly asks how he could possibly hide a bomb in the sole of his boot. I'm seriously regretting not discussing airport etiquette on the drive over.

"What's a belt?" I hear Zev ask the young female agent ushering travelers past the bag scanner.

"The hell you mean, 'what's a belt'?" she rightly fires back. "Put it through the loops, hold your damn pants up."

Zev looks confused, maybe even a little angry. Like the woman is toying with him. "Then how does it come off?"

"He's not from… here," I interrupt from the next row, hoping I can end this conversation before the woman gets growled at. "Zev, you don't have a belt, just walk through the thing!"

He might know a lot about earthly designs and have no trouble ripping through clothes, but now it's clear that werewolves can't handle belts.

"Just put it in the bin, sir."

Another TSA agent sounding more perturbed than usual alerts me to Darius refusing to put down his coat. It looks like she got as far as making him take it off, but parting with it makes Darius a little too uncomfortable.

Darius, I say in my mind. *How many knives are in your coat?*

Why?

The response has me thinking the number is somewhere between four and ten.

Tell Rune to create an illusion, you can't take those on the plane. My spoken thoughts are hasty, and I wonder if he can still hear them clearly.

Why can't I take them on the--

"Just do it!" I say out loud, then immediately hold my phone up to my ear so it looks like I was yelling at someone on the phone. Sort of.

I look over in time to see Rune nod at Darius and

then casually wave towards the conveyor belt. Once Darius' jacket passes through without any alarms sounding, I go back to my shoes.

With the biggest hurdles cleared, I do take a modest amount of pleasure in watching each prince walk through the metal detector and then stand still while a tired old man with no patience for bullshit runs his wand over their pockets. Rune has to go through the X-ray thingy three times before finally getting his pockets completely empty. One of the agents is about to confiscate some of his small containers when Darius steps in and forcefully changes the man's mind.

Shoes on and bags scanned, we head toward the boarding area.

"People live here?" Rune asks as we pass a couple of young travelers sleeping with their heads on their bags.

"No, probably just a long layover, waiting to board their next flight," I say.

"Why did they fly to the wrong destination?" Zev asks, but we thankfully arrive at our gate before I'm forced to answer.

I have my three handsome companions go ahead of me, and I feel like a mother escorting her children onto a plane for the first time. I snicker at the thought of putting them all on little child leashes. What a sight that would be. All the adrenaline from blasting magic out of my fingertips an hour ago has been replaced by a dull sense of responsibility.

When we finally get to the jetway and head for the airplane doors, I breathe a sigh of relief. I'll be able to sit back and rest for at least a few hours.

Naturally, no sooner has that thought passed through my head than Rain starts to cry. Poor little girl. She should be asleep in her crib and instead I'm hauling her across the globe on a mission I don't even understand.

The flight's about three-quarters full, which is nice for us late arrivals. We can get our bags into overhead compartments and find our seats without stepping over too many people. We get a mix of looks from the other passengers; some are annoyed to see a baby joining them for a red eye, others can't take their eyes off the strapping men moving down the aisle.

When we get to our seats, I sit between Rune and Darius, and Zev takes the row behind us, keeping Rain with him as he preps her bottle.

Let me know when you need a release, Darius whispers into my head. Instantly I'm imagining my last *near release* in all its glorious detail, despite knowing the vampire is talking about taking some of my magic blood.

But he looks at me and smirks. *Of either kind,* he adds, clearly picking up on my thoughts.

Heat pools in my belly at the thought of what that might be like and, despite the circumstances, I feel a burning need filling me. One glance at Darius' lap proves he feels it too. I smile. *I will, thank you. Ever thought about joining the mile-high club?*

The what?

Nevermind.

I turn my attention back to my baby, happily sucking down her bottle while a werewolf cuddles her. I hate that I can't hold her, that the thought of cradling her in my arms fills me with fear. I try to push those feelings aside, finding a tiny bit of comfort in knowing how well my co-travelers will care for her while I try to fix my broken, magical self.

Without a baby to occupy my energy, my thoughts return to Darius, and how fun it would be to have a stealthy fling while we're in the air. The plane is dark, passengers mostly sleeping. We could slip into the lavatory and then he could slip into...

The direction of my thoughts become too distracting, and when Darius takes my hand, gripping it firmly, his eyes dilating with need, I realize I've gotten him all hot and bothered too. To redirect both of our minds, I turn to Rune, wanting to ask a question I didn't get a chance to earlier.

"Why do you think the fae came after us first? I thought it was a council from all three realms."

Rune doesn't look at me right away, and it's clear these thoughts were already swirling inside his head. Finally, he speaks, though he still does not look me in the eye.

"It suggests, to me, that there was never any intention to discuss or negotiate a safe passage for you and the child."

"What do you mean?"

"A group of fae might be seen as a diplomatic envoy," he explains, "as we're largely viewed as the more trustworthy of the races. But those who attacked us went directly after Darius, not so much as speaking a word before blasting everyone with fire."

There's anger in his voice. Perhaps a sense of betrayal. It's funny, because these princes who have bound themselves in the common interest of my protection, they are surely viewed as traitors by their kinfolk. And yet that seems to be exactly how Rune feels about the fae sent after us this evening.

"Why would they go after him and not all three

of you?" I ask. "Or just come directly for the baby? Or me?"

"It's a coordinated attack," he answers matter-of-factly. "They intend to weaken us systematically until no one can protect Rain. Which is why..."

Rune looks worried, which makes me insanely nervous. He kept me calm when someone stole my baby in the middle of a storm, when things, at least to me, seemed much more dire than they are right now. Now he's struggling to finish a sentence.

"Which is why, once you are settled, and protected, and in control of your powers... Zev, Darius and I must return to our realms."

A tiny, shrinking sliver of myself has always known the day would come. Even as our bonds grew stronger and our love grew deeper, I knew my princes wouldn't just keep tending bar in a small town in Massachusetts. Still, the fae's words worm into the deepest part of my heart and plant a dark seed full of pain.

"But... I don't know if I can do this, if I can do anything without you three," I say, sounding exactly as needy as I feel.

Rune takes and gently kisses the top of my hand. "I don't think any of us are prepared to go on with a life that doesn't have you in it. Sadly, that's the exact reason we need to return. To put an end to this madness and stop the senseless onslaught."

"How would you do that? How could any of you get your kingdoms to stand down?"

He gives a thoughtful shrug. "We can't say with any certainty. Zev might have the easiest route, with the way wolf kingdoms establish hierarchy. Darius would need to convince a council of ancients who have never changed their mind about anything. I'd have to prove to my mother that the child is nothing without her bond to you." He looks at me, tenderness is his bright eyes. "None of it would be easy. Any success would be worth it."

I glance at Darius, whose mental presence caresses my worried mind. *Do not fear. We are oath-bound to protect you always. And if we have to bring down our kingdoms from within to do so, we will. But we will find our way back to you. I will find you always.*

Tears burn my eyes and clog my throat, but I refuse to let them fall. Instead, I twist in my seat to face Zev, who has remained quiet during this. His path may be the simplest, but Rune hinted at something that sounded much harder.

With the werewolf, I say nothing. I just dive into his forest green eyes, getting lost in them until the bittersweet bliss of his presence eases my heart. And I know there will be an unquenchable hurt inside me every day that I am apart from these men.

He leans forward so that we are forehead to forehead. "This war must end. For everyone's sake." With his free hand he cups my face, pulling away to make eye contact with me. "But we won't leave until you are safe."

That actually brings me a perverse kind of comfort. Since I seem to never be safe anymore, the chances of them being allowed to leave are slim.

Still, I know they're right. Eventually, they will have to face their families. I only wish I could protect them from the pain that will come.

As the plane starts to accelerate down the runway, I reach my hand into my pocket, gripping the fallen star tightly and sending some of my anxieties into its magical form. My nerves have nothing to do with flying and everything to do with where I'm flying to. *What* I'm flying to. And what I might lose when I finally gain what I'm so desperately seeking. Control.

I'm a witch.

I say that to myself probably twenty times each day, and every time it feels a little more real. Tonight it's stronger than ever before. I'm ready to take these powers, and then I'm ready to take on whatever comes my way. But first, I really have to pee.

I wait for the plane to get some altitude and then stand. I feel Darius' eyes on me as I scoot into the aisle, and I may or may not take a little extra time stepping over and straddling him as I go. It's possible I push my breasts against his face briefly as well, but that's only because the seating is so cramped.

In the row behind us, Zev has his eyes closed and is gripping the armrests fiercely, Rain strapped into her car seat next to him. I hope this is the last airplane experience we force on the poor wolf.

The bathrooms are empty since I'm technically still supposed to be seated, but that stuff is just a suggestion. I've been holding in a pee for the last five hours and don't give a shit about turbulence right now.

I'm just finishing up my business when there's a knock at the door. It's pretty ridiculous, because I know there's an empty bathroom a few feet away.

"Yeah, I'm in here," I say.

Instead of a response, I see the small lock on the door start to slide from *occupied* to *vacant*. Not exactly what a girl wants to see when she's plunked down on the toilet.

"Hey, I said I'm in--"

I know you are.

I stop talking and my fear turns to excitement as

Darius speaks into my mind. I scoot my feet back to make room for the door to fold in, and he quietly and quickly steps inside the cramped stall.

My eyes trail down to see that his pants are already unbuttoned and he's wasting no time pushing them down.

I stand, stepping out of my panties instead of pulling them back up, and bring his face to mine while his hand slides between my thighs.

I'd like to finish what we started, he says.

So would I, I answer.

Jesus Lord God, so would I.

CHAPTER FOUR

My body hums with energy as he presses himself against me, his hands sliding over my ass, and I don't waste any time. I pull his head down lower so I can reach his lips and kiss him with everything in me. Passionately, bruisingly, with such urgent need that I'm breathless from it.

I feel him in my mind. In my blood. In my soul.

And when he slips one of his hands between my legs, I feel him inside me.

I moan into his lips and he hardens against me.

I would question if this is prudent or safe, but my body is healed and prudent can go to hell.

I need this man.

Desperately.

When he turns me around to bend me over the toilet, I miss the heat of his lips but crave what's about to happen.

Are you ready? He asks in my mind, as his fingers dig into my hips and he positions himself against me.

More than ready, I reply.

"Excuse me," someone says, knocking on the bathroom door and totally ruining the mood. "Please return to your seats. The fasten seatbelt sign is on."

"I'm feeling sick," I say. "It'll be a minute."

Hurry.

I can practically hear the smirk in his mental voice. *As you wish.*

I doubt that he means to call to mind my favorite movie when he says that, but the effect is the same and somehow that's even more of a turn on.

Just as he's about to fulfill his promise to me and my horny body, the plane lurches, hitting an air pocket or a flock of flying bison, something with enough force to make everything in the bathroom shake violently.

I lose my footing and knock my head against the cabinet. As Darius tries to catch me, his... well let's just say his most-protruding body part has an unfortunate run-in with the sink.

He curses in my mind, loudly and creatively.

I feel a trickle of something on my head and realize I'm bleeding.

When I move to grab a paper towel to catch the blood now dripping into my eyes I trip over the underwear wrapped around my ankles and crash into the vampire, pushing us both into the door, which collapses outward under our combined weight, spilling us into the cramped hall where we land on the floor with our pants down.

Then three things happen in such quick succession it might as well be simultaneous.

Darius uses his super speed to set us on our feet.

He somehow gets both of our pants pulled up quickly.

And he speeds over to the flight attendant who witnessed all of this and uses his mind voodoo on her so she won't remember seeing what she saw.

The lights are out in the cabin and most everyone else on the flight seems to be asleep, so we've avoided the worst of the humiliation. We do, however, get a few knowing smirks from the nosier passengers as we walk back up the aisle.

By the time we make it to our seats, I'm dizzy and bleeding from my head. If it wasn't for the pain, I'd probably feel more embarrassed than at any other point in my life.

On top of all that, I'm still horny—a condition that feels like it's going to be permanent.

I do not like your aero planes.

Darius sounds like a sulky teenager in my mind and I can't help but laugh.

My smile fades when I see Rune's expression.

"What happened to you?" He asks as I take the seat next to him.

"Um. Turbulence."

Immediately he sets to work examining my head and dressing my wound with a smelly poultice that he snuck through security.

It stings but then a pleasant numbness sets in and I lean back in my chair.

I don't realize how tense Darius is until I take his hand, and the ripples of his hunger burn through my mind.

When I look at him, his jaw is clenched and he's facing forward, staring at the back of the chair in front of him.

You okay?

I'm. Fine.

Yeah, you sound fine. Do you need to feed on me?

No. It's too soon and you're too weak.

Well you can't stay like this the whole damn flight to Budapest.

I can.

You're a stubborn ass.

He has no reply to that. I smirk and make sure he can hear it in my thoughts.

When he glances my way, I tilt my head. *Do it.*

Darius narrows his eyes at me, then abruptly stands.

When Zev also stands and moves out of his seat I realize the two are communicating.

Are you serious? You'd rather change seats than feed?

You are too tempting and I will not risk your safety.

I expect Zev to sit next to me, but instead they approach the nearest flight attendant and within two minutes I'm being escorted to first class.

You did not tell me we had better options for our travel.

We didn't, I say. *I would have needed five more credit cards to pay for these seats.*

When we get to the other side of the curtain, the difference is night and day.

Zev takes a seat next to me and Darius and Rune sit together to the right of us, Rune now cradling my sleeping baby. The chairs are much larger and they recline into a nearly horizontal position. I'm informed by the flight attendant we will be served a gourmet breakfast in a few hours but if I need anything just ask.

I don't know why Darius thinks I can't handle giving him more blood. I'm touched by his concern but definitely feel he's making more of an issue of this than he needs to. It isn't until Rune's meds start to wear off and my headache returns that I reluctantly admit I hit my head pretty damn hard.

Zev seems to instantly sense my pain levels rise. "Do you want me to tear him apart for letting you get hurt? Because I will."

I roll my eyes at him. "You two will find literally any reason to fight, won't you?"

He shrugs and doesn't deny it. "It's in our nature."

He twists in his seat and encourages me to do the same so that I can lean my head against him. I close my eyes as he begins a gentle massage around my temples, carefully avoiding the part of my head I hit. The extra leg room of first class clearly has the werewolf feeling better about flying.

"Tell me about your life back on your world," I say. "Rune hinted at the wolf hierarchy but didn't elaborate. What's it like?"

"It's... complicated," he says, his voice soft.

"Being part wolf, pack is everything. We are, to some degree, ruled by the instincts of nature. But I am also a man, and so I must abide by the laws of man as well. My father is king and alpha of our pack. But he is also king of other packs, which creates conflict with those alphas. So there is always friction in our kingdom."

"What about you?" I ask.

"I have an older brother, Link. He's by rights next in line to be king, though our race is long-lived so that right will only pass to him if our father is killed in combat."

"I'm sensing a but," I say.

"But he wasn't born an alpha. I was."

"That must be complicated," I say.

"It is. Link and I were close in our youth, but as we grew older, as his future responsibilities came between us, a wall formed that I have never been able to break down."

"So what will happen? Will he ever be king? Will you be alpha?"

I feel Zev shrug. "Those are the questions on everyone's mind. The only way I can become alpha is if I leave the pack to form my own…"

"Or?" I ask as I slowly ease myself up to look at him.

"Or challenge my father and fight him to the death."

I flinch. "That's brutal."

"It is our way. My father killed his father. And his before that. It is a legacy born of blood and teeth."

I reach for his hand and squeeze it. "I'm sorry you have to live under that weight. Sounds like a real bitch of a burden to carry."

"I never gave it much thought. It's just the way it is."

"It's the way it's always been, maybe," I say, my heart hurting for him. "That doesn't mean it has to stay that way." I pause, afraid of the next question but unable to stop myself from asking. "Will you really leave? Once I'm... safe?" It's only now I realize what Zev will be going home to do, and what it will cost him.

Zev stares into my eyes, obviously conflicted. "It's the very last thing I want to do. But I will if I must."

There are no words I can offer that will bring comfort or change our paths, so instead, I squeeze his hand and adjust myself so that I'm leaning with my head against his shoulder.

I fall asleep to the sound of his heartbeat.

When I wake to the sound of the food cart

KARPOV KINRADE & EVAN GAUSTAD

passing by, Rune--who's taken Zev's place in the seat next to me--hands me a cup of steaming tea.

"Zev said your head was still hurting. Next time tell me," he gently admonishes as I sip the concoction. I nod, making a silent promise I'm not sure I'll always keep, and then look around the cabin. It seems Darius has mind-controlled everyone in our section to keep their windows closed so no sun gets in. At least I assume he has, because though I see one guy occasionally glance at his blind with a slightly confused expression, he never reaches to open it, nor does anyone else.

Rain is sleeping in Zev's arms, who looks half asleep himself, though I know from experience he'll be alert in a flash if there's a threat. Darius has his chair reclined and his eyes closed, but I feel his mind whirling, and know he's not resting at all.

It's not a familiar or fun way to travel for any of them. Only Rain, the happiest baby in the world, seems comfortable.

WE HAVE one quick layover and the rest of the flight passes uneventfully, with all of us sleeping in intermittent, restless bursts. When we finally land in Budapest a day has passed and it's nighttime again. Once we're off the plane and heading toward the terminal exit, it dawns on me that we're actually in Budapest. I also become aware that I have no idea what to do now that we're here.

"Does anyone have any thoughts about where we should go next?" I ask the group. "Anyone have my dad's phone number?"

Per usual, my sarcasm is met with frowns and raised eyebrows. I shake my head, which has become my go-to for telling them to move on with the conversation and not try to make sense of my jokes.

"I'd like to inspect my map," Rune says, "though I'd rather do it in privacy."

"We should get a room in the center of town," Darius says. "This land has old magic under the city streets. I'll look around once we have a place secured where Bernie can rest."

The word rest has me taking stock of how tired I am and how dizzy I still feel. Rune and Darius exchange knowing glances and, before I know what's happening, the vampire pulls me into a bathroom and locks us in a stall.

"Third time's the charm?" I ask hopefully, though honestly I feel too disgusting to do anything sexy at the moment.

"You're starting to glow," he says.

"Oh. Right." How had I completely forgotten my glow into the dark problem?

"But you're not strong enough to give blood," he says with a frown.

"Okay... so what's the plan? I assume you have one or you wouldn't have crashed the ladies room with me."

"You need to drink my blood again first. It will heal you and revive you enough to allow me to feed on you."

I swallow nervously. This wasn't what I was expecting. But I remember the instant healing I felt the last time I had a head injury, and I can't deny that would be real handy right about now.

So I nod and he quickly bites into his wrist.

I steel myself against the general unpleasantness of this, then place my mouth against the open wound and suck.

Like before, the viscosity coats my throat and I resist the urge to gag, but once it's in me I feel a zing of power and I can't help but suck harder.

Darius has to gently pull away before I take too much. I sigh, licking my lips, then tilt my head, offering him my neck.

The moment his teeth plunge into my flesh I sag

against him, held firmly in his arms, as I cling to him.

This time... it all feels different.

Like a bond that had been tentative between us, like a rope made out of smoke, has hardened into something unbreakable.

When he pulls away, licking the wound to heal it, I can't stop staring at him. At the perfection of his face and the depth of his eyes.

I feel overwhelmed by him and unable to let go.

"What happened between us?" I whisper. "How can I feel you... everywhere?"

He looks just as stunned, his grip on me tightening as if he can't bear to let go. "I didn't expect..." his voice trails off. "Nevermind. We must go. Before the sun comes."

Taking my hand, he guides me out and we catch up with Rune and Zev, who's just changed Rain's diaper.

We step out of the terminal and I start to see and hear things that come with foreign travel--different languages, funny license plates, interesting fashion choices. This is the first time I've ever been outside the U.S. and I wish I could just be a normal tourist. Maybe my estranged and possibly magical father lives in some cool ruins and I can live my Lara Croft fantasies.

Darius flags down a taxi and sits in front while the rest of us cram into the back. There's no room for the carseat, so Darius takes her and straps her to his chest. *She'll be safe,* he assures me mentally.

Once we all have seats, I pay closer attention and realize I'm hearing fluent Hungarian from the front seat and it's Darius doing the speaking. He gives our driver directions and we start weaving through traffic.

It's dark outside but my senses are heightened from feeding on Darius and I take in everything as we head to the hotel. The city is beautiful, with hotels and restaurants lining the central river. Modern buildings line the streets, but the sense of antiquity still has a firm hold on the landscape.

The car pulls up outside a beautiful building with a view of the water. It seems Darius opted for upscale lodging, so hopefully he has a plan for settling the tab.

I let Darius take the lead when we reach the front desk, since I definitely didn't master Hungarian on the flight over. Maybe he'll get us a discount with the whole sexy-as-sin-man-holding-a-cute-baby vibe he's got going. I'd give him whatever he wanted if it were me.

Before he can get more than a few words out to the hotel clerk, the young woman stares at me, her eyes narrowed like she's trying to place me. "You are Bernadette Morgan?" She asks in English.

I nod, surprised at being recognized, and surprised she was able to tear her eyes off of my vampire long enough to notice me at all.

She pulls a manilla envelope from behind the counter and hands it to me. "This was left for you two days ago. I was asked to give it to you when you arrived today."

I exchange glances with the guys, who all look as bewildered as me. Two days ago we didn't know we'd be in Budapest today. And two hours ago we didn't know we'd be at this hotel.

So who could have possibly found us here?

"Who left it?" I ask the clerk, who doesn't find any of this as unnerving as the rest of us do.

She shrugs. "It was left for my manager. I was just told an American woman named Bernadette Morgan with a baby would arrive today and to pass along the envelope."

I thank her for the useless information and move toward the elevator while Darius gets our room keys. As far as I can tell, the only people who know where we are--and possibly where we're going--are those who want us dead.

I'm lost in a trance until I find myself sitting on the edge of a couch in a fancy hotel suite. There's a common room with a couple lazy boys to go with the sofa, plus the TV, mini fridge and wet bar. Double doors lead to bedrooms on either side of the living room.

None of the Sexies speak, they all just stare, waiting for me to do something.

I nervously open the envelope.

Be careful.

Do you smell poison? I ask.

No.

A bomb?

No.

Then the greatest risk is a paper cut. Relax.

I do not, in fact, cut myself on the paper as I pull it out.

It's a thick cream card with calligraphed writing on it that simply says "9 pm Friday."

"What do you think it means?" I ask.

Zev growls. "I think it means someone will be coming for you tomorrow night."

"Is it someone who wants to kill us?" The question doesn't feel all that smart coming out of my mouth, and the looks I receive confirm my assessment.

"Most people with assassination plans don't set up meetings," Rune says, addressing my dumb question far too gently.

"So," the fae continues, "either someone who wants to help us will be here tomorrow night at nine… or someone else plans to kill us between now and then."

CHAPTER FIVE

"I just want one semi-plausible reason that anyone-- or anything--might know we're here."

Since opening the envelope and getting the incredibly bizarre invitation to my own hotel room for the following evening, neither Rune nor Darius nor Zev has been able to offer any sort of explanation. I don't expect *all* the answers, but I got us on the plane and to Budapest, and now I'd appreciate if one of these magical men could drop some knowledge on a poor little witch from Rowley, MA.

"I'll be back," Darius says, and then is out the door and probably in the street before I can tell him to sit his ass down.

"What's that shit?" I ask Rune, forcing someone else to deal with the anger I feel at Darius bailing.

"He's going to scour the city before he has to spend a day hiding from the sun," Rune says. "I know you want answers, Bernie, and this is the best way to get them."

Rune's right, but it doesn't calm me down. I walk over to Zev, who's putting Rain to bed for the night in the hotel's rollaway crib.

Hang on.

Why's there already a crib in here?

"Let's start at the beginning," I say, trying to keep my voice at a respectable volume while still presenting as much angst as possible. "Why Budapest? My dad is here, someone else knows we're here, my grandfather wanted us to come here when he found out he was going to be murdered. I know you can't solve any of those ridiculous riddles, but maybe someone can tell me why Budapest matters?"

"Oh," Zev says, a trace of confusion on his gorgeous face. "You don't know about Budapest?"

If he was closer, I swear to God I'd bite him.

"Of course I don't know about Budapest! What the hell am I supposed to know?"

Rune walks over and settles me with his calming touch, and not a moment too soon as I realize how tightly my fists were clenched.

"This is the first land," Zev answers, doing that

obnoxious thing where he says words that sound important but mean nothing to me. He senses his mistake when I grit my teeth and flare my nostrils.

"When the Fates created humankind, pooled from the three sisters' sweat, it began here," Zev explains.

"Hold up, dude," I say. I can tell he's about to keep talking, like he didn't just undo thousands of years of world religions with one casually tossed out sentence. "Humanity was created from witch sweat?"

Zev frowns. "Well, yes. Obviously."

I purse my lips. "Tell me how that is in any way obvious?"

He doesn't have an answer, because of course none of this is obvious. "There are thousands of religions in my world, and I'm almost 100% certain that none of them have an origin story involving witch sweat."

Zev clears his throat. "Okay. Well, now you know the truth. May I continue?"

I sigh, knowing they will just keep doing this. Throwing out super important, life-changing details like it's nothing. "Be my guest."

Zev nods and begins again like I never interrupted him in the first place. "Generally, of course. The land was different then, but the hills, caves and rivers never lost their importance. And witches have always kept this city as a stronghold, even when vampires pushed them to the brink."

"So," Rune says, assuming the sexy professor role that suits him so well, "for the Last Witch and her mother to be called to Budapest, by whatever power, stands to reason."

"Great," I say, pacing the hotel room impatiently. I'm sure it does stand to reason, as Rune says, but I'd sure as hell love to know what reason that is. And pooled from their sweat? I guess that's as good a primordial ooze as any.

"Either of you have an educated guess about what reason or power brought us here?"

My question is met with thoughtful silence, giving me a reflective beat to appreciate the change I've gone through in a few short weeks. From a pregnant bar owner with dashed dreams and limited prospects, to a single mother keeping company with paranormals who once meant to kill me and have since sworn to protect me, even if it costs them their lives. And also I'm a witch. A glow in the dark one at that.

While I wait for either Zev or Rune to spill the tea about Budapest and why it matters to me and my daughter, I delight briefly in the journey that got me here, commanding these gorgeous, powerful men, and knowing they'll go to hell and back if it means keeping me happy.

"I have a guess," Zev finally responds, his pensive voice rumbling in a low register that always makes me weak-kneed.

"Any witch with an understanding of her heritage knows of this land," the werewolf says as he takes a seat in one of the lazy boys. "We're living through the final stages of an ancient prophecy, one scribed by the Fates themselves after they came here and created life. I'd expect anyone looking for clues would search here. And that includes your father."

Finally, we have the semblance of a theory.

"So you think my dad is here, trying to interpret the prophecy?" I ask, Zev nodding along. "Any thoughts about Gramps' letter and why my dad bailed before I was born?"

"Imagine finding out you'd spawned a being with powers beyond your comprehension," Rune says. "That could certainly drive a man to go looking for answers."

It sounds a little too much like Rune is defending the deadbeat who abandoned me and my mother. My initial reaction is a scowl, but I have to remind myself I'm fresh off of killing my mother because she wanted to kill my baby. Maybe, *maybe*, the man who walked out on her had a half-decent reason. *Maybe.*

"As for your grandfather," Rune continues, "I can't say. I'm fairly certain he didn't write the letter, or wasn't in control of himself when he did."

"What makes you think that?" I ask.

"People can't write when they're dead," the fae states bluntly. It's not quite the insightful answer I'd hoped for.

"I'd say your father planted the letter," Zev says. "I don't know whether he's good or evil, but he's the most likely culprit in my mind."

I stand up and walk toward the window, trying to hide my frustration. I've grown so used to these men teaching and explaining, so to have them confused and searching for answers makes me uncomfortable.

"So what do we do?" I finally ask, hoping to find something to focus on to keep the questions from driving me crazy. "Sit in this hotel room until tomorrow night?"

Zev shrugs. "We'll see what Darius finds tonight, then Rune and I will look around tomorrow. If we don't stumble on some evidence that tells us to do otherwise, yes, we'll wait for our visitor."

"And while we wait," Rune says, walking over and placing his hand on the small of my back. "We'll turn this place into a magical fortress. Whoever means to meet you, whatever their intention might be, won't have an easy time of it."

The words are reassuring, giving me enough peace to notice how exhausted I am. This has been a long, travel day of shitty sleep, and it comes on the heels of a long, sleep-deprived night. Rune notices my heavy eyelids and guides me toward one of the bedrooms.

"Now's the best time for you to rest, Bernie. Zev and I will sleep and guard in shifts while we wait for Darius to return."

I nod, too excited about the prospect of sleep to engage in any more conversation. I give an unenthusiastic wave as I walk into the bedroom, kick my shoes and jeans off, and I'm out the moment my head hits the pillow.

It doesn't take long before vivid dreams consume my mind. I'm walking along the edge of the river, the Sexies trailing behind me, and in every doorway and on every balcony, a shadowy figure stands watching me. It feels like there are hundreds, if not thousands of eyes tracking my every move. I become more anxious with every step and keep looking back to see what my companions are going to do to help me, but they're just falling further behind. I try to slow down, but they can't catch up, and the slower I move, the more people I notice watching.

Finally, I dive into the river. I swim toward the bottom, thinking that the deeper I go, the harder it will be to see me. I hear a splash in the water above and turn to see several dark, faceless figures swimming behind me. I swim faster, going deeper, feeling my air running out but not knowing of any other way to escape.

At the bottom of the river, I'm faced with two different tunnels. I feel my lungs burning up oxygen but I still can't decide. I'm screaming in my brain to go either right or left, but it's like the choice has me paralyzed. *Which way do I go?*

Finally, before my lungs catch fire, I swim through to the right and hover at the entrance of a cave, though it's pitch black inside. I'm terrified to go forward, but more afraid of whoever is swimming behind me, and I cross the threshold into the darkness.

As soon as I swim through, I'm standing in a room. The water is gone, I'm completely dry, and a sense of calm washes over me.

The room is massive, so tall I can't even see the ceiling. Giant shelves stand against every wall, each packed with books. I finally notice the small tables scattered about the room, and all the people who sit at them, casually reading and studying. I'm in some kind of enormous library, and I've got the sense that everyone in here is a student. They're all trying to figure out who the Last Witch is, and I'm suddenly afraid of being seen.

I turn around to see if I can get into the water again, but there's no cave or river to be found. I'm trapped in a room filled with people trying to find me--to find Rain, and sooner or later they will.

As if reading my thoughts, the strangers' eyes start to drift upward, looking away from their texts and discovering me. The mother of the Last Witch.

And then, Darius is there. Right in front of me, staring into my eyes, a smile on his lips. I want to tell him that we're in danger, but I don't want to speak. I step toward him, getting as close as I can to whisper in his ear. Just as our bodies touch, before I can warn him, I feel his teeth sink into my neck.

I feel an immediate release. A release from the fear and the tension.

A release from the dream.

I'm in bed, in the hotel, the fog of sleep lifting. However, one thing from the dream remains.

Darius.

His body hovers over me, his teeth in my vein, my blood flowing through him.

My hands reach up to his sides, and I feel exactly what I hoped I would--no clothes.

I slide my fingers down, gently tracing along his rigid, flexed form, traveling down to the curves of his naked ass and digging my fingers into his flesh.

I'm left wanting as he pulls his teeth out of my neck, but find a new pleasure as his lips meet mine while his hands make quick work of my clothing. After so many failed attempts, I know I'll finally have him.

I reach down and grab his hardness, causing him to moan into my mouth. I'm already on the edge, the passion having built for days, and I just can't wait any longer.

Please, he whispers into my mind, showing he also can't hold off another moment.

I guide him, he pushes, and the most explosive pleasure I've ever experienced fills me. The world melts around us as he goes deeper, forcing my back to arch and my body to shiver. My hands move furiously, trying to touch every inch of him, to bring all of him into me.

I wrap my legs around his back, our hips finding the same rhythm, his pace increasing, my climax building. Darius' short breaths make it clear he's nearing his own precipice, and I contract around him to move him over the edge.

Time freezes. My body convulses uncontrollably and I feel like my skin is on fire. Even with my eyes squeezed shut, I notice the glow of my skin intensifying as wave after wave of pleasure crashes through me.

I float on the swell of that wave for what feels like hours but might have only been minutes, and I'm dizzy and trembling when the hum in my loins finally starts to subside.

I open my eyes only to lose myself in the vampire's dark, penetrative gaze. Never have I felt so intertwined with another soul, so connected to someone outside myself, and I know in my blood that he feels the same.

He leans in and brushes his lips against mine, then trails feather-light kisses down my jawline to my neck, flicking his tongue over his bite mark.

I sigh and fade into his arms, lost to the world until the next morning when the sound of a bird chirping outside our blacked out windows wakes me.

My brain wakes up slowly, processing where I am and what's happened with sluggish reflexes. I'm still naked, so I know at least part of last night wasn't a dream. Darius is still asleep next to me, his naked body exposed after I apparently stole the covers. I don't know if he gets cold when he sleeps, but I gently tuck him in, freezing when I hear my baby cry. In a panic, I dash out the bedroom and, still naked, poke my head out into the common area.

Zev is sitting on the couch, drinking coffee and reading a newspaper, somehow managing to look like a dad on vacation waiting for the rest of the family to wake up. Rain sleeps in the crib next to him.

He eyes my naked figure and gives me a smirk. "Need any help, love?"

A mix of relief and self-awareness pushes me back into my room, where I grab my clothes off the floor and quickly dress. Moderately presentable, I head back out to talk with Zev.

"I imagine that's the best you've slept in weeks," the werewolf says, and I'm not sure if he's talking about the duration of my sleep or the sexy interlude in the middle of it.

"Yeah, I was out pretty hard and fast." *Jesus, Bernie. Word choice.*

Zev lets out a small bark of a laugh, then throws his paper down on the table.

"Darius will sleep for the next two or three hours and then sulk in a closet until the sun goes down, and

Rune's off getting some sort of tree bark or frog skin, I can't remember which."

Zev's almost bored description of his magical counterparts makes me laugh. In some ways, he's the most human of the three. He relies on his mind and physical abilities instead of spells and manipulative powers. It gives him a little perspective and sense of humor the other Sexies can't quite muster.

"So," the werewolf continues, "fancy some breakfast? I heard of a great cafe down the street."

Zev stands and extends his arm with an inviting smile that makes my stomach flutter. I smile back. Food sounds amazing, as does a little bit of sun on my soon-to-be-glowing skin.

He straps Rain to him as we head out and I finally get a good look at the city for the first time since we got here. Our hotel is right on the water, and the streets bustle with people on foot, in taxis and on bikes. It's a brisk, sunny morning and I'm immediately drawn to this historical place. I've always been enamored with the famous European cities--Rome, Paris, London and the like. Budapest never made the fantasy list, but clearly it should have. The baroque architecture and beautiful bridges make the city feel like a 360-degree painting, every view pulled off an artist's canvas.

Zev and I settle at a little cafe along the river. It takes exactly one sip of my Hungarian coffee to turn me into a coffee snob who will never go back to the instant garbage I've been drinking up to this point. Why was I never told coffee could be good? I blame not having a father and my mother being a psychopath.

We drink coffee and nibble pastries in silence. Zev seems equally enchanted by our surroundings, though he might be focused on reading whatever smells waft by his nose. Either way, it's as pleasant a morning as I've had in a long time.

When the magic tingle in my skin becomes more of a burn, I know we need to head back to wake Darius. I've got the star in my pocket which helps keep me from lighting up like the marquee outside a strip club, but I still probably shine more brightly than is normal for a human. I've definitely gotten more compliments from random strangers on my beautiful skin since this started.

Zev drops some Euros on the table, which he either stole or just had on hand because he's hip like that, and we walk along the river back toward the hotel.

At first I assume the knot in my stomach has to do with the unchecked magic surging through my body. But as we walk, I realize I'm having a strong bout of *déjà vu*. This path along the river's edge is eerily similar to the route I took in my dream. I pass the same buildings, see the same windows and balconies where cloaked figures watched as I ran along.

I look into the water, and it seems to change color before my eyes. It goes from a dark blue that's nearly opaque, to a more translucent turquoise. The longer I stare, the clearer the water becomes, and now I swear I can see nearly to the bottom. Past the fish and kelp and rocks--to a dark, underwater cavern.

"What do you see, Bernie?" Zev breaks me out of my trance. "You've been locked in on the same spot of water for about a minute."

I don't know how to respond. I see... a memory? A vision from a dream that I can't really define, nor do I think is real?

"I'm not sure. The water... does it look clear to you?"

"Not particularly," he says, making me even more unsure of what I'm seeing. "But," he continues, "I don't have your powers, and this isn't the city of my people. So if you say the water looks clear, I'm inclined to believe you."

. . .

WHEN WE GET BACK to the hotel, Darius is awake and hiding in a blacked-out room. My insides turn to jelly the moment our eyes meet, and I feel nearly feverish at the memory of last night and the promise of more nights to come.

But now is not the time for such thoughts.

There is always time for such thoughts, the vampire says, speaking directly to my mind. *And soon there will be time for more than just thoughts.*

I suck in a breath at the promise, but push it aside as I turn my attention to the fae. Rune has the right idea and is busy creating illusions around our suite so whenever our guest or intruders arrive, they'll have some work to do before they can murder us all.

Despite my protests, the three of them gang up on me and force me to nap--at least for an hour or two--so that I'm well-rested for whatever the night brings.

I insist I can't possibly sleep with so much to do-- though we all know there's nothing I can do. Sleep gets the last laugh and I manage to doze for a bit.

I wake feeling refreshed and grateful, and after a shower and a cup of coffee, I'm ready.

Ready to wait for a really long time.

During the remaining daylight hours, I teach the

three princes of magical kingdoms poker. Then I proceed to destroy them at it.

They teach me a game called Jokers, and I annihilate them.

Convinced I have a new super power, they all refuse to play more with me, so we each fall into our own rhythms, them taking turns playing with, feeding or changing Rain while I try to read the same page of the same book one thousand two hundred and sixty six times.

After the sun goes down, my heart rate kicks up a notch. Seconds feel like hours and yet each tick of the clock happens too fast, bringing us nearer to whatever's lurking on the other side of 9 pm.

It's now 8:30 pm and I want to throw up. I wish I could just buzz the front desk and ask the clerk to make a few calls and have the mystery visitor come early.

Darius is equally on edge, rapidly darting between windows every time he hears a noise. If we had more time, I might push him into the bedroom for a repeat of last night and take care of some of this excess energy.

8:40 pm.

The room around us has had a magical remodel. Rune created a labyrinth of walls and mirrors to conceal us, at least momentarily, from anyone that dares enter.

8:47 pm.

Zev morphs into wolf form and sits on the small balcony outside the french doors. He keeps an eye on the street to see who might be coming or going.

8:52 pm.

Rain lays in her crib in the center of the room, as far as possible from any windows or doors, and at the middle of Rune's illusionary maze. I wish I could hide her in a closet or something, away from whatever action might take place, but I've learned from harrowing experiences that she needs to be in my sight always.

8:59 pm.

I stand with the Sexies surrounding Rain, ready as we'll ever be. I face the main door while each of the others faces in a different direction. No reason to believe our guest will come through the front entrance.

At 9:01 there's a knock at the door, which both startles the living shit out of me and makes me feel a little less like we're about to be ambushed. As planned, Darius silently glides to the door, looks through the peephole, and turns the knob.

"Oh, hi," a male voice says from outside. He has a

trace of a Hungarian accent but not so much that he's difficult to understand. "I'm looking for Bernadette Mor--"

He can't finish his sentence before Darius grabs him by the sleeve and jerks him into the room. Now that I can see the source of the voice, I honestly feel underwhelmed.

A man in his thirties with shaggy brown hair and ill-fitting clothes stands next to Darius. He might be 5'8" or so, but he looks tiny compared to the strapping vampire. He also looks terrified.

"What's your business?" Darius asks, not even trying to dial back the hostility in his voice.

"I'm here to see Bernadette," the man answers with a tremble. "I left a note, I came alone, I'm not here to cause trouble. Is she here?"

I realize the illusions are still around us and the stranger has no idea that I'm just a few feet away.

Let him go, I say to Darius.

No.

Do it, I insist. *He's not dangerous and you know it. Tell Rune to drop the illusion.*

After a few moments, Darius relaxes his grip and the man's eyes dart over to me, the layout of the room clearly having changed from his point of view.

All the fear I felt earlier has faded, and I can't tell

exactly why. It helps that the man isn't at all menacing, but there's something more than that. A connection I never could have felt before, but now registers within my magic spirit.

"Who are you?" I ask, taking a step forward.

"I'm Andor." He smiles as he looks me over, like he's arrived to take me to prom and thinks my dress looks nice. "You're Bernadette?"

I nod and then push past the formalities. "Did my father send you?"

He shakes his head and looks past me, like he's searching for the right response. In the end, he just goes with, "No."

"Then why are you here?"

Andor looks from me to the men standing on either side of me, then up at Darius. He swallows, clearly fighting some nerves of his own, then looks into my eyes.

"I'm, um... I'm your designated lover."

CHAPTER SIX

"My what?" My shock turns to laughter. I can't help it. I'm simply overcome. I have no reservoir left for this conversation. I'm tapped out.

And so I laugh.

The princes are less inclined toward hilarity. They each look ready to rip poor Andor to pieces. He's about 20 seconds away from sharing a fate with my bestie's ex asshole.

Andor turns a bright shade of pink that burns his whole face as he fidgets with sweaty hands. "Err... surely you've been told about this. That is why you have come?"

"Told about a... designated lover?" I purse my lips like I'm thinking, then shake my head. "Yeah, no

I'm pretty sure I would have remembered that. What the hell are you talking about?"

"Oh, um, this is very awkward. Not at all how it was supposed to go," the man stutters, desperately avoiding eye contact with me. "Well, you see," he glances at the kitchenette. "Um, could I trouble you for a glass of water?"

Rune steps in his way, turning the kitchen into the illusion of a desert. "Answer the lady," the fae says with a severity to his voice that is always shocking and always effective.

Andor looks as if he wishes the floor would open up and swallow him.

I almost feel pity. In the past, I probably would have. But present-day me is slightly jaded by A: all the people who have tried to kill me, including people I thought I knew; B: all the lies I've been fed like sugar my whole life, sweet until it kills you; and C: all the people who were supposed to be dead who weren't and who weren't supposed to die who did. Sadly, all this has made me more cautious in my empathy.

"Speak!" I say, and though I do not shout, my power fills the room like thunder trapped in a bottle.

The Sexies aren't rattled by my force, but poor Andor looks like he's about to shit himself.

"Right, well, um," he tries to stand a bit taller and he holds out his sweaty palm to me for a handshake. "I'm Andor Maldone, from the *Kő Sorrendje* and I am here to claim you as my own and offer myself to you in service of your magic."

Darius curses under his breath in a rather creative blend of English, French and a bit of Hungarian, which makes our guest's eyes bulge.

You are not going with him, the angry vampire hisses into my mind.

No shit.

To everyone else he says, "The Order of the Stone. I thought your pathetic numbers died out ages ago."

Andor simultaneously puffs his chest in pride and averts his eyes in fear. It's a strange combination of reactions that makes him look like a chihuahua trying to mimic a wolf.

"We did not. We simply allowed the world to think so, in order to protect our ranks and the witches we are pledged to."

I huff in annoyance. "How about someone fill me in on the missing pieces of this conversation, real fast, before I lose my shit."

Darius turns to me, his face shifting from anger to almost amusement. "The order is a society of men employed as the chosen protectors and guides to witches. Through a sexual alliance with those women of power."

My jaw drops as the pieces do in fact come together. "So y'all are basically magic penises."

Zev bursts out laughing. Darius snickers. Rune grins.

Andor loses even more color. "Um, not precisely, no. For the most part, we do not possess magic. Each witch is given a mate--"

"A designated lover," I say, throwing his own words back at him.

"Yes, er, a designated lover, who is meant to protect her and help her control her power."

"Through sex," I add.

"Well, yes, how else?"

"So... powerless magic penises." AJ is going to absolutely die when she hears about this. She'll also be pissed she missed it.

"Thanks for the offer, Andor, but as you can see," I wave to indicate the three increasingly possessive and incredibly sexy men surrounding me, "I'm all stocked up on magic penises. I won't be in need of yours, as lovely as that sounds."

He doesn't need to know I've only actually sampled one of said penises. But there's enough sexual tension between me and all three guys that I feel pretty safe asserting my claim. At least for purposes of dissuading Andor from his hopeless mission.

"Yes, um, well, that's not really how it works."

I cock my head. "How what works?"

"Witches and their mates," he says, as if he's the expert here. "You must mate with a member of the order. That bond will strengthen your power."

I laugh. Again. "First of all, I'm not taking an assigned lover. That's not how *I* work. Second, I do not need to strengthen my power."

"Oh, well, I know it might *feel* like you're strong. It's always a rush when a witch's power comes in, and yours was held back for so long, judging by your age."

Oh hell no he didn't.

Completely oblivious to the quicksand he's walking into, he keeps talking. Poor fool.

"But given how little magic is left in the world, and how weak the witches have become… it is instrumental that you, that is… you will only feel the true reach of your magic--"

"Let me guess, when I sample the magic penis."

He blushes, but he also nods.

"I'm going to let you in on a little secret." I step forward, staring him down as my skin begins to glow again. "Women don't like being told who they're supposed to have sex with. And we definitely don't like being mansplained to about our own bodies and powers."

With my anger comes a surge of magic, though with a different intent and energy than before. I don't feel like I'll hurt anyone, but rather just flex my powers a bit.

As much as I fear my lack of control, I make no attempt to hold back in front of this stranger who's trying to stake a claim in me. I am super tired of secret orders trying to control me. I'm walking into this situation packing... in a manner of speaking.

As the glow in my skin and the magic in my veins reaches boiling point, I don't really know what will happen. I'm as much a spectator as an actor, and I look on as I light the place up.

Literally.

As my hands glow brighter, hundreds of sparkling lights float up from them and hang in the air like fireflies on a warm summer night. It takes me back to when AJ and I would catch them in jars and run around pretending we were magic fairies with the power of light.

If only we'd known then what we know now. Turns out we weren't too far off.

I keep my eyes unfocused as the flying stars of light dance around me, then my fingers move instinctively and begin to shape the light into an ancient symbol that feels familiar and entirely new all at once.

Andor falls to his knees, his eyes wide, his hands pulled up into a prayer supplication. I have no idea what just happened, but I don't want to let him know that.

"Get up, will you?" I say, holding my hands behind my back to hide how badly they're shaking. "I don't want to make a big thing out of all this. Just tell me how you knew I was coming and where my father is. That's all I want from you. Not your magic penis or whatever else you and your creepy order have planned."

When he doesn't rise, Zev steps over to him and jerks him to his feet. The werewolf growls at the man, letting it rumble up from his chest like a predator on the hunt. "How did you know we'd be here?" he asks.

Andor trips over his tongue answering. "We are connected. I had a vision of you in my dreams."

That reminds me of my strange dream and the sense of strong *déjà vu* as we walked through the ancient streets of Budapest, but I don't want to create any shared connection with this stranger, so I hold my tongue. The less he knows about me, the better.

"Do you know my father? His name is…"

"Timót," he says, interrupting me. "Of course I know him. He's the leader of the men in our order. Has been for decades. At least, until he disappeared."

"Disappeared?" The Sexies and I all ask in unison.

"Yes. A few weeks ago. He said you would be coming," Andor gestures to me. "And that you would need a wand more powerful than one we've ever seen. That kind of wand would require a dragon's scale. So he went to retrieve it. And he hasn't been seen since."

Minutes, hours, days... who knows, maybe months? I'll never know how long I sat in stunned silence after Andor describes my father's disappearance, because I think time stopped working.

Reading Gramps' letter caused my brain to fracture, learning that my father was alive after years of believing otherwise. At the same time, I was almost ready for it. Mom was supposed to be dead, but that wasn't the case. Tilly was bedridden but could still freeze time and give me her powers. Hell, grandpa's letter only came to me because he knew he'd be murdered, so the existence of my father wasn't that big a leap.

Hearing Andor say my father's name, the

Hungarian version, shakes my reality in a whole new way. People here *know* him. Until very recently, they were *with* him. I'll be able to ask questions and get answers, and that's a little overwhelming for me.

Sensing that I might be trapped in my thoughts for quite some time, Rune picks up the conversation.

"Are you saying Timothy Trendle was killed by dragons?" the fae asks.

Andor gives a weak shrug. "We don't know. Those caves certainly aren't a safe place to visit, even for someone powerful like him."

"What do you mean, 'powerful'?" Darius cuts in. "He was human, was he not?"

"Yes, he is human," Andor answers, though there's a hesitancy in his voice. "But he is also one of the strongest members of the *Érintett*."

The word means nothing to me, but it prompts Darius to pace toward the window, staring at the floor while his mind probably races through centuries of memories and learning. I don't have that kind of time, so I just request the Cliff Notes version.

"What the hell is an *Érintett*?"

"The Affected," Darius answers from across the room, stealing Andor's chance to be useful.

"Witches exclusively women," the vampire says, "but certain men, over time and with the proper training, have been said to absorb or inherit their magic."

Comparatively speaking, my dad being a little bit magic doesn't seem like a very big deal.

"So, dad was, what, like a JV witch?"

"Who is JV?" Andor asks, and I instantly regret my ultra-American analogy.

"Nevermind," I say. "What's the deal with the Quartet of Erins? Or whatever you called them."

"There haven't been many," Andor answers. "Those with enough inherited power have brought strength to the *Kő Sorrendje*, defending witches from would-be attackers."

"Not all in your ranks are so friendly," Darius says, as he remains facing away from us. Seems like the vampire still has some past beef with witches that needs to get sorted out.

"Has anyone gone to look for my father?" I ask. "Another Airy Tut, maybe?"

Andor looks at his feet and shakes his head. "No one dares tempt the dragons. Timót was told to stay back, but he refused."

This all hits me a little harder than expected. Assuming any of it is true, which is a sizable leap of faith, I may have come all the way to Budapest to meet my father and realize my powers as a witch, only to be thwarted by dad getting all cavalier and going to fight dragons so he could give his daughter a wand.

"Where are the dragons?" Zev asks. Leave it to the werewolf to get excited about a dance with death.

Andor thinks about his answer for a moment, looking between all of us as he chooses his words.

"Well, since, um… since we won't be consummating our--"

"No, we won't, so just get to the next part." I can't wait to meet whoever *assigned* this man as my lover so I can fireball them through a wall.

"Right, since that won't happen," Andor says, "would you come with me, Bernadette? I'm meant to lead you to the Grand Hall."

The moment Andor singles me out, each of the Sexies inches closer to me. There's no chance I'm going anywhere without them.

Andor takes the point, but makes one last attempt to push back. "I was told by a very powerful witch that only--"

"We will explain to that witch that you were given no choice," Darius says. Andor immediately nods his understanding, possibly due to some mind control, more likely just because Darius could kill him in milliseconds.

"What's at the Grand Hall?" Rune asks.

"Well, it's hard to explain in English... or any language, really," Andor says. "I suppose the best answer is, everything."

I watch the Sexies exchange glances, perhaps doing a little mind-speaking as well. I'm sure they're discussing whether or not this is a trap and all the other logistics of following a stranger into the night.

While they have a silent conference, I stare at Andor. Perhaps he came here with shitty intentions, but I don't think he can take much blame for the shittiness. He seems like a nervous little man caught up in a cause much bigger than himself, and I can't help but feel he probably isn't trying to kill us and may be trustworthy--to an extent. It's not just a judge of character, because that's not a reliable metric in my new magic life. It's an instinct that seems like it's rooted in my powers. Like ancient witch knowledge inherited through Tilly and my mom is guiding my brain.

"Yes, we'll go with you," I say before anyone else can take the lead. I'm not sure where my certainty comes from, other than I'm not leaving this country without some answers, and this seems our only way of getting them.

"Bernie," Rune starts.

"No," I shut him down.

Bernie, Darius tries the mind-speak approach.

"Nope," I shoot back audibly, throwing a glance his way. "You three be on high alert in case there's funny business, but I say we're going with Andor."

The Hungarian man looks at me with a smile, and maybe a sense of hope that I feel inclined to squash, so I add a qualifier: "My designated lover who will never get to do any of the loving."

Andor deflates immediately, but does so with a nod to show he understands. Rune dissolves the remaining illusions and packs Rain into a carrier that he straps to his chest. Zev carries the diaper bag. It's all quite the vision of what modern male parenting should be.

We follow our guide down through the lobby and out into the night. It's a little past 9:30 but the city still buzzes with activity. Bars and restaurants are in full swing with people enjoying the brisk winter evening from covered patios.

After a block or two on the main drag, Andor leads us down a smaller street paved with cobblestone and lined with charming old street lamps. It gives off such a quaint European vibe but also makes me think Jack the Ripper is lurking in the shadows.

The smaller street leads to another busy road, across from which is a large, open square. People mill about in the space, sitting on the edge of the fountain or coming and going from nearby cafes.

"We're headed to the center of that square," Andor explains before leading us across the street. "When I stop walking, everyone please gather close to me."

He doesn't wait for our consent, which is good because I'm not sure Darius would ever acknowledge any sort of obedience to my Hungarian wanna-be lover.

We get to the other side of the street and move into the center of the plaza. Hundreds of people are coming and going from the area, and I'm starting to wonder what exactly Andor has planned.

Meanwhile, my Hungarian man-bride has his eyes glued to the ground, inspecting each slab of cement he steps on. Finally, he seems to approve of a standing area and comes to a stop.

"Gather, if you would," he says. "Stand with shoulders touching, we need to be in a tight little circle."

The Sexies hesitate, as expected, so I take the lead and stand next to Andor. He smiles when our arms touch, and I'm finding him more harmless and adorable with every passing minute. I'm glad I didn't accidentally kill him with magic back at the hotel.

KARPOV KINRADE & EVAN GAUSTAD

"Join us please, if you want to go to the Grand Hall." Andor has a little more confidence in his voice now that I'm following his lead and he has some leverage. With a trio of scowls, Zev, Rune and finally Darius move into our five-person cluster. Six if you count Rain, who's still conked out and strapped to the fae's chest.

When Andor's happy with everyone's positioning, he glances around quickly to make sure no one's watching, then pulls a small pouch from his jacket and, in a quick flourish, throws a little dust into the air around us. The powdery substance filters down on our hair and shoulders, but nothing seems to happen. Andor watches each of us closely, seeming to observe something the rest of us aren't. Once he sees whatever it is he needs to see, he stomps on the stone in the middle of our circle three times.

There's a grinding noise, distant at first and then louder as it seems to come up toward the surface below our feet. I look around, wondering if the people nearby can hear the sound, but no one seems to notice or care.

"There we are," Andor says, bringing my attention back to the ground where he stomped. The stone he pounded with his foot is no longer there--it's been replaced by the first step of a narrow staircase leading into the earth below.

"Quickly," Andor says. "The dust casts an illusion to hide our descent, but it only lasts a few moments."

I start to move, but Darius grabs my arm and stops me before I can get to the opening.

"No, not you," he says. "Not first."

Zev growls in agreement and moves into the lead, throwing a look back at Andor right when he reaches the first step. "You go behind me."

Andor nods, his confidence reduced again. He steps in after Zev, then Rune and the baby, and finally I enter with Darius behind me. The grinding sound starts again and we hurry down the first few steps to avoid getting pinned by a closing stone.

Once I'm well below ground level, I look back up to see the night sky disappear. I listen for sounds of the bustling city above, but hear nothing. It's like we've stepped into another world.

I look back down, expecting darkness, but the stairs are lit by torches along the narrow wall.

"So none of the people in the square could see us?" I ask Andor. "Did we just disappear in front of their eyes?"

Andor shakes his head, then starts walking down the stairs behind Zev. "Our shadows lingered and then walked off. To anyone watching, we stopped for a moment and then walked into the darkness. No one expects a secret entrance in a crowded place, which is why this door has remained for centuries."

THE STAIRS WIND around a central column for quite a while, making me wonder how deep we're going. Through our blood bond, I know that Darius is on edge. Each step makes him a little more agitated, and I reach back to take his hand.

Are you okay? I ask.

I've had bad experiences with witches in hidden buildings, he responds. *I'll be fine.*

Not exactly the answer I wanted, but I don't have time to unpack it as the stairs come to an end in front of a large, stone door. Andor fumbles for a second with the chain around his neck, then pulls it from under his shirt to reveal a long, grey object that looks like a fang or a claw. He sticks it into a hole at the center of the door, and the stone slides back. Andor starts to enter, but Zev grabs his shirt and takes a moment to sniff out danger before letting anyone proceed.

We go in the same order, Darius pulling up the rear as the stone door slides shut.

"This is the Grand Hall," Andor says. "I'll fetch those who can answer questions about... Bernadette? Are you alright?"

His words barely make it to my ears, as too many thoughts and feelings are rushing through my head. As soon as I stepped through the door, my skin started glowing more brightly than ever before.

And, as if the burning in my blood and my glow-in-the-dark skin aren't enough to cause worry, fate scores another point in this game that is now my life, solidly cementing my panic.

"This is the room," I whisper, speaking more to myself than the guys.

The room from my dream.

Vaulted bookshelves climbing walls that seem to go forever.

Tables scattered throughout the space, where people are reading and studying.

And, just like in my dream, all eyes are on me.

CHAPTER SEVEN

The more I look around the room, the stronger the sense I'm reliving that dream. It's not just the similarities of the space, but also the feeling that my legs can't move--that I couldn't get away if I tried.

Everyone is silent, from the men I came in with to the strangers staring at me. The spectators all wear black robes with their hoods drawn, really laying into the eeriness of the moment.

I feel my body moving toward the center of the hall, even though I'd swear my feet aren't doing the walking. It's like I'm being pulled by a magnet, and yet I know it's the magic swirling inside me that's doing the moving.

Before I know what's happening, I've fallen to the

ground and Zev is immediately beside me, catching all my weight in his strong arms.

"Your powers are surging, Bernie. Don't try to move."

I want to explain that I'm not trying to move, but speech evades me. From the corner of my eye, I see Andor running through the hall. The hooded faces turn to watch him go, then slowly look back at me. That trust I felt for Andor back in the hotel room is fading fast, as I can't help but think he's led us into a trap.

Darius...

I only need to think the vampire's name and he's at my shoulder, knowing what's needed and ready to take my blood. Still, I feel a hesitancy that's not normally there. He's usually so quick to drink me, but now I feel his face hovering inches away from my neck without making contact.

What's wrong? I ask

"Your skin is burning, Darius."

It's not the vampire who answers my question, but rather Rune. I turn my head back to see Darius' agonized face, smoke rising from his lips as he tries to help. I put my hand against his chest, trying to push him away even as he resists.

I must, he says. *You need me.*

He's not wrong. Whatever pain he's experiencing, I'm confident the burning in my body is worse. Nevertheless, I know his bite won't solve this. I don't know how I know, but it's clear to me.

I put my head down against the floor, trying to concentrate. Maybe I can control this shit, a little mind over matter. Though, it's not really matter, is it? Mind over inexplicable witch powers coursing through my veins trying to kill me from the inside. That's what I'm up against.

Zev and Darius stay close to me, each lending me their strength the best they can as I think of Tilly, how strong my Nanny was the last time I saw her. The calm grace she possessed while controlling an infantry of witches and saving my life. She was so old and frail, but she summoned her powers and made everything okay. *C'mon, Bernie. Just be more like Tilly.*

"*Távolítsuk.*"

The unrecognizable word comes from an unspecified source. My forehead is still against the stone floor, so I don't have any idea who might be around me chanting in Hungarian. While I don't know what's happening, I do know that a tight knot is forming in my chest. It's like a muscle is contracting, but also growing. Maybe I'm having a heart attack? Whatever it is, it doesn't feel great.

The knot grows and the pain magnifies. Just as it reaches an unbearable level, I lift my head off the floor to scream out, but it's not a sound that leaves my mouth. Instead, a ball of light bursts from my throat and into the air above my face. It shocks me into silence, and I'm mesmerized as I look into the shining, floating orb of power.

Because that's what it is. I know beyond a shadow of a doubt that I'm looking at my magic.

The orb of light floats away from me, and as my eyes trail behind it, they settle on the person who must have brought the powers out of me.

A beautiful elderly woman stands before us, her wand extended, pointed at the glowing circle, a look of thoughtful concentration on her face. She has red hair with streaks of silver, light gray eyes and strong cheekbones. If I'd been asked as a child to draw the prettiest old witch, this woman is exactly who I would have envisioned.

Andor stands beside her, a look of relief on his face as his eyes move between me and my floating powers. I glance down at my hands and see that the glow from my body has completely dimmed.

The burning is gone.

But there's an emptiness in its place.

"Hello, Bernadette," the woman says, her eyes still focused on controlling the light.

"You've taken her magic," Zev says, stating the obvious but with a little vinegar in his voice making it clear how he feels about the witch's intervention.

The woman shakes her head. "No one could take her abilities. Not so long as she and the baby are alive." Her wording is very particular and a little frightening. The way she speaks makes me wonder what side she's on. Is she about to kill me to prove her point?

"I've only pulled the magic out of her body," she goes on. "It will return to her the moment I release, and then we'll have to find another way to keep Bernadette from succumbing to her gifts."

Darius, who had been kneeling beside me to this point, rises.

"I'm able to help her. We have a blood bond that-_"

"That doesn't work in this Grand Hall," the woman responds, cutting him short. "I imagine you felt quite the discomfort when you tried to feed earlier. This room and the surrounding chambers are guarded by Fate spells as old as time. Perhaps as old as you."

If push came to shove on neutral ground,

Darius could probably take this woman down. In this room, however, it's clear who has the upper hand.

"Besides, you shouldn't be here in the first place, Darius."

The old witch knowing my vampire's name throws me for a loop. It's fine if everyone in the witching world knows who I am because of this prophecy bullshit, but I'm not ready for people to be calling my Sexies by name.

When I glance up to see how Darius is reacting to the unexpected recognition, he looks shocked. As I read his face and open myself to his feelings, I get the impression he's not surprised that she knew his name. I sense that he recognizes her as well.

I turn back to the witch, whose focus remains on the powers she's harnessed out of my body. "Bernadette," she says, "I'm going to return your strength to you. When I do, I want you to look to the sky and yell."

I reflexively look up, wondering if I can actually see the sky. Did she mean to say sky, or is she just generally referring to an upward direction--

My scattered thoughts disintegrate as I feel an explosion of magic hit every wall of my skeleton. I'm not sure if I've actually imploded, but I guarantee this is what spontaneous combustion feels like. Clearly, I've been regranted my powers.

As for yelling skyward, it's funny that she even bothered giving me that direction. The jolt of pain hits me so hard I have no choice but to throw my head back and cry to the heavens. When I do, it's like I've fired a flare out of my mouth. It shoots upward, a beacon of light moving through the darkness of this cavernous hall. The blaze continues on until it dwindles to a tiny speck and disappears in the abyss.

I take stock of myself, noting that there's a glow about me, but not an offensive one. Things appear to be in check… for now.

The woman seems happy with how this turned out, walking over and looking me up and down.

"You'll be better for the moment," she says. "But those moments will be fleeting until you learn your powers and find the tools to control them."

Naturally, I have fifty thousand follow-up questions, but the witch has already turned back to the Sexies, who still look like they've seen a ghost.

"Trying to remember the last time you saw me?" She poses the question to the group, indicating the familiarity doesn't stop with Darius.

None of the men answers for long, deafening

seconds. At last, Rune slightly bows his head. "Hello, Queen Erzébet."

My head snaps toward the fae. "Wait. How the shit do you know her?"

"Because," the witch named Erzébet says, "these three princes went to school with my daughter, Cara. We met a few times during those years. Then the race wars started. And then Cara was killed."

It takes a moment for my brain to piece together anything Erzébet just said, but the memories finally come trickling back. The sexy princes had schooled together and there was a fourth in their ranks, a woman from the witching realm. Something happened to her and that's when their relationships fractured.

Darius, Zev and Rune are all as stunned as I've ever seen. They're usually at least a little prepared for everything, but standing next to their old friend's mother apparently wasn't something they foresaw.

"And before you ask, Darius," Erzébet goes on, "I don't blame you for my daughter's death. Nevertheless, you can understand if we witches don't welcome vampires with open arms."

At this point I'm reminded that, throughout all of my recent trials and tribulations, we haven't been alone. The Grand Hall still has a few dozen onlookers, and it's being hinted that some of them may hate my vampire, which makes them instant enemies of mine.

"Needless to say," the witch queen says, "a vampire prince inside the final stronghold of the witching realm might put some of our order members on edge. Which reminds me..."

She turns away from Darius to look at Andor, who's been standing about ten feet away since running off and returning with help.

"Andor, for the love of the Fates, why did you bring three hostiles here?"

Andor, who had been in the midst of changing from the street clothes he wore to our hotel into his black robe, freezes. He slowly crosses his arms over his chest and it looks like his goal is to squeeze until he compresses to the size of a bug and can make an unseen getaway.

"I, um, I was not told there would be others with Bernadette," the little man answers. This day just hasn't gone to plan for poor Andor. "I was outnumbered, and they seem very... protective. So... I'm sorry."

Erzsébet fires a last disapproving look, then turns back to us. "Members of the Kő work to protect our shrinking numbers, though they have no powers of their own and are often put in situations for which they are outmatched."

"And then they turn us witches into concubines with their magical members?" I ask the question with an extra side of sass, thinking back to why Andor scheduled our 9 pm meeting and getting bothered by it all over again.

The witch queen raises an eyebrow, and it seems we have different opinions about the matter. "It's more the opposite, Bernadette. The status remains with the witch, while a man with allegiance to our cause helps to provide a child."

Provide a child doesn't quite jive with me, and I'm sure Erzsébet can tell.

"When you've lived through centuries of vampires and fae trying to infiltrate and decimate your species," she says, taking great care to look at both Darius and Rune as she makes her point, "you begin to take extra precautions with relations."

And with that, she walks off toward a corridor at the other end of the hall. We all waste zero seconds following, even though we've no clue where she's headed. We came here for answers, and we've finally found someone who might have them.

The Grand Hall is not lacking in grandness, as the walls stretch on forever. It's a never-ending series of bookshelves, and each shelf is packed. As we go, I see men and women walking through the space and giving us quick glances. It's only the men that have the hoods pulled over their heads, while all the women are more exposed. The women are also able to summon books from the shelves, the materials floating directly to them on command. The men, meanwhile, have to jump on floating ladders in order to reach whatever book they need next.

"So, is this just study hall?" I ask. "Witch school? The grown up version of Hogwarts?" A flutter of excitement replaces some of my worry. "What's everyone reading?"

Erzsébet keeps walking, answering over her shoulder without breaking stride.

"Spells," she says. "If a witch has created a spell, good or bad, useful or not, the record is kept here for future generations to learn. Normally you'd find more Kő members in here assisting the witches, but as the prophecy has come closer to fulfillment, their numbers have dwindled, for reasons I don't fully understand."

She reaches the end of the vast room, standing at a small entrance leading to a long, narrow hall. She finally turns back, looking into my eyes and, seemingly, all the way into my witching soul. "Nevertheless, our remaining women and men are studying and preparing for the hardships on the horizon. Most witches start to develop their magic at the age of eleven, twelve at the latest. You're behind."

And she's off again, walking briskly down the hallway as the rest of us trail behind.

At the end of the corridor, we reach another stone door. With a flick of Erzsébet's wand, the door slides open and we follow her through the threshold.

For some reason, I'd been expecting an office. This woman is clearly important, she knows a lot, so surely she's going to sit behind a desk, lean into her leather high-back chair, and tell us things. Now, on the other side of the door, it's clear I still have a very human way of thinking about things.

The small stone doorway has led us into a vast, magical, underground garden. Ferns and ivy and money trees with deep green leaves grow everywhere. Above us, sparkling crystals hang from the ceiling. Brightly colored birds fly from tree to tree, while an enchanting stream runs through the center of this spellbinding landscape.

Rune leans over next to a small fern that looks like it's been bedazzled. Tiny diamonds line the leaves, giving it an impeccable shine. "Amazing," the fae whispers to himself.

"Many witches use Asplenium crystals to tip their wands," Erzsébet says. "It's a small but powerful stone, magnifying light and strengthening spells."

I can't help but feel a child-like excitement when she talks about wands. I really hope she's about to give me one, and I hope it looks badass.

Erzsébet senses my anticipation. "You, however, are not most witches."

My dreams are momentarily dashed. I was about to run over and pluck a diamond off a plant, but I guess I'll hold off.

"Wands help us to control and guide our powers. They aren't a source of strength, but a means of focusing it." She stops to look at me, giving another thorough inspection that makes me feel important but also severely judged.

"You'll get nowhere if your magic overpowers your wand whenever you try to employ it, and that's exactly what will happen if you use the normal ingredients."

She steps away from us, the water coming up to meet her feet as she crosses the stream. When she reaches the center of the garden, Erzsébet waves her wand above her head, and as we look up, I see the most amazing display I've ever witnessed.

My mom conjured images from a fire, and in the

moment that was pretty dope. But now I'm staring at a ceiling covered in crystals, colors flooding the translucent spears to create a more vivid, HD image than any screen could ever present. A 3D image comes to life above, and I nearly fall backwards as I tilt my head back trying to take it all in.

Erzsébet first conjures a view of the Grand Hall, looking just as we'd left it.

"Is this right now?" I ask. "Are you able to see anywhere in the world?"

The witch smiles. "Universe, child." With another swipe of her wand, the view morphs to a familiar, worn down room, with a most familiar face wiping a spill off the copper countertop.

I gasp. "AJ."

There's my best friend in the world, larger than life on a screen made of crystals. And of course she ignored my pleas to stay away from my haunted pub. Bless her. She's just tending bar like the world is normal, though she knows better and is probably worried sick about me. God, I wish I could just teleport over there to give her a hug. Can witches do that? I'm going to need to schedule more time with this witch queen to ask questions unrelated to my current quest.

Erzsébet has a distant look on her face as she

watches the image she's conjured. "We've spent many an hour watching over Morgan's and Rowley. Watching Lauren devolve from a ray of hope to a breath away from the collapse of all witches was quite harrowing."

Yeah. Imagine what it was like being there.

"If you could see what was happening, why didn't you help?" My question is pointed, but I'm expecting a sensible answer. Erzsébet doesn't disappoint.

"We're not the only ones with powers, dear girl," she says with a trace of regret, like she wishes she could have done more. "Sending an envoy to you would have surely brought attention from others, and it's not like you weren't already in enough peril."

With that, she flicks her wrist again, dissolving the image of AJ and intensifying my heartache. The picture that takes its place, however, forces me to shift gears in a hurry.

We're now looking at the inside of a cave, also covered in crystals, though this one is much larger and without the beautifully tended garden.

"Jesus!"

I can't help but scream when a massive dragon flies through the image. It settles down in a corner of the cave, curling into a ball like an enormous, winged, fire-breathing dog.

"Where is that?" I ask, shock stifling my voice.

"Aggtelek Karst," Erzsébet answers. "Caves in the northern part of Hungary. Many people visit to see the beautiful formations within. If you look a little deeper... you find dragons."

"That's where my father is?"

Erzsébet pauses for a moment in thought. She searches the image in the crystals, like she's looking for him.

"We don't know," she finally says. "If he is, he's masked by a spell. More likely..."

"He's been eaten."

Zev doesn't always display tact when talking about death. This is one of those moments.

The witch nods and sighs, the crystals returning to their normal state as she offers a final flick or her wand and walks back to us. There's an elegance to her movement that reminds me of how my mother moved. I always thought it was the dancer training, but I'm beginning to think women with incredible powers just glide with confident grace.

"It was dangerous for your father to leave, and we told him so," Erzsébet says. "But he's spent more than twenty-five years preparing to help you, and there was no talking him down. Plus..." she starts, then hesitates as her eyes meet mine. It's a look I've received quite a few times in the last couple weeks. The look of a powerful being with powerful secrets, who's wondering if I'm strong enough to hear what they have to say. So far, I've been up to the challenge.

"Go on," I say.

"Your father wasn't wrong to go," she says with a shrug. "It may have cost him his life, but you'll get nowhere without dragon scales."

"What do you mean? Why not?"

"No other wand core can endure your force," Erzsébet answers. "We've seen but a fraction of your power, Bernadette. It will only get stronger until it kills you or you learn to control it. It would take years to master the right spells, so a powerful wand is the only solution. And dragon scales are the only foundation you won't immediately destroy."

Aside from the gentle babbling of the magical stream, there's complete silence. I look to Rune, who's doing nothing to hide his concern. Zev stands next to me, so close that our bodies touch, as is his way of offering comfort. I'm struck by the fact that this progress--meeting a powerful witch and beginning work on my wand--only pushes sand through the hourglass more quickly. It only brings me closer to the moment when my princes will leave. It's almost enough to make me want to stop trying.

I turn to look back at Darius, and his eyes are on the ground, though his thoughts mingle with mine.

I wish I was enough, he says.

You are, my prince. And more.

He looks up at me. I know that neither of us have felt a connection like this before, and I'm sure he's never been as helpless as he is in this moment.

I give him a soft smile, the most comfort I can offer, then turn back to Erzsébet.

"How do I kill a dragon?"

CHAPTER EIGHT

"My kind has a saying." Zev is the first to speak after a lengthy silence. Apparently there's no easy answer to my dragon-slaying question.

"If you want to kill a dragon," the werewolf says, "find an egg that's about to hatch and crush it."

The visual makes me a wee bit nauseous, and I try not to imagine this man I care so much about stomping dragon hatchlings to death.

"That's, um, pretty savage and awful," I say.

"I agree," Zev answers. "But it's the only way to kill the beasts, as far as we werewolves can tell."

"Is there no magic?" I ask Erzsébet. "A spell I can cast or a potion I can use?"

She shakes her head. "Any spell that might kill a

dragon is not one we wish to invoke. The creature need not die for you to get a scale."

Oh. I kinda wish she'd led with that. "So we just zip in, grab a scale and leave?"

Again, the witch's head shakes. "The dragons don't readily want to part with their protective plates. If you looked down and saw a mouse removing your toe, things likely wouldn't end well for the mouse."

Solid analogy, Erzsébet. Feels like she may have used that one before.

I'm about to give the queen props for her word-play when a deep red hue falls over the room, shining down on us from the crystals above. I'm immediately reminded of the shifting colors when I was in the woods with my mother and the Order, and I know this can't be good.

Erzsébet waves her wand toward the ceiling and an image appears of the square above ground where we first came in. There's the normal flow of pedestrians going about their evening, some locals, many tourists. It's the small group standing near the stone that gave way to the staircase who give me pause. They are all clad in black cloaks with black breeches and shirts beneath, and they are studying the humans like they might be dinner. Their skin is pale, almost translucent under the moonlight. And their eyes look just like Darius' when he's about ready to feed.

I suck in my breath. "Vampires."

"Darius..." Erzsébet says, her eyes still on the vision above.

"I've taken an unbreakable oath," the vampire answers before an accusation can be leveled against him. "I'm bound to Bernie, as are Zev and Rune. Any visitor from my realm wants me dead as much as they want the baby."

Erzsébet remains focused on the ceiling, the vision traveling through the cement and earth, looking to see if any assailants have discovered the entryway. By my count, I see ten or eleven vampires, none underground yet.

"Well," the witch says, turning around after she's seen all she needs to in the crystals. "Let's hope this one is stronger than the pact you three made with my daughter."

She leaves us with that parting gut punch and glides out the door and into the hallway. I turn to look at the men, none of whom have started to follow.

"Do we fight?" Rune asks, glancing down at my child's head resting against his chest in a nap.

"If we do," Zev says, starting for the doorway,

"best we do it in these halls where the Fate's magic is on our side."

Darius nods in agreement, and then is out the door before I can blink. The three of us rush after.

"We're under siege, and you all have jobs to do."

I hear Erzsébet's voice echoing from the Grand Hall, loud but controlled. She doesn't have to say anything else before the men and women in her order are on the move. As I get to the end of the hallway, I see dozens of bookshelves lifting like garage doors, allowing witches and Kő members to quickly come and go from the main room.

Some witches grab books from shelves before they exit. Others command books with their wands, bringing them under their feet and turning them into antique, literary hoverboards. They fly on books into the vast space, and it's undeniably cool.

I stand in a tight group with the Sexies, and it takes a moment before I notice Andor is also by my side.

"Don't you have a station or whatever?" I ask.

He just looks back and offers a weak smile. "Here," he says. "Protecting you."

As the activity settles and everyone gets where they need to be, a quiet falls over the hall. It's the kind of deafening silence that makes you wish someone would speak.

Maybe they can't get in? I think to Darius.

Perhaps not as fast as they like, but they'll get in.

A loud bang sounds through the room, coming from somewhere above. Moments later, another one follows. Then another.

"They're breaking through the walls," Rune says softly.

"It's just the ten or eleven we saw, right? Or are there more coming?" I ask. Since we survived the first onslaught of fae, I'm a little worried we're about to be outnumbered ten-to-one by the undead.

"Probably not," Darius says, calming my nerves a little but quite possibly lying to make me feel better. "They'll send more if this mission fails, but none of the kingdoms wish to leave their homelands unprotected. Warriors for all of us are in short supply."

Makes sense, and I guess I'll take the short-term good news over the long-term bad.

Another loud thud sends dust fluttering down from the wall over the main entrance. Seems like the wall thumping vampires are making some headway.

"What will the Fate's magic do to protect us?" I ask, a lump of fear in my throat making me almost inaudible.

"Probably just make the vampire's hands burn while they rip our limbs off."

And with a little parting gallows humor from Zev, the wall above the Grand Hall entrance explodes into the room.

Before the slabs of stone have hit the ground, bursts of light shoot toward the entrance and turn the room into a fireworks display. I notice that Darius has left my side, but before I can freak out about it he's back.

"Rune, cover Bernie," he says. "They're moving around the room trying to find--"

Before he can finish, two fangs are in my face, attached to a terrifying face with bloodshot eyes. I feel hands on my belly, like the creature's searching for my child. The way his fingers dig into my flesh, he might think the baby's still inside of me.

The invasion of my space, the chilling sensation of the fingers on my body, and the general horror rooted in our situation all lend themselves perfectly to some accidental magic. I shove my hands forward and the vampire in front of me both catches on fire and flies through the air in the opposite direction. I look down at my hands, wishing I understood what I did and could do it again.

"Let's get Bernie and Rain out," Rune says. "No

need to press our luck and hope for another burst of power that might not come."

I don't try to argue. It's my child the vampires are after, and I've got no control over these crazy hands of mine. No reason to think I'll avoid killing the people I want to keep safe.

"Back through the opening?" Zev asks. "The vampires have given us plenty of room--"

He stops talking just in time to dive out of the way as fire shoots past us. Bodies are running and flying through the room, though most are Kő members thrown violently by vampires. One flailing figure lands with a sickening thud at my feet, the life instantly crushed out of the poor man.

"Wherever we're going, let's do it sooner than later," I say.

"Go back to the garden," Andor says, still a few feet from my side. His face is ashen as he looks down at his fallen comrade. Something tells me this is the first time Andor's witnessed death and I very much empathize.

"There's a tunnel that leads further underground." Andor finally looks up and meets my eyes, his own brimming with tears. Just as he opens his mouth to give more guidance, he's swept off his feet by a blurring figure. He screams, the sound rapidly growing distant as the vampire races Andor toward the exploded entrance.

"Go," Darius says to all of us. "Get to the garden and find the tunnel. I'll guard the entrance."

I'd protest, but I'm learning that's just a waste of time. With Zev and Rune at either side, we break for the hallway. I look back to see if Darius is following, but he's already in a scrape with one of our attackers. He's quickly got the lesser vampire lifted above his head, making me feel good about his odds of coming out on top.

Before we can reach the exit, two vampires flash in front of us, blocking the path.

"Left," Rune says, walking forward with my baby clasped tightly under one arm. I'm not sure what he means or who he was talking to, but before I can think on it, a shifted-Zev pounces on the attacker to the left. At the same time, Rune approaches the other vampire, walking over calmly as though he's going to ask for directions.

Just before the vampire can lunge at him, Rune divides into eight different bodies. I'm sure he doesn't actually do that, but my eyes are very convinced of the existence of seven extra Runes.

Mine aren't the only deceived eyes, as the vampire spins in a circle, swiping at the fae that now surround him. Each strike simply passes through the illusion, the vampire growing more confused and furious by the mystified attack. At last, the real Rune sweeps his leg under the vampire, knocking the teetering adversary off his feet. As the vampire falls, the fae throws a fistful of powder into his face. A horrifying shriek fills the hall as Rune's foe tears at his burning eyes.

By the time I look away from that match, Zev's attacker is already scurrying in the other direction, and it looks like he's holding his own detached arm. When the situation calls for it, my werewolf goes off.

He stays in wolf form and rushes over to me, crouching so I can climb onto his back. Rune has already started down the hall, the two princes working with a coordination that reminds me they've known each other for a really long time. It's like Zev and Darius' sexy striptease, except not sexy and Zev bit off a guy's arm.

I grab hold of the wolf's fur and he sprints toward Rune, catching up to and passing the fae in seconds. When we reach the stone door, it's immediately clear that we've got a new problem.

"How do we open it?" I say, staring at the hole where a magical key would go. Zev's still a wolf, and probably doesn't have much experience picking locks with his paws. I look at Rune, who's already scanning the hallway for another way into the garden. It's comforting to know the witches have strong defenses, but it's a real bitch being on the wrong side of one of their doorways.

This corridor that once felt like an escape route now seems like more of a death trap. Without access to the garden, we're just stuck here, waiting for the vampires to attack.

I look down at my hands, hoping to see charged fingertips ready to pry open a can of magic whoopass. The glow is there, but I don't feel the surge.

Maybe if I aim my hands at the door. Who knows, my magic might just need some clearer intention before it does my bidding. I try pointing my fingers and then lifting my palms, testing different angles that might let out some zesty light.

Nothing. I don't know what my powers are, much less how to control them. I'm the only hope we've got, and I feel absolutely hopeless.

And then the door slides open.

For a brief moment, I credit my pity party. I got so scared and sad that my magic did what I wanted. When I see Erzsébet's face on the other side, I know that's not the case.

"Inside," she says. "Quickly."

Zev rushes us through with Rune and Rain on

our heels. The door flies shut right after Rune gets in, crushing the outstretched arm of a vampire as it closes.

"Those pesky monsters are so fast," Erzsébet says, showing she's flustered in the most charming way.

"Bernadette, you already know where you're going," the witch says, announcing something I don't believe to be true. "Rune, you and I will shield the child. I expect they'll make it into the garden, but at that point we'll manage."

"Hang on," I say, climbing down from Zev's back. "I don't know where I'm going."

Erzsébet smiles at me. The calm she keeps while her world gets attacked and her proteges get killed makes no sense, but that's probably why she's been alive forever.

"But you do know," she says with a wink. "Because I showed it to you in your dream."

She offers no other information, just takes my hand and gives me a reassuring squeeze. I glance down at her fingers wrapped around mine, and I really don't want to let go. I'm terrified of witch life without this woman here to guide me, even though we just met. As I'm staring at our hands, I notice she's placed a small piece of paper in my palm.

"For the dragons," she says with a final smile.

After that, she rushes toward Rune. "Let's conceal here," she says to the fae. "Hide me until they start searching the walls, then the others will flood in."

I guess Rune doesn't need any more detail than that, as he and Erzsébet instantly disappear into a mesh of ferns and flowers.

The garden is suddenly very still, the trickling of the stream the only source of sound.

Until the vampires start slamming against the wall.

Having seen what they did to the Grand Hall, I know the garden door will be crashing down in no time. That means I've got seconds to figure out how the hell to get out of here. I shove the piece of paper into my pocket and start searching the room for something that will spark my memory.

It's not that I don't remember the dream--it's as vivid now as it was this morning. But it didn't lead me to the garden, just from the river to the main room.

The river?

I walk over to the stream, peering into the waters. Instead of a shallow creek, I'm looking into a deep trench. The water flows gently, but it goes much deeper than I expected. As I stare into the depths, the water stills and clarifies, just as the river did earlier in the day. I see all the way to the bottom of the trench where there are two separate tunnel entrances.

Just like the dream.

I turn to Zev, who's got his hackles up as he faces the door. There are now cracks in the stone; it's not going to stand up to many more blows.

"Can you swim?"

He looks over his wolf shoulder, first at me and then down to the water. In answer to my question, he moves to me as he morphs back into human form, now naked by my side.

"I hate water as a wolf," he says. "I'll tolerate it as a man. Guide me."

I'm about to describe my plan when the wall starts to crumble. Instead of speaking, I just grab Zev's hand and jump into the narrow channel.

We splash through the surface and swim down. Once we're below the banks of the stream, the walls open up and it's like we're in an underground swimming pool. There's plenty of room to maneuver and small silver fish swim around us, creating a shimmer that's obviously meant to light our way. This is without a doubt the world's best pool.

I flip around and start kicking, swimming as fast as I can toward the bottom. In my dream I went into the entrance on the right, so that should take us back to the river entrance next to the city street.

That's not where I want to go, though.

I want to go find dragons.

I also don't want to pop up with a naked werewolf in the heart of Budapest.

Unlike my dream, I'm not afraid of passing into the dark entrance. The only thing pulling me back is that my little girl is in a room full of vampires, and I'm just leaving. I know it's the right choice, and I trust Rune with all of our lives, but that doesn't make it easy.

I feel Zev swimming alongside and just behind me, and with a final push through the water we go into the cave to the left.

Even though we'd been swimming downward, I burst up through the surface of the water as we come out on the other side of the entrance. There's a subtle blue glow coming off the water, otherwise it's completely dark. I don't know where we are and I definitely don't know where we should go.

Zev bursts through the water next to me, inhaling deeply as he does. I hear soft splashing as he looks to the left and the right, trying to get his bearings.

"There's only one direction to go," he says, his wolf vision much sharper than my lame, human sight. He pulls himself up onto solid ground, and the glow from the stream gives me just enough light to watch water cascade down his naked form. His body is perfect, and its perfection is further magnified when wet.

He reaches a hand down and helps pull me up, my momentum carrying me into his body. His arms immediately wrap around me, and it would seem this hug was no accident.

"Where do you think we are?" I ask, keeping myself pressed against him. The warmth feels good with my clothes soaking wet.

"You tell me," he says. "According to Erzsébet, you know exactly where you're going."

As much as I want my powers to manifest fully, I'm not ready to move on from having these princes guide me and carry me and answer all my questions. Now that we're in witch territory and I'm having dreams planted by the witch queen, my responsibilities are on the rise and it scares the shit out of me.

"We're in a cave, trapped between vampires and dragons," I say, doing my best to imitate Erzsébet's calm.

Zev smiles, our faces just inches apart. Despite how often it's happened since these three beautiful men came into my life, I'm still surprised with how quickly fear turns into lust. Of course it's more than that with Zev, our connection running much deeper than our physical beings.

"What do you suppose we should do while we're here?" the werewolf asks with a sly grin.

"Probably find some dragons so I can build a wand before I incinerate," I joke back.

"Sounds like a fine plan," Zev says, stepping out of our embrace but keeping my hands in his. "If nothing else, their fiery breath will warm us up after that swim."

We turn, hand in hand, and start walking into the darkness. I can't see, but I know where I'm going. My clothes are drenched, but the touch of Zev's hand keeps me warm. I miss my girl with all my heart, but I know I'm doing what's right for both of us. Everything is chaos, danger, and uncertainty, and yet, in this moment, I'm right where I want to be.

CHAPTER NINE

I have no idea how long we've been walking or what time it is. A handful of hours have passed since Andor showed up at our hotel, but I doubt it's light out yet in the real world. I'd ask Zev if he has a guess about the time, but I'm sure he doesn't know or care.

"What did Erzsébet give you back in the garden?" he asks.

This is the first I've thought about the paper, and I immediately panic because it's stuffed in the pocket of my sopping-wet jeans. I reach in to retrieve it--and pull out a miraculously dry piece of parchment.

"Oh my God," I say. "It's not wet."

Zev laughs. "It seems as though the witch knew we'd be going into the water. Would have been a dastardly move to give you an important paper that couldn't handle the trip."

I unfold the note, though there's no reason to do so as it's too dark for me to read. I hold it out for Zev to inspect.

"Looks like an incantation," he says. "Let's put it back in your pocket until we can read it properly. I think we should take our time when you cast your first spell so you don't turn me into a goat."

I laugh, and grip his hand a little tighter. It's unfair for a man to be so handsome and so charming. And on top of that, he's mine, fated to me. It's all a little too much to handle, frankly.

"So… Erzébet," I say, opening up a discussion we didn't have time for in the Grand Hall. "You all know her?"

"Somewhat," Zev says with a shrug. "We knew her daughter very well, but met the queen only a few times. The last time we saw her was right before Cara and Darius traveled to meet the king of the vampires, Darius' father."

Zev's voice is barely above a whisper by the end of his sentence, and it doesn't take a genius to piece together how Cara died. If Darius was the last of the three princes to be with Cara before the vampires killed her, that explains the dissolving of any friendships.

I'm yanked out of my thoughts--physically and mentally--when Zev stops walking but keeps holding my hand. I look at him, his eyes glued to mine, a curious look on his face.

"We need to stop here," he says.

"Why? It's pitch black and we don't know where we are."

"We're getting close," Zev says. "The air's getting thicker. Dragon's breath."

I trust the werewolf's senses, even if I can't sense these things myself. And how freaking thick is dragon's breath?

"And, a more important reason..."

He trails off as he steps toward me. I can barely see him, but I can absolutely feel him.

"I need to warm you."

Just the words leaving his lips light a fire in my belly. *Mission accomplished, sexy wolf.*

My heart is instantly aflutter, beating against my ribcage with a rhythmic force that feels almost alarming. Zev circles behind me and slips his hands around my waist. I lean into his chest as he bends his neck to whisper into my ear, his lips teasing the tip of my earlobe, sending shivers down my spine.

"No sense being uncomfortable now that we're safe," he says softly.

I snort in a very unladylike way. "Safe?" I say, my voice growing serious. I twist in his arms so that I'm facing him, his hands gripping my hips now, my arms resting on the hardened muscles of his chest. "Just because we're closer to the dragons than the vampires?"

He doesn't answer with his voice, but his gaze says yes. Wherever we were and wherever we're headed, this is the calm of the storm. Zev's green eyes darken as they stay locked with mine, becoming clouded with a need that pierces straight through all of my defenses. He tightens his grip on me, pulling me closer to him. I raise my arms, letting my hands fall to his neck, pressing my breasts into him, wishing we had far fewer clothes between us.

And then I notice the darkness around us brightening slowly, but distinctly, and it takes me a moment to realize I'm the cause. I'm literally lighting the cave up with my glowing skin.

I attempt to step away from Zev, worried I might hurt him, but he refuses to release me, and instead closes whatever microscopic distance remains between us. I suck in my breath, my mind and body at odds with each other. I want to protect Zev from... well, from me. But I also am desperate to be closer to him. A primal need has been growing between us, amplified in ways impossible to ignore after he bit my shoulder during that bath. It feels like that was a lifetime ago, yet the memory is still so fresh.

"Why do you pull away?" he asks, his gaze demanding and intoxicating.

"You saw what I almost did to Darius." Even now, the thought of his lips burning as he tried to feed from me makes me sick to my stomach.

"I can handle your heat," he says gruffly.

I'm trying to think of the perfect comeback for his perfect line, when he silences whatever I would have said with his lips against mine.

His hands spread over my back, working their way down my hips to my ass as his tongue pushes open my lips and his kiss deepens.

I moan into his mouth, momentarily forgetting my fear of blasting him with my witch magic, as I wrap my hand around his neck and pull him closer still.

His heart beats against my chest, our bodies in rhythm to each other as our passions grow.

Before I get swept away by him, I try to grasp any remaining coolheadedness I might still have access to.

This is insane.

I can't do this in a random cave with dragons God knows how close by, while my baby is with Rune and Darius in a fight for their lives, while everything hangs in the balance of me not blowing myself up.

Zev seems to notice my shift in mood, and he lifts his head, breaking contact with my mouth, which is a real disappointment if I'm being honest.

He lifts his thumb and traces it along my forehead. "You've got too many worries, love," he says. "There's no point in dwelling on what's out of our control."

"But--"

He kisses me again, this time pinning me against the cave wall as he does. "But nothing. Rain is safe. I trust Rune with my life--and hers--and yours." He kisses my forehead, where he just ran his thumb over. "Darius is safe. That man is frustratingly hard to kill. He also has something...someone...to live for now." He pauses, his eyes scanning my face for signs that I understand what he's saying.

"Me?" I ask, surprised.

"Of course you. And Rain too. We are all devoted to her. But you, my love," he kisses my cheek this time, and the five-o-clock shadow framing his jaw tickles my skin. "You, we live for." And then his mouth finds mine again, and the passion between us explodes into fireworks in my soul as Zev's fire burns out of him and into me, both of us burning from within.

Any trace of cold leaves my body the second Zev starts to undress me. He works slowly, deliberately, taking his time to peel the wet fabric away from my skin. As he does, I admire the view in front of me, drinking in the sculpted chest and abs I will never tire of seeing.

As he unbuttons my blouse, he somehow snaps open my bra at the same time. My eyes widen in surprise and he chuckles, his hands exploring the shape of my breasts, starting from my ribcage and working up until he's cupping them both.

I reach down and hold the hardness growing between his legs as he rolls his fingers over my nipples, sending shivers of desire and pleasure into the core of my body.

I arch into him, wanting more of his hands on me, needing to feel him everywhere, to quench this desire.

While I don't want his kneading to stop, I also want something more. I move my hands to his hips, dropping to my knees as I do, letting my hair, then my mouth tease the hard length of him.

He growls, the deep thrum of it echoing throughout the cave, and his fingers dig into my hair as I flick my tongue out tentatively.

I feel a whole other kind of power rise up in me with him, the kind that comes from a connection that defies logic or reason. A connection that cuts straight to the soul.

When I take him in my mouth, his pleasure is mine, his ecstatic need is mine… and I feel our destinies knot together into something that can never be broken.

With a jerk, Zev pulls away, and I nearly topple over, as I was precariously balanced on the balls of my feet as I knelt.

He catches me, helping me stand, his eyes a storm. "I'm sorry."

"Did I… did I do something wrong?" Even as I say the words, I regret letting them leave my mouth. I sound too… desperate. Too insecure, and I don't like that.

But Zev grabs my arms and pulls me to him. "Nothing could be further from the truth. But I need to… tell you something."

My stomach clenches in fear of what he's about to say. It seems serious. And so I do my best to prepare for a broken heart.

"Did you," he begins, seeming unsure of his words. "Could you, could you feel a connection forming between us?"

My breath hitches. "Yes." If he's asking me this, he must have felt it too. I can't help but feel hope rise in my chest.

"I've told you that you are my mate."

I nod. I've been wanting to have this conversation since he said that to me, but I've been too scared of what it all might mean--with him and with the others.

"You need to know what will happen if we..." his voice trails off, so I nudge him along.

"What will happen if we...?" But even as I ask the question, I feel the answer within. It is already happening. The bond has already begun to form.

He nods as if reading my mind. "It might already be too late to stop it," he says, looking pained as he speaks. "But if you want to stop it, I will try." He's gritting his teeth now, as if this conversation is really causing him harm.

"Do you not want that with me?" I try to make my voice sound big, strong, confident, but I don't think I succeed even a little.

"Not at all. That's not it. I don't want you to feel forced. For those of my kind, our wolves mate with their Chosen in a primal way. I have no control over it. But I am also a man, and that I do have control over. So I will not force you to be my mate."

My heart feels brittle, and I try not to take everything he's saying as a rejection, but I'm a bit too fragile to pull it off entirely.

"I don't want you to feel trapped in something because of your wolf," I say, feeling suddenly far too exposed half-naked in a cave with a werewolf.

He growls again, and I can feel the rumble in his chest as he pulls me closer. "Are you daft, woman? I want you. I'm... apparently very badly, asking if you want me. If you want this. If we keep going, our fates will be sealed to one another for life. There will be no breaking it."

I shiver at the promise in those words and I have no fear of sharing fates with him. I have only one fear that needs to be addressed. "What about Darius? And... Rune?" I don't know what's going on with me and Rune, but there's a connection there I cannot deny, even if it hasn't been acted on.

He frowns, and I fear the coming response. If I had to choose between them, what would I do? Picking only one would mean breaking other pieces of my heart. There's no way I come out whole from this.

"Normally," he says, "a wolf doesn't allow other mates to his Chosen."

My stomach clenches in worry of what his next words will be.

"However, a normal Chosen wouldn't be a witch. And I wouldn't share a pledge with your other suitors. You... you are different. For all three of us. And when we bound ourselves to you, we bound ourselves to each other as well, as a byproduct of the sacred oath."

My stomach flips, my mind rushing to piece together the meaning of his words. "Are you saying..."

"I'm saying that Darius and Rune are now part of our pack, love. The three of us have already spoken about this. I'm saying, you don't have to choose just one of us if you don't want to."

And just like that, a great dam is released inside me, and this time I claim his lips, pouring into him everything I have been holding back out of fear.

He accepts my answer, spoken with my body rather than words, and wraps himself around me, trying to move us both closer to each other.

But I need to not have pants on for us to make any progress with this goal, so I begin to slip out of them, with Zev quick to help in pulling them down.

I kick them away as Zev guides my last remaining

piece of clothing off my hips, his fingers lightly brushing between my legs, where all the heat and ache is gathering in me.

I bite my lip and try to keep my body relaxed as my underwear drops to the floor and Zev cups my ass and positions his mouth at the perfect spot between my legs.

I'm nearly undone with one flick of his tongue, and I lean against the cave wall, ignoring the stone scraping my skin raw, as Zev treats my body like an all you can eat buffet. I'm writhing in pent up need and nearly at the edge of the cliff about to fly off when he pulls away and raises his body to meet mine.

"You're evil," I breathe, everything in me desperate for the release he promised with his mouth and his fingers.

He slips his arms behind me to support me more, so I don't get torn apart by the wall, and as he nudges my legs apart with his knee, he kisses and nips at my neck and shoulder. "Are you ready?" he asks softly.

I nod. God am I ever.

He bites my shoulder as he thrusts himself into me and I can't help but scream from the delicious blend of pain mixed with the explosive pleasure he offers. My arms are wrapped around him, my nails

KARPOV KINRADE & EVAN GAUSTAD

digging into his back as our bodies unite as one. His thrusts are strong, deep, and powerful, and I hold on to him harder. His hands grip my ass tightly, fingers digging into my flesh, keeping me positioned for the most optimal angle.

I feel the waves crashing and am lost in the forest of his eyes, the feel of his skin against mine, the feel of him inside me. Nothing else exists, and when we both reach the edge of that cliff together, I sink my teeth into his shoulder and bite, and together we fly.

IT'S NOT until the pulsing of pleasure in my body slows, until we are holding each other on a smooth stretch of stone floor, until the quietness returns, that I feel what is new to feel between us. It is a binding stronger than blood, a soul connection so powerful I know to my core I am changed because of it.

Just as sharing blood back and forth with Darius has made us part of each other in a way that just sex could never do, so too has this experience with Zev been so much more than mere physical pleasure--as mind-blowing as it's been. There is a tether between us that cannot be broken. And I feel a warm sense of belonging that is growing stronger with each of these beautiful men. He is also glowing slightly, his skin casting the same sheen as mine is, though not quite as brightly. My glow, and the pain caused by it, has dimmed since we made love, which has me wondering how this will affect him, being bound to a bomb waiting to explode.

As our heartbeats settle into a new, slower, more relaxed pace together, I finally muster the courage to ask him the question that has been weighing on me, making me feel--unworthy, perhaps. Undeserving, certainly.

These are not emotions I enjoy having exposed to the light, reflected in the most polished mirror of love's pure shine.

And yet to ignore them altogether, to turn a blind eye to my darker thoughts, would be to fester them into something truly terrorizing.

So I expose my heart and I ask. "How is it I can be your mate, when I'm not a werewolf? Won't you be missing something... not being mated to your own kind?"

This question holds so much fear that I am not enough, not enough for Zev, the passionate, deep, unexpectedly brilliant man who is also part wolf. That I am not enough for the mysterious, dark and dashing vampire, with hidden secrets in his past and eyes of a depth I could never escape from. That I am not enough for the beautiful fae who has lost so much and even still gave up more to save me and my daughter. Who has been nothing but kind and pure. Who holds within him so much power, and yet does not use it with ill intention. That I--a silly normal human--am not enough.

And yes, maybe I'm also witch, and maybe I can sometimes shoot lightning out of my mouth, but it doesn't change who I see when I look in the mirror. And it is not a person that could capture the hearts of three incredible beings of magic.

"I may not be a vampire, but that doesn't mean I can't tell what you're thinking, love." Zev's words are soft, kind, as he cups my face in his hands.

We tangle our legs together, our bodies still craving each other too much for either of us to consider moving away.

"What am I thinking?" I ask, wondering if he really can tell.

He shakes his head, then leans in to kiss me. "You are more than you know. And not because you're a witch," he says, kissing me again. "And not because you're part of a prophecy." Each sentence is punctuated with a tender brushing of his lips against mine. "But because of who you are at the core, Bernadette Morgan." He caresses my cheek, his deep forest green eyes penetrating mine. "Darius has been feeding on you. Rune has been in your mind. I have bonded my soul to you. We each have glimpsed parts of your core, your truth. We know what we see when we look at you, and if you can't see that person, you need to take a closer look, because you're missing out."

I can't help the tears that leak from my eyes, and I try to avert my head, to hide my sudden burst of emotion, but Zev holds my face in his hand as he swipes at my tears with his thumb, gently drying my cheek. We both move in at the same time, our lips seeking each other. And this time, as we claim each other's bodies with only the old stone walls as witness, we take our time, exploring every inch, memorizing every curve, tasting and pleasuring and enjoying each other for the few remaining hours of the night.

When morning comes, and the urgency of our quest weighs upon us once more, I stretch and roll over, facing my lover.

His eyes are still closed and I take a moment to study his face. I long to crawl into his arms and never leave, but I know sooner or later, he and the others will have to go home without me. What will happen with our mate bond then? Will we be in pain? Will the loss eat at us? I want to ask, but I also don't want to know. So when he smiles and opens his eyes, I smile back at him, pushing away the dark thoughts for a later time. I can't change what will be, but I can stay present long enough to enjoy what I have now. And right now, I have my werewolf mate in my arms.

"Ready to sweet talk a dragon out of its hide?" he asks.

I grin and kiss him more deeply, speaking into his lips, my breath mingling with his. "Ready as I'll ever be."

CHAPTER TEN

It's a small piece of paper, insignificant and insanely powerful at the same time.

The spell Erzsébet gave to me before we left sits in my palm, a bit of thick parchment with two Hungarian words scrawled across it in a very inky and fancy font: *felfed* and *pálya*. "Reveal" and "path". All I can do is guess how casting this spell works and what it will do. I assume it's going to guide us through the maze of caves to the dragon's lair. And if I'm wrong… well, surprise is on us.

It's also technically my first official spell as a witch. Which is kind of exciting and makes me feel accomplished, like I've finally graduated junior high after years of not making grades.

I stare down at the small slip of waterproof paper,

trying my best to stay focused on our mission. And to not think about how my daughter is doing, feeding from a bottle without her mom there to help. Or how Rune and Darius are doing, if they even survived the attack.

They did. I have to believe they did. I feel like I would sense if something happened to them.

Zev walks up behind me--still naked since he refuses to accept any of my clothing, arguing that he's more adept at keeping himself warm and can always shift to wolf form when needed--and pulls me against his chest, his hands gripping my hips. "Soon we'll have the scale and then rejoin the others by this evening. She's okay."

I bend my head back to look up at him and smile. My expression clearly gave away my thoughts. "I know. It's just..."

He kisses my head. "Hard," he says, finishing my sentence. "Of course it is. It's by design. Some moments must be hard, must have weight, must make us fight for them. That is how we know we have found something of true value in our lives. That is how we know what's worth living for."

"What if I can't control my magic for that long?" I ask, expressing my other super stressor.

"Our mate bond is helping siphon some of the

extra energy," he says. "It should be enough until we get back to Darius. And maybe between the two of us, you'll have an easier time."

I seal those words with a kiss, then reluctantly pull away.

Zev nods that he's ready, so I take the slip of paper and read aloud the Hungarian spell.

At first, nothing happens. I look at the words and the accent marks, making sure I'm pronouncing it correctly. I can't think of what I did wrong. Two words in and I'm very frustrated by being a witch.

"Try, um…" Zev seems tentative about telling me how to use my powers, as he should. I do appreciate his effort to avoid full mansplaining, or were-mansplaining, as the case may be. "Try saying the words like you mean them. Not like you're reading Hungarian for the first time."

It's annoying, condescending, incredibly accurate advice.

When I try a second time--thinking about the words, our mission, my goals-- the sound of my voice ignites a glowing ball of light. It's about the size of a baseball, pulsing with the ebb and flow of its essence. It bounces twice in the air, then moves forward a bit.

"I think it wants us to follow it," I say, checking if Zev sees what I'm seeing.

He nods and gives my arm a gentle, affirming squeeze. "Let's be off."

The glowing light keeps pace with us. If we speed up, so does it. If we slow down, it does as well, but if we stop for too long, it starts to bounce again until we pick up the pace.

That could get real annoying real fast, but fortunately, we're in a hurry and it seems, based on Zev's sniffing, that we're not too far off.

It brings some small comfort that we don't have to kill the dragon. I'm far too fond of their mythology to harm a real, live one. I can't believe I'm even going to be getting this close to a real freaking dragon! My life is bananas.

We are both quiet as we walk, lost in thoughts as vast as this new world I've found myself in. When I left New York--along with my dreams of a career in music--I thought I knew what every day for the rest of my life would look like, more or less.

Some people may find that comforting, but for me it felt claustrophobic, like the constraints of my narrowing world were suffocating me. Now, I always seem to be one step away from dying, but I'm so much more alive as well.

I smile to myself as I realize how much happier

I've been since the three of them walked into my bar, despite all the craziness.

"What's brightened up your somber mood?" Zev asks, breaking the comfortable silence. He slips an arm around my waist as we walk, pulling me closer. "Perhaps memories of earlier?" He nuzzles my neck with his nose and I laugh and shove him away playfully.

"No… but now that I think about it, yes," I say. "I was just thinking that I can't imagine my life without you. Any of you."

My joy in the moment is shadowed by the understanding that the closer I get to mastering my powers, the closer we come to saying goodbye.

Zev senses the shift in my mood and pulls me into an embrace even as our guide ball bounces in place impatiently.

"You'll never be without me. Our mate bond will always connect us, no matter the distance. And I will come back to you. All that I do, I do so that we can be together and so you and Rain can be safe."

His lips find mine, and I am lost in him once again, the taste of his fire in my mouth consuming me.

We are both breathless when the kiss ends, and I

grip his hand as we continue our walk together, lost in thoughts of what if.

Lord, what a beautifully messy bed I've made for myself.

After a few twists and turns through narrow passages and enormous, cavernous rooms, our little guide begins to change color, first turning a very pale pink, then slightly darker the further along we follow.

"I think we're getting close," I say, and as if to confirm my suspicion we feel a growing heat fill our lungs. The air is thick with the scent of burnt wood, smoke, and something else. "Please tell me I'm not smelling what I think I'm smelling," I say, covering my nose with part of my shirt and gagging at the stench.

Zev nods, surely having noticed the scent a mile back. "That's the smell of burnt flesh."

Suddenly my excitement about seeing my first dragon is overshadowed by my fear of being a flesh-kabob. The fear for my own safety is compounded with a worry that I'm about to see the charred corpse of my father.

We continue walking much more slowly now, creeping and staying to the walls like we might blend in better that way. I can tell Zev is on the edge of shifting at any moment. I glare at my hands, willing them to produce magic on demand, but I feel nothing to indicate they might obey.

The tunnel we're walking through begins to widen into a larger cavern where sections of the stone wall are charred with ash. This cave is no stranger to fiery dragon breath.

The smells intensify, and my eyes burn from the noxious fumes permeating the air. Let's hope Rune has a potion for whatever damage this is doing to my insides.

Ahead and to our right another narrow pathway widens into a cavern, and the long tail of a dragon peeks out through it, winding around itself.

We both freeze.

I can hardly breathe.

And not just because it stinks in here.

"Let me have a look first," Zev whispers. He doesn't give me a chance to respond, going straight into wolf mode. The grace and ease with which he moves along the uneven floor make it clear he's relieved to be in wolf form for this part.

A sharp and unexpected ache seizes me as I realize this is a part of his life I'll never be able to share. I will always be a witch, never a wolf. He'll never run with his mate through the forest under a full moon; or howl in harmony at the edge of a cliff; or share that bond that must be so special.

I shake my head, pulling myself back to the present circumstances where I'm less than twenty feet from a very real dragon and my mate is about to get close enough to it to become its next appetizer.

I clench my teeth and take deep breaths, praying to whatever gods, goddesses or magic beings are listening that my power will work if we need it. I send out unspoken thoughts to Zev. *Be careful. Come back to me whole.* My heart constricts at the thought of something happening to him.

I don't expect an answer of course, not like with Darius, but I know on some level the words will find him.

Still, I'm stunned when a voice that sounds suspiciously like Zev replies.

I will always come back to you.

Hang on. You can mind-speak?

Zev sounds very pleased with himself when he replies. *Perks of being mates.*

The wolf then disappears into the shadows, his fur spiked out like an animal on defense, his movements cautious, the pads of his paws making no noise.

I don't want to distract him and get him killed, so

I hold my three million questions for when we aren't trying to take a piece of dragon.

Our plan, such as it is, involves scouting around the legendary creature, hoping it lost a scale the way a bird might lose a feather. When we find one, use our super stealth skills to take it and leave without being seen, smelled or heard.

That's Plan A, and requires us to be in an action adventure movie where the hero never dies no matter how many times he's shot, stabbed or blown on with dragon fire.

Plan B involves one of us distracting the dragon while the other physically plucks a scale off its hide, which requires us to be actual well-trained NAVY Seals or some shit. I don't even know. Just... like... a real life badass, ya know? This one is not my favorite plan. At all.

Plan C is to die and spend our time in the afterlife discussing what went wrong with Plans A and B.

It feels like ages that Zev is gone, and when he returns and quietly shifts back into a man, my nerves are beyond frayed.

I throw myself into his arms and kiss him fiercely. He responds with abandon, tucking me against his chest as he explores my mouth with his.

Finally, I pull away, breathless and relieved. "You scared me."

He grins, his green eyes twinkling with mischief. "If that's my reception when I scare you, I'll have to do it more often."

I lightly slap his arm, careful to not make any noise. "I'll happily greet you that way for *not* scaring me. Did you find any spare scales lying around? Mission accomplished, time to go home?" I ask, crossing my fingers.

"No," he says with a frown.

"Well, that sucks monkey balls," I say, even though I knew it would never be so easy. "Looks like it's Plan B? Which one of us is gonna be bait?"

"Also no to Plan B," he says, his frown deepening.

"What do you mean? We need to get the scale, one way or another. Or I'm going to blow us all up."

"We don't need bait," he says.

"Okay… do you want to just fill me in on what's going on or are we playing a really annoying game of twenty questions?"

"The dragon is dead," he says finally.

My jaw drops. "Dead? But I thought it's super hard to kill a dragon. You can only kill them while they're still in the egg or whatever."

"It is. You do."

"Then… how? Who?" A horrible thought settles on me and my eyes widen. "What if… what if my father found the dragon first and… and somehow killed it to get the pieces for my wand?"

Zev's eyes soften and he reaches for my hand. "I don't think that happened. Bernie, there's another body in there."

"The smell…" I gently pull myself from Zev and make my way to the dragon.

"Love, wait. It might not be safe."

I don't stop, letting him catch up with me instead. "If everything in there is dead, what do I have to fear?"

I pause at the entrance, stepping carefully around the thick tail and look in, shocked despite myself. The dragon is massive, the size of a house, and fills the cavernous space with its bulk. It's covered in iridescent scales that shimmer and cast rays of blue and green light, despite having no obvious light source.

Near the mythical beast are the remains of a man, leaning against the stone wall and holding something in his hand at his chest. Beyond his human form, he's unrecognizable. I guess this is how I meet my father.

As disturbing as the scorched corpse is, the most

startling bit about the whole scene is the fact that the dragon is also charred to death.

Zev leans in, whispering against my ear. "What we both should fear is whatever killed that dragon."

RIGHT. That's definitely the thing to be scared of right now. My mind spins, trying to sort out what I need to do before I can get the hell out of this place. "We need a scale. Then we should go."

Zev takes the initiative, wrapping his strong hands around a scale on the right forearm.

I turn away, uncomfortable seeing its poor dead body desecrated like this.

My eye is drawn to the charred human body that is slumped to the left of the dragon. I edge toward it, my curiosity overriding good sense.

"Bernie," Zev says, growling a soft warning deep in his throat.

"I just need to know," I say. It's an almost trance-like state I find myself in as I near the body. I fight against my own gag reflex and lean in to examine what he's clutching in his hand.

Using a bit of my scarf I pry the object out of his fingers and hold it up.

It's a pendant, silver with gold trim and an intricately carved design of an eye with a crystal as the iris.

It feels warm in my palm, even through my scarf, and I wrap it and stick it in my pocket. Just as I do so, I hear the sickening sound of the scale coming free.

Tears burn my eyes and I force myself to look at the dragon's face, into one of its reptilian eyes, which remain open despite its eternal slumber. "Thank you. I know we're not giving you much of a choice, but thank you nonetheless. Your gift is helping save more lives than you'll ever--."

I swallow a scream and fall back when the eye blinks slowly.

"It's not dead," I whisper, dread filling my chest.

"Stay still," Zev hisses. "Don't move."

I've fallen on my ass, so I stay put, trying not to breathe. Or to move. Or to emit any kind of scent.

Puffs of smoke shoot out of its nose like a sneeze, and its body shifts and shuffles just enough to make the stone around us groan and crack as if it's about to cave in.

I can see that Zev did manage to remove the scale. That's a meaningless fact if we die here, but will be awesome news should we somehow manage to survive

173

an encounter with an injured and probably very pissed off dragon.

As the monstrous creature shifts, its long tail unravels a bit, revealing something that breaks my frightened heart.

A massive egg, about six feet tall. Cracked. Hatched.

"I thought you said you crushed the egg," I say to Zev, my eyes never leaving the giant shell. "How the hell does that get crushed?"

"With a very big foot," he responds.

"How big are dragon babies?"

Zev looks at the broken egg, then back at me. "Big enough to do damage when they're a few minutes old."

My eyes well with tears as I look back at the wounded mother. She's nearly dead because she wanted to protect her baby. And now she's here, dying, having lost the thing she valued more than her own life.

I feel like I'm going to vomit.

"I'm so sorry," I say to it, stepping forward timidly as an unbidden tear rolls down my cheek. I've got no reason to believe that this dragon and I can communicate, but I feel an overwhelming need to show my empathy.

"I don't know who--or what--did this to you, but I am truly sorry for your pain and suffering. And for your loss." I swallow tears and continue, as the eye blinks once again at me. "I'm a mother too. Not being near my child hurts so much, I can't imagine the pain of losing her."

It might have more to do with pain than hearing my words, but a tear pools in the corner of the dragon's eye. As it falls, it begins to sizzle from the heat of itself, turning to steam before it can get too far.

My gut sinks when I realize the shared pain is too deep, that this dragon has become something so much more than an ingredient for my wand. She's the most majestic creature I've ever seen, only feet away from me, more concerned with a shattered egg than her injuries.

"We can't take the scale," I say.

"What are you talking about?" Zev asks, definitely annoyed, and I don't blame him. I'm annoyed at myself. But I'm also not wrong.

"She's a mother, I say. "And she's grieving. And dying. I won't treat her like she's anything less."

I stand there, not sure what my decision means for our quest, but already having made it. Zev, meanwhile, isn't giving up on the original plan. "We're taking the scale, Bernie. I'm sorry if it makes me heartless, but I don't give a damn about anything other than saving your life."

My heart swells at his words, but it's not his choice to make.

"I can't explain it, but I know I'm right," I whisper, my throat suddenly very dry. "If I steal this piece of her, if I rob a dying mother of part of her body, my wand will be tainted. It won't work, Zev."

"Then what do we do?" he asks, approaching gently.

"How do you think I ask for permission?"

Zev thinks about my question, looking from me to the dragon. When he turns back to me, his eyes show pure admiration. "Just make her believe in you. The way the rest of us do."

He might as well be reading off a motivational poster in a doctor's office, but the words still strike me. If I can get a tear out of this dragon, I can show her my worth.

I take the scale from Zev and step forward, close enough to the dragon to feel the heat of her breath. Sweat immediately beads on my forehead, but I step even closer.

"You're saving my life," I say, holding the scale in front of the dragon's big, beautiful eye. "And with that, you're saving my child, and countless other souls."

At this point, I've reached the end of my speech. I felt genuine saying those things, but it still feels like I need more. I look at the charred body next to her, the remains of who I can only assume was my father. A man I never met, never knew, and yet somehow brought me to Budapest and sent me on the craziest journey of all time. I return my gaze to the dragon.

"I can't repay you, but I swear on my life I will find and kill whoever, or whatever, did this to you. I will do everything in my power to find your baby and bring it home."

There's no way the dragon understands. There's no way I can make and keep such a promise. And yet, there's something to be said for the power of a sentiment, for the truth of conviction. Another tear trickles and steams off the dragon's cheek--then she lowers her head and closes her eyes.

I shed a tear as well, watching her take what I know will be her last breath.

"She says it's okay," I say to Zev. "I can have her scale."

My gaze stays on the magnificent creature while Zev moves to me and wipes away my tear. "You're brave, powerful, and the most magical being I've ever met."

He gently kisses my head, then whispers in my ear, "Let's get back to your daughter."

Those words spur me into action immediately, and Zev shifts into wolf and pushes into my legs so I'll ride him. It's faster than my running, and I lean into him, wrapping my arms around his wolf torso. I cry some more for the fallen dragon, my tears matting down Zev's soft, white fur.

He doesn't need our guiding magic to find the way back, instead using his nose to retrace our steps. I can't see in the darkness, but I feel the power of these incredible caves. When she's old enough, I'll bring Rain here to meet a dragon.

It feels like it takes mere minutes for us to get back to the watery portal, and Zev shifts back to man as we dive in.

We swim from one underground tunnel to the next, avoiding the garden stream and instead taking the exit that leads to the river running through downtown Budapest. I don't want to walk us straight into the vampire's arms in case they decided to stay the night.

Unfortunately, this means my naked wolf man is going to be a problem.

We push through to the other side and pop out in the middle of the river, right where I swam in my dream. The evening rush is underway, and we're just a couple of tourists swimming in the river.

We get plenty of looks from passersby, wondering where we came from and why we're swimming in the frigid waters. Wait till they see the swimming trunks that Zev definitely isn't wearing.

Hungarians, it turns out, are fun-loving people, as we're met with hoots and hollers after we climb up the ladder of an anchored boat and step onto the sidewalk next to the water. Zev stares at the men and women who whistle and clap for him. He doesn't seem to mind, but I've got too much social conditioning. My face turns bright red as I take my sweater and try to tie it around his waist.

Do I embarrass you, love?

In response, I give his ass a swift, open-hand slap. Dozens of people break into applause. *Not at all,* I say. *But we don't have time for this. Where will we find Darius and Rune?* I close my eyes and think of Darius, imagining our connection, the way our blood sings to each other.

Darius? Are you okay?

I feel his utter relief mentally pour over me. *Thank the Fates you are safe. Across the street from our hotel, there's a narrow alley. Take it until you reach the cemetery behind the church. We will meet you there.*

I break into a jog and Zev quickly follows, waving goodbye as strangers continue to clap.

It feels like perpetual night in Budapest, though I know that's only because I spent the day underground.

Still, it's spooky to step into the sacred and holy ground that is the resting place for so many as the heavy moon casts its silver light over us.

I see Darius first, and nearly trip over my own feet getting to his arms.

Our embrace is passionate and too short, as I pull away to look for Rune. "Where is he? Where's Rain?"

Darius frowns. "They are safe. Given the attack, we felt it best he keep her hidden while I find you two and bring you back, making sure no one follows us."

My heart sinks. I've been away from her for nearly a full day. I know the precaution is justified, but I can't bear to be without her any longer.

Before I can protest, Zev begins to growl as someone walks out of the shadows.

Erzsébet stands in the moonlight. She's dressed in black with her long red and silver hair cascading down her back in waves. She looks more magical than anyone I've ever seen.

"Did you find what was needed?" She asks.

There's something about her tone, her slight surprise at seeing us that gives me pause but I set it aside, rightly blaming it on exhaustion and the stress of the situation.

"Yes, we got a scale," I say, patting my pocket. I remember my other take from the cave and pull it out, unveiling the pendant to the queen. "But the dragon was already dead. Her tail was wrapped around a broken egg shell, so she died trying to save her baby."

Erzsébet cocks an eyebrow. "The dragonling was gone?"

I nod. "There was only the dragon and a dead body. My father."

I study the queen witch's face carefully as she looks at the pendant for a second, then averts her gaze back to me. "How do you know it was your father?"

Huh? Based on everything Erzsébet and Andor have said, this seems pretty obvious. Dad went to get the scale. There was a dead guy next to the dragon. Therefore, dead guy equals dad.

"Did someone else go to the cave?" I ask.

She takes a moment, her eyes never leaving mine. It's not the longest pause, but long enough for me to recognize she knows something. Something she's keeping hidden. Powerful as she is, helpful as she's been, there's something about this woman I don't yet trust.

"I can't say if another accompanied your father," she finally says, "or if they perhaps met him in the cave. But if you say there was a dead dragon, and a dead man next to it, and a missing dragonling…" she trails off, again looking at the pendant before snatching it from my hand and putting it in her own pocket. "It seems as though they had company."

CHAPTER ELEVEN

Without another word, the witch turns and starts walking back into the shadows. Since I didn't pick this meeting place, I'm not sure if we're supposed to follow her or not. Which reminds me: "Why are we in a graveyard?"

Darius takes my hand--the feel of his cool touch somehow warming me from the inside-- and we fall in behind Erzsébet with Zev close on our heels.

"And where are they?" I ask Darius, referring to the fae and my baby.

"Nearby," he reassures me, though the fact that they're near the cemetery isn't all that comforting. We're walking along a narrow path, gravestones on either side. I always have a compulsion to read each headstone I pass, like I owe it to the deceased to take a moment and honor the life they lived rather than treating their final resting place like decoration. But this cemetery is massive and we've got places to be-- hopefully someplace not teaming with the ghosts of the dead, even though I'm pretty sure Erzsébet brought us here for a reason.

At a certain, unremarkable spot, the witch stops and casually looks around. Despite the fact that it's nighttime and we're surrounded by the dead, I still see a surprising number of people walking about. There are dog walkers and happy couples cruising around as if this were a park like any other. It's a combination of off-putting and charming.

When there's a lull in foot traffic, Erzsébet flicks her wand and the ground in front of a headstone slowly opens up, leaving a hole in the earth about the size of a garbage can lid. With a final glance over her shoulder, Erzsébet steps forward and falls into the ground.

I, for one, have some apprehension about diving into a grave. Darius doesn't share my concern and lets me know it.

She's not leading us into a coffin, my sweet.

I bet you wish she was, I say back, stalling before I'm forced to take the plunge.

Darius flashes a quick smile.

It would be nice to get a decent night's sleep.

The vampire steps forward and drops out of sight, leaving me and Zev to follow. The werewolf takes my hand and gives me a brief, loving kiss, sending sparks of fire through me. I can now always sense our mate bond, but when we are touching it is so much stronger.

"I'm not fond of the under-earth in cemeteries either," he says. "But I've got a feeling your daughter's waiting for you."

He's good at motivating me, this one. With images of Rain in my mind, I repeat the mantra 'I will not die, I will not die, I will not die,' and then take the plunge, my nerves frayed as I step in after Darius and feel gravity give way. What I expect to be a short drop lasts for excruciatingly long seconds as the air leaves my lungs. Just when it starts to feel interminable, my feet finally plant solidly on the ground. I don't stumble, fall, or even land with a jolt. I'm just standing.

As I open my eyes, Zev lands to my side. Darius and Erzsébet are a few feet away, looking back at us. We're all in the middle of a large, underground chamber, light coming from torches stationed along the stone walls.

And there's Rune, standing next to a crib, which

looks so incredibly incongruous in the middle of an underground tomb of a cemetery.

I push past Darius and Erzsébet, literally shoving a witch queen who's thousands of years old to the side, so I can go to Rain. I still don't feel safe enough to touch her, and the ache to do so is nearly overwhelming, but I lean over the crib and devour her with my eyes as she sleeps. She looks so peaceful, so content. I hope she always feels this way.

Rune watches, tears brimming in his eyes. His affection for both Rain and myself is palpable, especially when he sees this special mother-daughter connection. I move over to the beautiful fae and bury my face into his chest.

"Thank you," I say while wiping my wet eyes on his shirt. "Thank you for always taking such good care of her."

He wraps his arms around me and speaks softly into my ear. "You two are my reasons for living. It's my pleasure."

When I finally pull away from the sexy fae, I look around to see all four magical, powerful people staring at me.

"Hi," is all I can think to say. "I'm pretty tired and haven't eaten in a day, so does someone else want to do the talking?"

My own mention of food makes my stomach growl. My body goes on auto-pilot, moving around the room in search of some water. I find a table with a pitcher and glasses on it, and Zev is instantly by my side pouring us water. As I chug a first glass, then a second, then start on a third, Erzsébet does some wand work and mutters *"ünnep,"* which makes a platter of bread, cheese and fruit appear out of thin air. I practically trip on myself running over to it. I need to learn that spell before I learn anything else.

"You should rest," Erzsébet says as I shove half a baguette in my mouth. "Your journey continues as soon as you wake up."

I hadn't thought much about the next step in my wand-making quest, which is silly. I knew there was more to my wand than a piece of dragon, and it would be foolish to assume the other ingredients can just be found at a craft supply store. Unless there's a magical craft supply store hidden between ancient buildings somewhere? Or underground? A black market for magic folk? That seems like it should be a thing. Someone should make that a thing.

I also hadn't noticed, until right now, that I'm hardly glowing, even though Darius hasn't fed on me and Zev hasn't... fed me... in quite a while.

"I don't feel like I'm about to explode," I say to no

one in particular. "Is that because I have the dragon scale?"

Erzsébet shakes her head. "This room is keeping your powers under control. We're inside an ancient witch's tomb, built ages ago before the vampires came for us. The spells inside these walls are made to keep the power of a fallen witch in equilibrium, allowing their souls to live on without their bodies."

The room feels more like an unstaged wine cellar than a creepy crypt, but it sounds like they've had a lot of years to renovate.

"Does that mean there's a spirit floating around in here with us?" I ask, thinking of the ghost we left AJ alone with at the pub. Shit. She's gonna be pissed I haven't called her.

"Indeed," Erzsébet says, then just moves right along as if that's not something worth addressing. "As long as you're in here, you should be safe from yourself. It's also a good place to practice spells, like the food summoning I just did."

The prospect of making food appear whenever I want pushes the thought of a long-dead roommate right out of my head. Still, I'm sure I can't just take a long holiday in this magic chamber.

"What happened with the vampires?"

"They'll be back," Darius answers. "We'll be ready, but more *Kő* members will die."

Sounds like we won the battle but still have a long way to go before claiming victory in the war. My thoughts flash back to Andor, ripped away by a bloodthirsty vampire last I saw him. We didn't get off to the greatest start, but I wish he hadn't died.

He lived, Darius says into my mind, responding to my thoughts. *Saved by another Kő.*

I smile with my eyes, happy to hear at least a shred of good news.

Erzsébet bows her head, her beautiful hair draping over her face. "The Grand Hall had been safe for so many centuries. I knew this day would come, but it still feels so unexpected."

It's not lost on me that Rain and I are the only difference between the centuries of peace and the day of devastation. There's a council of paranormals tracking me, combining their efforts and resources to find me and take my baby. And I led them right to the epicenter of witch power.

Erzsébet looks up, reading my thoughts like everyone else always does, because apparently my mind is an open book for anyone to read. "This isn't your fault, Bernadette. I share in the responsibility for bringing you here."

"How so?" I'm still under the impression that my dad lured me here through the words of my soon to be murdered grandfather. What role did the queen witch play in all that?

"There are ways to direct a person to a place without making that intention known," she says. "When I learned you left for Budapest, I set some bits of magic in motion that would lead you to the right hotel at the right time of day. I wasn't going to rest until you were under my watch."

I open my mouth but decide to hold my tongue. It's very suspicious that she makes no mention of my grandfather's letter, the original catalyst for this whole trip. The idea that two parties have been orchestrating my travels makes me uneasy, but I don't feel like opening up about that just yet.

"Let's discuss the matters at hand before you sleep," she says, moving the conversation along.

"Right," I say, tabling my concerns to bring up later with the Sexies. "My wand."

Erzsébet holds her own wand forward and ushers me over with her hand, prompting me to take a closer look.

"The ordinary wand features a wood casing, or sometimes an exterior made of tightly woven feathers," she explains while turning her wand from side to side.

Getting a closer look, I see that hers has thin lines throughout, as if it's made of thread.

"Mine is made of the baleen from a leviathan. That's what gives it the strength to contain the phoenix ashes within."

While the wand sounds very cool and powerful to me, I sense that her words have shocked each of the Sexies.

"Your wand is alive?" Rune asks, a dark concern taking over his light eyes. The fae clearly has some opinions.

Erzsébet nods calmly. She doesn't seem overly surprised by the reaction she's getting.

"In my realm," Rune says, trying to be judicious in his word choice, "some would describe that as dark magic."

"I daresay many witches would agree," Zev adds.

The witch meets their gaze, absorbing the accusatory tones and firing the sentiment right back at them. "To that I would say: when a witch queen, a direct descendant of the Fates, combines her blood, the blood of her fallen daughter, and the ashes of a phoenix in order to cast the spells necessary to save the worlds… one finds the gray area that exists between dark and light magic."

I can't help but enjoy the irony of standing in a tomb and it being deathly quiet.

These princes, once friends before tragedy tore them apart and then I brought them back together, have never been able to mourn their fallen friend. Now they're faced with the girl's mother, made incredibly powerful, seemingly invincible, in the wake of her daughter's death.

That's some heavy shit. I don't know if the Sexies will be able to process it. I don't know when they'll find the time.

"Is that how you, ya know, keep on living?" I ask. It feels a little tactless, but it's the best word combination I can come up with at the moment. Rest is sounding more and more necessary.

Erzsébet nods, and there's a pain in her eyes. "That's the darkest part of all. No mother wants to outlive her child. Certainly no mother wants to outlive her child for all of eternity."

"Was she, um… was Cara born through the designated lover program you have here?"

There was probably a more tactful way of asking that, but I'm too exhausted to think of it.

The witch cocks her head and studies me. "No,

that *program* was created many, many years later when we realized the need for protection and tighter ranks. I was past my childbearing years by then and had already mastered my magic. I did not need such a lover. Cara's father was my husband and greatest love. He died shortly after she did."

As I struggle to find the words sufficient for such tragedy, the queen glances away, walking over to Rain's crib where she stares at my baby in solemn silence.

The sight almost gets me emotional, but instead I yawn, overcome with exhaustion. I need to sleep in a bad way, ideally in the arms of a vampire. Tired as I am, I'd love to give Darius a quick feed and see what happens next. My body and blood have missed him.

I'll prepare the bed, the vampire thinks into my mind, hearing and sharing my needs and disappearing through an opening into what looks like a smaller chamber. I almost follow immediately, but decide to wrap up this conversation.

"Where do I find a leviathan?"

"You can't," Erzsébet says with a shake of her head. "They're long since extinct. Perhaps one or two still swim in the greatest depths of the sea, but we chased them away from the surface more than a thousand years ago."

"Okay," I mutter, my patience wearing a little thin, especially now that my mind has drifted to the bedroom. "So what am I looking for instead?"

"Something natural," Erzsébet says. "The dragon scale gives you great strength, but you need a living element that will transfer power from your hand to the wand's tip."

Annoyed by all the riddles, frustration and impatience builds up in me. I just want to lay my body down and have someone else do all the thinking for a little bit.

"I don't understand," I say with a whimper, my nerves frayed.

"Rest," Zev says, wrapping his hand in mine, letting our mate bond fill me up. "We'll deal with this in the morning."

Rune runs his hand along my back, accomplishing his usual transfer of calm. "I've studied wands, Bernie. I'll find the answer."

I trust the fae with Rain, so of course I trust him with my wand ingredient list. I hug him, kiss Zev, and tiptoe over to the crib to look at my sleeping infant one last time. She flops her tiny arms above her head, a source of pure cuteness in a world that's otherwise a little too ugly for my liking.

After a few moments, I shift my focus to Erzsébet,

standing by my side, her striking gaze giving me that conflicted feeling. I trust her, but not implicitly. I need to know more of her secrets. At least I've learned that her immortality comes from a wand full of bird ashes and dead daughter blood. Nothing freaky about that.

"Bernadette," the witch says, her face inching closer to mine until our noses almost touch. "I trust you learned something in the dragon's lair, or else you wouldn't be here with a scale in your pocket."

She might know everything that happened from watching on her big, crystal TV, or she knows nothing and is speaking in relatable platitudes that always ring true. Either way, she's got my attention.

"Your powers found you, but not without your help. Others can only offer so much guidance before your instincts have to take over."

She turns her attention from me to Rain, a warm smile coming to her lips. "Goodnight, my light."

Her face lingers on the baby for another moment, then Erzsébet walks back to the center of the room, stares at me, and flies into the earth above her, like a canister getting sucked into a tube out of the mailroom.

I'm too tired to dwell on anything she said,

though I know her words will play over and over in my head as soon as I wake up.

With a wave to the others, I head off in the direction of my vampire. Something about the blood bond makes me need him in a way I can't deny, no matter how tired I am or how connected to Zev I might feel. And though this whole situation of having more than one lover is totally new for me, none of the guys seem to mind, and honestly, it's the lowest concern on the list of strange new things that have happened. I'll probably have to sort out how this will work functionally in the long term, if there is a long term for us. For now, I need them all too much to change anything.

The tomb has different rooms, each barren except for the light furnishings magically conjured or summoned; a table here, a chair there, a few more pitchers of water. We sure don't have the amenities of a hotel, but this charmed room suits us just fine in the given circumstances.

When I round the corner into the room Darius took, he's standing beside an assortment of blankets spread about on the floor. He's already disrobed and is very, *very* ready for me.

My heart lurches at the sight of him. His body sculpted to perfection by a master artist. His eyes dark orbs that pull me into their fathomless depths. I shiver at the prospect of what we are about to do, and heat collects in my center, my body more than ready for him.

I shed my clothes as I move toward him, half-naked by the time we embrace and full-naked by the time we hit the blankets. I guide him inside me, our bodies immediately finding our rhythm, ecstasy overcoming me almost instantaneously. As he sinks his teeth into my neck and he drinks from me, I fully embrace the throes of pleasure, releasing the stress and trials I've faced over the last twenty four hours.

When our passions are spent, I curl up in his arms, my head on his chest, his lips grazing my head.

I have missed you, he says softly into my mind. *I have not known what it means to miss someone in a very long time. And never with this intensity.*

I sigh into his chest, tears pooling in my eyes. *I've missed you too.*

And then my eyes close, and I sleep the sleep of the dead. My mind and body submit fully to unconsciousness, recharging so I can wake up and face another day.

Just before waking, I step into another dream that has the same feeling as my prophetic dream from our first night in Budapest. I'm in a dark tunnel or cave, it's impossible to know because the room is pitch black. I feel my way around, my hands finally sliding over an opening in the rock wall. When I climb through, I'm in the Grand Hall.

It doesn't look the same as it did before; now there's rubble strewn about, and instead of studying from books, the witches are carrying bodies out of the room. My dream is no doubt walking me through the aftermath of the vampire attack.

I feel crippling sorrow as I step through the space, thinking about the lives and history lost to the violence. I hope the Grand Hall can be rebuilt. I hope future witches can learn from it as they have in the past. But I know, even in my dreaming mind, those hopes rest on my ability to keep Rain alive.

Erzsébet stands in the center of the room, tears staining her cheeks while she looks at the spell books on the enormous shelves. She slowly turns in a circle, looking at every wall in the spacious room.

"He can't be trusted, Bernadette."

The witch speaks to me without looking my way, her eyes continuing to search the shelves.

"I knew it wasn't safe to show him, and now the book is gone."

"Who? And what book?" I ask, starting to scan

the walls myself as if I might be able to find what she's looking for.

"Bernadette..." I hear a new voice coming from behind me, and turn to see Andor. He approaches cautiously, his eyes darting between me and Erzsébet.

When he reaches my side, he smiles. It's genuine and friendly, making me feel a little bit of peace. He holds out his hand, gesturing for me to take it. He's going to guide me somewhere, show me something. I think I'll go with him.

As I'm about to take his hand, I look up at Erzsébet. She stares at Andor, shaking her head, her face contorting in anger. Why is she so mad? He only wants to help me.

"Come, Bernadette," Andor says, extending his other hand as well. I start to turn to him, but notice Erzsébet has raised her wand.

"Meghal lélek!"

Before either of us can react, a ray of light bursts from the tip, knocking Andor to the floor. He lies motionless, his eyes open, smoke rising from the hole in his chest where the magic blast hit him.

I look back at Erzsébet, her wand now aimed directly at me. Light shoots forth, striking me in the chest, delivering the same fate to me as it did Andor.

And waking me from the dream.

My eyes open, taking in the soft flicker coming from a torch just outside the room. Darius no longer lays with me, and I have no idea what time it is. Mostly, I'm just happy to be alive after my brush with death in that very vivid dream.

I rise quickly and dress, then rush out to check on Rain.

In the main room, Zev and Rune sit near the crib, Rain laying on a blanket between them. She's cooing and squirming about while the magical men just watch her. It's the most heartwarming scene imaginable.

"Good morning," Zev says, the sexiest of smiles on his face.

"How long did I sleep?" I ask, having zero concept of time. It could be ten in the morning or three days later.

"A few hours," Zev answers, shocking the shit out of me. "It's four or five in the morning, still dark out so Darius is patrolling the grounds above."

"Only a few hours? I feel like I was out for days."

Rune rises, walking over to me with a steaming mug of tea. We could be trapped at the bottom of the ocean and this man would still find a way to make me a warm, herbal beverage.

"I've wondered about your sleep since you

reclaimed your powers," the fae says. "It might be that your mind and body rest more quickly, as ours do."

I hadn't thought about that, but it makes sense. I've been averaging somewhere between no sleep and a tiny bit of sleep since before we left Rowley. I definitely get tired, but my mind hasn't really failed me yet.

"You're saying my magical brain is better than my old, stupid, human brain?"

Rune dissects my sentence for a moment before smiling, having learned a little bit about how sass works over the last few weeks. "Yes, Bernie. That's exactly what I'm saying."

I sit next to my baby, watching her discover her toes, all while trying to shake the lingering uneasiness from my dream. I want to talk to Zev and Rune about it, and tell them my feelings about the queen witch, but I don't know what to say. So I opt to move the day along instead.

"What did you come up with, Rune?" I ask. "What's the next part of my wand made of?"

"There's an ancient forest a few towns away," he answers. "I can't say if we'll find the element in question there, but I'll be able to better understand the magic of these parts if I visit the elder trees."

"Sounds great," I say. "I'll come with you."

Rune's eyebrows drop to a scowl. Zev growls. Predictable reactions from both.

"I have to be there," I explain. "I have to find the material myself. Zev, you saw how I became connected to the dragon. I can't just give you a shopping list, not for a wand as powerful--and personally connected to me--as this."

Neither speaks, because they know I'm right. I'm silent as well, a little surprised by how confident I am in my words. Especially given that this means I have to leave my baby behind again. Mother of the year, right here, folks. Is this how moms who have to go straight back to work without maternity leave feel? Only… with dragons and werewolves instead of glass ceilings and cubicles?

"What's happening?"

Darius joins us, speaking before any of us had noticed his entrance and causing me to spit tea directly into Rune's face. I apologize, then laugh while I mop it up with my sleeve. He's a very good sport about the whole thing, and I enjoy a few seconds of getting lost in his silver eyes while drying his cheeks.

Meanwhile, Zev explains to Darius that I'll be leaving with Rune, and we all watch the vampire clench his jaw so hard I'm worried he'll bite through his own face. After a few seconds of processing my determined stare, Darius gives a slow, understanding nod.

"I'll have to prepare extra formula," Rune says, pouring a glass of water while he takes a small pouch from his coat. "Zev, you've given Rain a bottle before, correct?"

The fae is going into full worried-mom mode, and I'm a little concerned that I'm being too casual about everything. I've come to trust these men so completely, with such enduring confidence in them, that once I resign myself to the fact that I'm leaving Rain behind, that's the end of my worries. It seems Rune doesn't have the same belief in the others' co-parenting abilities.

He spends another half hour getting everything set up just right, and I keep thinking he's going to end with giving them a post-it note with phone numbers for poison control and the fire department. It's a strong display of neurosis that only Rune could make charming.

I spend those precious minutes giving one last feed and a thousand kisses to my baby, then settle her into her crib. I'd love a shower and a change of clothes, but at least I got to swim in the river last night. And I'm sure Rune will find me some leaf in the woods that will make me smell and feel very clean.

When we're ready to go, I spend a moment in Zev's arms, promising him I'll be safe and return as quickly as I can. Then I embrace Darius, holding him tight and presenting my neck for a final visceral moment. He takes his time to lick my wounds, and I have to pry myself out of his arms when it's time to leave.

With a few supplies loaded on our backs, Rune and I step into the center of the room, ready to get sucked into the human world above, then travel into the unknown, searching for the mysterious.

Before we leave, Darius gives a serious, somewhat ominous look.

"Watch out for vampires," he says.

"And wolves," Zev adds.

I nod, and then, right as I feel my body start to lift, I'm compelled to yell back, "Watch out for the witch."

CHAPTER TWELVE

With Darius, he carries me and we sprint at ungodly speeds to wherever we need to be.

With Zev, he shifts into wolf form, takes me on his back, and he runs with amazing grace and balance.

With Rune, we get into the back of a truck, and he creates an illusion to make it look like we're not in the back of that truck.

And honestly, with a life that's changed from no magic to way too much magic, I'm enjoying the shit out of a casual car ride to the forest.

I look at the passing countryside as we go, enamored with the old architecture that shines through in even the most inconspicuous buildings. New England has some good history, and I grew up in a family bar that was more than a hundred years old. Before visiting Europe, I felt like Rowley had some old buildings. This trip makes clear what a baby America really is.

While I take in the sights, Rune's eyes never leave me. Nor does the look of contentment on his face.

"Yes?" I ask when I finally return his gaze. "Do I have something on my face?"

"Just your normal magnetic beauty," he responds, dropping a line like they're going out of style. "It was very difficult being away from you yesterday. I don't think I fully understood how addicted to your presence I've become."

Words that might sound trite coming from another mouth have my heart all a flutter when Rune says them. His sincerity is off the charts, and such things said by a creature so beautiful, it makes me feel like I really am the most important girl in the world.

"I know… I know I'm not as forward in my affections as Darius and Zev," Rune says, not looking away from my eyes as he speaks. "It's… complicated. I want you. I crave you. I need you. And I haven't felt those things for anyone since my betrothed died. It feels almost disloyal, and yet I know she would want me to find happiness. I have mourned long enough, but these things take time."

I take his hand and nod, emotion clogging my throat. "You don't have to explain yourself to me. There's no hurry. I'm here." I don't add, *for now*, because that feels too much like a blade in the heart for both of us. The words still sit between us, unspoken but all the more present because of it.

We drive on in silence for a few more minutes while our eyes never leave each other. It's like a makeout sesh for our souls, just staying locked in without our physical forms getting in the way. It's one of the most stimulating, arousing connections I've ever felt, to be honest. Turns out extended eye contact is hot.

It finally gets too hot and I have to break away before my body tries to join in. We both have a lot to process without lust getting in the way, especially him.

When I pull my eyes from the fae's, I look down at my chest, rising and falling with each accelerated breath. And then I remember my dream. Erzsébet killing Andor, then firing a spell at me. The dream is disturbing enough on its own, but knowing that the queen witch has the power to control my dreams makes it even more disconcerting. Is she announcing that she plans to kill me?

"Did you spend much time with Erzsébet yesterday?" I ask Rune. He's now looking at me with some concern, having noticed my shift in demeanor.

"We spent an hour or so concealed in the garden," he says thoughtfully. "Once she'd disposed of our attackers, she brought us directly to the tomb through underground passages, then left until we met up with you last night."

"Did she... did she kill all the vampires?"

Rune nods. "The ones that didn't retreat, yes."

I'm struck and concerned by that kind of power. From what I've seen, vampires are pretty hard to kill when there's just one of them. A dozen seems like way too many.

"She has immense power," Rune says. "The strongest witches are the most feared by vampires, which is part of what led to the wars that have raged all these centuries."

"Vampires attacked the witches because they felt threatened?"

"It depends on who you ask," Rune answers with a wry smile. "Vampires originally served as powerful protectors of all races, invincible defenders against anyone who might wish to harm the Fates or their children. But then the protectors became the provocateurs."

"Why? What changed?"

"They grew dissatisfied with their position, and at the same time realized how much power they possessed." Rune's eyes survey the passing landscape, but he's clearly looking back in time, recalling horrors I'm glad I never witnessed. "The witches developed fiery spells to target the vampires' weaknesses, and the conflict escalated. That's when the fae capitalized on the upheaval, seizing witches' land and trying to take some of their powers for our own."

He talks about events from hundreds of years ago as if they just happened. Things he wasn't even alive for still have a profound impact on this thoughtful man. It seems like quite the load to carry.

"The prophecy was self-fulfilling in that regard," Rune continues. "Witches created everything. Erzsébet herself descends from those with the magical fortitude to bring planets and people into existence. But it was their own creations that brought us to this point."

We sit in silence as I try to wrap my mind around all this history, and the fact that I'm now such an integral cog in the story. My daughter, a tiny baby who's only just discovering she has toes and fingers, is the final piece in this enormous, cosmic, magical puzzle.

"Do you trust her?" I ask, finally breaking the silence and bringing the conversation back to the witch queen.

Rune takes a long pause before answering. "More than most. Less than some." He turns to me, moving so his forehead rests against mine. If his goal is to make me feel the profundity of the moment, it's working.

"Dark magic leads to some of our greatest sorrows," he says. "You saw it with your mother. However, elements of the same magic that nearly killed your child are what brought Tilly's power to you and allowed you to save us all. So, while I fear the powers that run through Erzsébet and her living wand, I know that darkness colors your powers as well. And I trust you with my eternal soul."

I'm glad our bodies are so close, because I don't know if I could deal with the idea of possessing dark magic without Rune's tranquilizing touch.

"Erzsébet trusted the vampires to meet with her daughter," Rune says, pulling his head away from mine as he dips into what must be a painful memory. "Cara wanted to reach common ground, to explain the prophecy as a means of keeping the peace instead of a motivation for war and murder. Erzsébet put faith in her daughter, and faith in goodness."

I know that this story ends with the death of the witch princess, and it seems Rune is struggling to get through to the end of it.

"They opted to go with a simple magic," he says, the slightest quiver in his voice. "They asked for trust. And it worked on Darius... but not his father."

I take Rune's hand again, needing his touch as much as I figure he needs mine. We spend the rest of the drive into the woods in silence.

WE PASS through dozens and dozens of tree sentinels lining both sides of the road, and they all look the same. The repetitive scenery makes Rune's decision to stop seem very random to me, though likely he spied some subtle shift in algae on every other tree or some shit. Rune squeezes my hand and indicates it's time to go. I'm about to ask how we're getting off a moving vehicle without injury when the truck pulls over and stops.

Huh. Problem solved, I guess.

Rune and I grab our packs and I groan under the weight of mine, which is sort of pathetic. I had no

KARPOV KINRADE & EVAN GAUSTAD

trouble carrying around a twelve-pound baby, but this fifteen-pound backpack has me feeling overloaded. Nevertheless, we make quick work running into the woods as the driver gets out of his truck and studies the road before him, scratching his head in confusion.

When we're far enough away not to be seen or heard, I stop running and turn to Rune, my breath hitching as I try to slow my inhales and exhales. "What... how did you get him... to stop?" My words come out with exhausted puffs and I slump against a tree, my body drained of all adrenaline.

"I created the illusion of a fallen tree in the road. He will be very confused when it suddenly disappears."

"Poor guy. He's going to be questioning his sanity forever." It makes me wonder how many crazy stories people have told over the years are a result of a run-in with a paranormal and they never knew it.

Rune hands me a little vial of blue liquid. "This will help with the exertion."

"Yes please," I take it, not at all ashamed of my enthusiastic support for any herbal cheats the talented fae is willing to provide. I throw it back like the pro drinker I am, only to gag on the disgusting taste that coats my throat like tar. I start spitting and try hard not to vomit. "What the hell?"

Rune hands me a water jug. "Apologies. It is not the most pleasant tasting, but it is very effective."

"Not the most pleasant?" I ask incredulously, looking up at him even as I know my face is blotching from the gagging. "It's the worst thing I've ever put in my mouth."

I rinse said mouth again, spitting the tainted water out. I repeat this, hoping we have a way to get more water, until the taste has faded enough to function.

"I will carry that putrid taste into my night-mares," I say.

He doesn't seem repentant at all as he patiently waits there, watching me.

"What are you--?" I cut off my own words with a relieved sigh and a smile. "Ah okay. I see now."

Rune grins. "Impressive, yes?"

I nod. All my muscles feel extra pumped, my lungs feel unstoppable and I've suddenly got the energy to run a marathon without a single break. I hitch my pack, straightening it on my back and smile even wider. "I'm stronger!"

"For a time," Rune says. "Do not be careless. You

are still working with a human body and can be injured."

I nod. "Where do I trade this one in for a fancier magic edition?" I ask.

Rune scoffs. "Your body is perfect. Do not trade it in. Ever." The heat in his eyes and need in his voice strips me down to my bare emotions, turning me into a puddle at his feet.

But we have work to do and don't have time for sexy sex against a tree distractions, plus I'm giving him time to process his complex emotions. Sexy tree sex can wait.

"Where to?" I ask, trying to break free of his spell long enough to focus.

He shakes his head, like he's clearing it, and coughs, causing my insides to warm knowing I'm just as much a distraction to him as he is to me. "I don't know," he says, making me panic a little. "A decade ago, near here, humans uncovered trees that were millions of years old. They offered a few scientific explanations for the trees' longevity, but I expect there's more to the story."

"So we're just looking for old trees?" I ask. "And if humans already found them, don't we know where they are?"

Rune nods. "We are looking for old trees, but it's

not so simple as looking on a map. The earth and power beneath the tree is just as important as the trunk."

"Great. Let's start walking and hope we trip on some magic." Even though Rune's potion makes me feel like I could hike forever, I still can't handle being away from my baby, and from Darius and Zev for so long. I miss my child something awful, and I am determined to get this wand made as quickly as possible so I can hold her and nurse her again. The separation is breaking my heart.

I hitch my bag a final time and Rune and I start walking into the ancient woods of Hungary where who-knows-what awaits.

It's hard to imagine what the fae might be feeling, now that he's in his element, and about to connect even more deeply with nature. He's always moved with impeccable grace, but now there's an added live-liness to his step as his eyes dance around the passing woods.

We hike around for an hour or so, and Rune's potion makes it feel like minutes. We talk of our lives before he walked into my bar, of our interests and dreams and ambitions. Rune tells me about how he learned to play the harp--from his great grandmother who is a renowned musician amongst his kind.

"You two must be very close," I say, stumbling over a root because I took my eyes off my feet for more than three seconds. It's really clear who's got the spirit of the woods in him and who doesn't.

Spoiler: The woods hate me.

I'm bitten by all the bugs, rocks and twigs jump up from the ground just to trip me, and I can't stop sneezing because apparently the air up here is made entirely from allergy powder.

"We were," he says, his gaze drifting to the past. "My parents were busy running our kingdom, my grandmother was killed in a skirmish before I was born, so my great-grandmother took on the task of entertaining, teaching and guiding a little boy full of mischief and questions."

I smile at the image of Rune as a child and can only imagine the fairytale life he had as a prince raised in a forest palace.

"She taught me secrets of the forest and herbs and of the earth that she learned over many hundreds of years, sacred knowledge passed down only to those intended for Master Alchemy."

I glance over at him, my hand sliding into his, hoping the physical contact helps him as much as it helps me. He smiles and squeezes my hand.

"Was that your destiny?" I ask. "Before all this?"

He nods. "Since I am not the eldest, I was freed of the burden of rulership. My sister has that privilege and took to the training and lifestyle it required with enthusiasm, leaving me to enjoy my passions in peace. Until the wars started, and then there was no peace."

"And then you got sent on a hunt for a fulfillment to a prophecy," I say, sympathetically, as it sinks in even more how much this must have disrupted all of our lives, not just mine.

"And then I got sent to find a new destiny," he says, his gaze lingering on mine, his silver eyes shining like the moon. "One by your side to the end of days."

I gulp, suddenly nervous at the enormity of that promise, but also filled with heat at the safety and joy his words fill me with.

"I, for one, am glad you come packed with all that knowledge. It makes modern medicine look pathetic."

He grins. "I'm happy to be of service."

The forest smells of cold and mulch and all things green and natural. I inhale the pure oxygen as we stop for a brief break.

I shrug out of my pack gratefully and find a place to relieve myself, then take a couple minutes to pump my breasts dry as I pray my milk continues to come in while I'm keeping my distance from Rain.

When I return, Rune pulls thin slices of a dense bread from his pack, handing me a square. "This is an ancient fae recipe. It's packed with nutrients."

I eye the tiny bite of food doubtfully as the fae pops his into his mouth and takes a long swig of our water.

I do the same and am pleased by the taste. It's nutty and sweet, like honey and berries and something else I can't quite place. I chase it with water and lean back against a tree, closing my eyes. I'm not tired per se: the concoction Rune gave me is still in effect, but I am weary on a soul level, and I can feel my powers ramping up again as my skin begins to glow too brightly.

A headache pounds at my skull and a nervous energy zips through me.

"I have an idea to help you on this trip," Rune says, shuffling around in his pack.

I peek my eyes open and see him using a stone mortar and pestle, crushing some herbs in it. He then stands and looks around, studying the trees as if waiting for one of them to tell him something.

Who knows, maybe they will.

Frankly, I'd be disappointed if my magic fae boy couldn't talk to trees.

After a few long moments, he nods and walks

over to a nearby cyprus. With deft fingers, he plucks a piece of bark from it and returns to his mortar to grind it down. When it's all a nice fine dust, he glances at me. "I need one more ingredient for this," he says hesitantly, and I know instantly he needs my body fluid of some kind.

I sigh. "Blood, urine, sweat, tears or saliva?" I say, listing off as many readily available options as I can think of.

He raises an eyebrow in surprise. "Blood, if you don't mind."

I hold out my arm. "Have at it."

Rune nods and brings the mortar over, along with a very sharp knife.

First, he pours something over the knife and it glows then dies down to normal metal. Then he makes a swift, clean, cut, releasing a thin line of my glowing blood into the mortar. I flinch at the pain, but it's gone quickly enough.

When he has enough, he rubs a salve on my cut and it heals nearly instantly.

"I always assumed all fae knew how to do what you do. Is that true?"

He shrugs as he mixes my blood with the herbs. "All fae have some connection to the earth that they can use to manipulate their environment. You'll never find a fae who doesn't have a green thumb, unless they've been cursed. Even a drop of fae in your ancestry will guarantee a proper, thriving garden," he says. He stops speaking for a moment and closes his eyes, holding one hand over the mortar, while the other holds it. In that ancient Elven language I've heard a few times now, he mutters some words under his breath. The concoction flares before disappearing into smoke.

I expect him to scrape it out and make a tea from the paste, but instead he surprises me by dipping his fingers into the mortar and pulling out what looks like a small, black pearl.

Before I can ask, he answers my next question. "This should let the forest itself absorb your excess power, to give you control and ease the burden while we are here."

Damn, I'm going to be sharing my magic with ancient trees? That's wild.

"Do I just hold it?" I ask.

He shakes his head. "You ingest it."

Right. Of course.

He drops it in my hand and I feel a thrum of power connecting me to it and it to the forest trees. It's not much bigger than a pill and it's smooth, so it should go down easily enough. I take a swig of the water, then plop it into my mouth and swallow, taking another swig to help ease the journey.

The effects take a few moments, but when it works, I breathe a deep sigh of relief, my body ten times lighter as the stress of carrying that much power disappears.

"Shall we move along?" Rune asks once I've settled into the effects of his magic pill. "I sense we're getting close."

I hoist my pack off the ground and follow him, moving deeper into the woods. Now when I pass each tree, it looks so much more like a living spirit. I can see their wooden bodies exhaling oxygen and absorbing sunlight through their leaves. Trees are goddamn awesome.

When we reach the top of a hill, Rune stops. I come to his side and join him in looking over a strange, stunted cluster of trees. It looks as though all the trunks were chopped down about ten feet from the roots, but there's no cut line from an axe or saw. And I still sense the base of the trees are alive.

"Is this it?" I ask.

Instead of answering my question, Rune comes up behind me, his hands gripping my shoulders to give me a massage.

It seems like an odd time for this tenderness, but

I'm not going to fight it. If the fae feels like I need a backrub, then I must need a backrub. To my surprise, he wraps his arms around me and pulls me against his chest as his mouth settles near my ear.

I'm expecting words of comfort, or words of seduction even, but what I'm not expecting is words of warning.

His voice is a harsh whisper full of urgency. "There are wolves behind us, a pack of five. I need you to stay calm, and if I tell you to run, you must promise you will."

I freeze, my body on high alert and in serious adrenaline overdose panic mode. If Rune tells me to run because he thinks we're losing the fight, I don't think I'll be able to leave him.

I feel Runes' hands leave my body as he steps away. With a deep breath, I turn around to face our newest adversary.

The wolves are still about a hundred yards away, crouched and slowly slinking toward us. As strong and cunning as the fae may be, I've got my doubts about these lopsided numbers. I don't think I can fend off even one wolf, and that would leave Rune to fight four on his own. Also...

"What kind of wolves?" I dread the answer, as one

option presents a much greater danger than the other. "Like, earth wolves, or... you know."

We've been attacked by the fae and the vampire. Werewolves are the logical next wave.

His eyes stay locked on the approaching beasts as he reaches behind his back and drawers his sword.

"There's only one way to find out."

CHAPTER THIRTEEN

As Rune draws his blade, the wolves attack.

All five rush toward the fae, leaving me safe for the moment but absolutely helpless. I flinch as the first wolf lunges through the air, sharp teeth bared, ready to rip through flesh and bone. At the last second, Rune punches with the hilt of his sword, strong metal connecting with the wolf's jaw and sending the creature crashing to the ground.

At the same moment, another wolf approaches from behind. Rune displays some uncanny awareness, thrusting the blade back into the shoulder of an attacker I was sure he didn't see. The wounded animal limps away, one paw held off the ground.

I have no idea what types of wolves these are. Each is smaller than Zev in wolf form, but he's also an alpha prince and I just assume he's larger. They're certainly not small, and I see no reason why they'd shift into their slower, human forms mid-battle.

The remaining three wolves slow their roll a little, circling Rune cautiously after seeing how quickly he neutralized the first two attacks. They close in tentatively, but still with the same violent intent, their chests rumbling with deep growls.

As fear ramps up in my chest, I feel the familiar burn of my magic reaching its boiling point. Whether or not I'm connected to nature, the energy in my blood is on the rise and needs somewhere to go.

"Rune..." I barely manage to whisper as I lift my glowing hands. I know what's coming, so I'm going to do my best to stay a step ahead of this power surge and maybe, in some way, use it to our advantage.

Whether Rune hears me or senses a magical explosion I'm not sure, but he suddenly does an aerial cartwheel over the wolf behind him, hitting the ground and rolling away. As soon as he's out of my direct line of sight, I stop trying to hold back and expel the energy built up within. The power bursts from my chest and through my arms, forcing an emphatic gesture from my shoulders through my wrists as a brilliant wave of light and fire crashes into the scene before me.

The wolves yelp as the heat burns their fur and the energy knocks them to the ground. Behind them, a row of trees ignites, the smaller branches immediately turning to ash while the trunks burn bright blue.

When my hands have drained of the explosive magic, I look over to see Rune lying in the dirt, seemingly unburned. I rush to him and help him stand.

"Thank you for the warning," he says as we watch four of the five wolves retreat. The fifth, the one Rune stabbed, lays against a rock, its breathing labored and its fur smoldering.

"Those were earthly wolves," he says, returning his sword to its sheath. "I'm glad your spell only took the one. We've come to their home. They've every right to attack."

He walks over to the creature, which makes no effort to escape. Rune kneels next to it, placing a hand over the puncture wound by its shoulder. The wolf whimpers at first, then starts to pant. As Rune reaches into his pocket for one of his many ointments, he suddenly freezes and looks at the burning trees.

"Hurry," he yells to me as he abandons the wolf and runs toward the flames.

I fall in line without hesitating, though I can't

imagine what we're going to do with the fire I started. I certainly feel bad about any woodland casualties, but I can't very well suck the heat back into my fingertips.

The fae reaches the edge of the blaze--too close for comfort if you ask me--and flings a handful of bright yellow powder into the air. As it starts to float down toward the ground, Rune circles his hands with incredible, Darius-like speed, summoning a breeze that carries the dust into the flames. He's like a fire-fighting plane doing a chemical drop, but from the ground and with magic.

I stand next to him, completely at a loss for how I can help. He's working too hard to give me a job, and so far all my powers are good for is lighting shit on fire. I start to feel the dismay settling in; the one time I try to control an outburst and I've torched an ancient forest that was once the home of magical elves and fairies and spirits. This is why humans don't deserve to have nice things.

"Bernie, look at me," Rune says, and I realize that the fires have almost completely extinguished while I was being sad for myself. The fae reaches for my hand and gives me a small vial, this one full of a thick, amber liquid. It looks a lot like tree sap.

"This sap comes from regenerative trees in my

kingdom," he explains, confirming my obvious but still correct sap assessment. "One drop at the base of each tree. No more than that, do you understand?"

Instead of answering, I scamper off to one of the burning trees, intent on undoing what I've done. I start at one end of the smoldering grove and Rune starts at the other. There are eleven trees that took the brunt of my force, which doesn't feel like too many, but the haste with which Rune moves makes me think we've got seconds left before the effort becomes futile.

I uncap the vial and tilt it carefully as I stop at the first tree. Heat still emanates off the charred bark, but I don't care about my face getting a little toasted if it means I can make amends. I'm being super careful about letting just one drop fall, and at the same time the viscosity of the sap makes it take for freaking ever to pour.

I'm about to start shaking the vial when a drop finally releases, hitting one of the exposed roots at the base of the old tree. There's a slight sizzle as the sap gets absorbed into the root, and I watch to see what will happen next.

"Keep moving, Bernie," Rune says from across the grove. "They're dying from the inside, you won't be able to see if the remedy works or not."

I pull my eyes off the first tree and rush to the second, keeping the vial tilted so the next sap drop is ready to go. I notice that Rune's already tended to five members of the grove, so it's no wonder he's politely urging me to go faster.

The second drop of sap comes more quickly, and this time I waste no seconds moving on to the next tree. This one is stouter than the others, even though they're all short from whatever event cut off their top halves. I aim the sap droplet above the largest root I can see, my feet already poised to carry me off to the next tree as soon as the sticky liquid hits its mark.

But when the tree lets out a blood-curdling scream, my feet fail me.

I fall backward at the sound, my heart jumping out of my throat because the noise so shocks me. I manage to keep the vial in my hand, but the sap misses the root and settles into the dirt and ash a few feet from the tree.

Rune has a look of horror on his face, though he still manages to get to the last of the burning pillars before rushing over to me. As he arrives, another shrill screech pierces my ears and ripples goosebumps across my flesh.

"What is that?" I ask, even though I know the answer. Rune's pearl has me connected with the natural world in a way I could never have imagined. And while the surrounding trees helped steady my powers before the wolf attack, now I'm hearing the pained wails of death from one of their family members, because I can't control what flows through my veins.

"We've hopefully saved the others," Rune says in an attempt to comfort me. "For this one, I fear it's too late."

There's a tear in the fae's eye as he stands, walking from my side to the smoldering trunk. As upset as I am, Rune obviously feels this on a deeper level. Nature is a part of him in a way I will never fully understand. But it feels akin to the loss of a close family member, and that breaks my heart.

He comes to the trunk and, in defiance of his own nerve endings, places his hand against the scalding tree. Rune grimaces in pain but leaves his palm on the bark, absorbing the hurt or communing with the earth or something that he clearly believes is worth doing despite the intense pain.

As he stands there, I notice a shift in the tree to his right. There's a slight ripple within the bark, quick but noticeable. From the flattened top of the trunk, a body starts to emerge.

Rune stays focused on his searing palm and the

dying tree, so I'm alone in watching an indescribable figure grow out of an ancient stump. It looks like a pile of kindling in motion, but as more of the form comes into view, it starts to take a human shape.

I look back to Rune to see if he's noticed yet. His head is turned to the side where another figure is climbing out of a different trunk. Now, with the exception of the tree I couldn't save, every blackened stump has a body crawling out of it.

Rune backs up to join me. He keeps his eyes on the creatures moving toward us, but he doesn't unsheathe his sword.

"These are dryads," he says to me in a low voice.

"They live in the trees?" I ask, a lump in my throat as I face down nearly a dozen homeowners who might now be homeless.

"They live *with* the trees," he says. "It's a kinship humans could never understand. A deeper connection than most beings ever experience."

Each dryad stands nearly ten feet tall, and they slowly form a semi-circle around us. They have legs, arms and faces, sharing many qualities of a human body, but they're also like walking trees, with leaves and branches giving them shape. With each step, roots flow from their feet into the ground, keeping them constantly connected with the earth.

"I guess they're pretty mad at me?" I try to sound lighthearted because I'm 100% scared shitless. It's a different kind of fear than when wolves or vampires attack; this is the feeling of getting caught doing something wrong and awaiting judgment.

Rune doesn't answer, only takes my hand as the tallest of the tree people steps forward.

"You've slain one of my own," the dryad says, its voice like a loud gust of wind. The sound is horrifying and beautiful at the same time.

"I'm so sorry. I didn't... mean to," I say, stumbling on my tongue as I try not to cry. "I tried to save it. Him. Her." A squeeze of my hand from Rune indicates it's time for me to pass the microphone.

"Are you the queen?" Rune asks the dryad that approached. It, or rather she, gives a subtle nod, the leaves around her head rustling as she does.

"We were attacked by wolves, who we fended off without harm." Rune points to the injured wolf, still panting over by a rock, it's wound now mostly healed.

"You've entered the home of Cupressus without invitation," the tree says. "You've used dark magic to kill one of our family. Of the two, which shall pay the price?"

"Who two? Us two? What's the price?"

Rune squeezes my hand again, imploring me to shut the hell up. He's very right to do so.

"Neither," the fae answers, stepping toward the dryad queen in a way that could be perceived as either defiant or reverent. I guess we'll find out the queen's take soon enough. "My name is Rune, prince of the fae realm, long friend to the dryads and all growing life."

All the tree people lean forward to look more closely when he says his name. I'm really hoping his ancestry gives him some celebrity status in the forestry world.

"I've come on a quest, along with Bernadette, mother of the Last Witch."

Now all the wooden, leafy faces turn to look at me. For some reason I'm surprised to see recognition from trees, but I guess word of this ancient prophecy has made the rounds.

"Where is the child?" the dryad queen asks. It seems she wants proof of the claim, which is totally fair, but I'm guessing Rune didn't pack Rain's birth certificate or immunization card when he was loading up our bags.

"With our companions, princes from the other realms and the witch queen, Erzsébet," Rune answers, craftily name dropping. "We're bonded to save the baby witch and her mother, to keep any kingdom from acting on the prophecy."

"And why is that?" the dryad asks, stepping forward and towering over the fae. "Do you not wish to save your kind? Or are you spellbound to this witch?"

"Only by our own spell," Rune answers, standing his ground. "There's a magic within Bernadette, and surely within her child, that can't simply be sacrificed to a single race. I have seen this and it is why I willingly risk my life to protect her even against my own kind."

The queen of the tree folk turns and moves toward me. I don't have quite the same gumption as Rune, stumbling back a few steps as she approaches. Her face is exquisite but intimidating, with skin that looks like smoothed bark, eyes like shining knots, hair a woven mess of twigs and leaves.

"What is so special about your magic that you can kill?" she asks. "Wherefore do you get the right to strike down a tree soiled by the Fates themselves?"

Goddammit. I killed a tree that's as old as the planet. Thanks for making me feel even worse, tree lady.

"I... I don't have that right."

I don't know what else to say. I also know my

riffing hasn't been great thus far, so I just turn back to Rune, hoping he can help.

He takes his cue right away, stepping back to my side. "She bears a burden none of us could understand. Magic only recently came to her, days after she learned of her daughter and the prophecy. Our quest, that which fated this moment, is to help Bernadette control her powers so that she may protect her child and save this world, as well as the other realms."

The dryad keeps her gaze on me as she takes in Rune's words, seeming to consider it all for an extended beat before speaking again.

"Nevertheless, her magic is dark. What answer do you have to that, to ensure the safety of my kingdom?"

Rune looks into my eyes, his face warming as his expression softens with love and admiration.

"She has the powers of her mother within her, which, as you can sense, brings a shadow to her light. But there is only good in her heart, and only kindness in her soul. I've spent nearly every waking second in her company since coming to this world, brought by a prophecy that should have pitted us against one another. And yet there is no way not to fall in love with this woman's entire being. The care with which she treats all those in her presence. The love she provides for her daughter, even in the direst of moments. She brings constant light to a world in which there's a constant effort to extinguish her glow."

I've entirely forgotten why we're here and the point of Rune's monologue. His words are striking so deep in my core that I just want to kiss him and then live in his arms forever.

"Whatever darkness exists in Bernadette has no measure against her light," he says, turning back to the dryad. "This I promise you, and it's why you must be compelled to forgive."

The queen's eyes haven't left my face the entire time Rune speaks. Her expression hasn't changed either, but that might be because her face is mostly wood. I can sense the slightest shift in her perception of me, thanks to Rune giving the most inspired introduction in history, but I have no idea if it will be enough.

The dryad leans even closer, bending down so that the leaves atop her head nearly touch me.

"I sense the magic you describe, fae," she says. "But I must feel it for myself."

At those words, she starts to lift one of her gnarled arms, the tips of her branchy fingers directed at my chest.

"My queen, I implore you--"

As soon as Rune starts to speak, I raise my hand to silence him. I can't quite explain why, since his words have very much kept me alive to this point. Still, something in my witch's intuition says it's time for the dryad to commune directly with me.

"Bernie, you mustn't," Rune pleads. "You don't know what you're about to experience."

"I know that," I respond truthfully. "But neither do you."

He shakes his head, but now it's the fae's turn for words to fail him. He might understand what's about to happen, but he doesn't know what I will feel. And my gut says that the queen of the dryads, who has every right to consider me a murderer, will find the goodness she's hoping to see, through whatever method she uses to see it.

I raise my chin and take a deep breath, standing ready for the queen to do her bidding. Her arm inches closer to my chest, hovering above my heart, the pointed branches of her hand pushing past my clothes to touch my bare skin. And then I feel the worst pain I've ever experienced in my life.

Pushing out a baby hurts like hell, but I prepared myself for that and could understand the agony. As the queen spears me with her arm, puncturing my flesh and sticking her wooden fingers directly into my heart, I'm lost entirely to the excruciation.

Somehow, my body understands that this horrifying experience is not meant to kill me. My arms remain at my sides instead of flailing and trying to end it. My head tilts back but doesn't thrash. My feet stay planted and don't try to get away.

Through it all, the hurt doesn't dull a bit. I feel like pain receptors are supposed to go numb after they cross a certain threshold, but I'm getting no such treatment. I only feel it more intensely, like my heart is pumping anguished blood into my veins.

And then there is another layer of a new kind of pain as her magic plunges into my very soul. Waves of emotions overwhelm me, spiraling me into the darkest corners of my heart. Flashes of moments from my past flicker in my mind: lies I told, hurt I caused, all the ways I inflicted pain on others or myself over my lifetime. I feel sure I'm going to die, that I am being judged and found wanting and I am now seeing the worst parts of my life flash before me until finally I will come to the afterlife and discover where it is we all end up, if anywhere.

I feel myself tumbling into the darkness of eternity only to be pulled back to my body when the queen speaks.

"Hmmm," the queen murmurs, leaning her face even closer to mine. "I know you," she goes on. "Yes… I know this blood."

It's definitely what a serial killer would say while eating a still-living victim, but it has a different meaning coming from this ancient, powerful tree-being. If she recognizes the blood that flows through me, that has to mean something, right? Hopefully a good something.

As fast as it started, the pain retreats when the dryad pulls her branch hand out of my chest. I look down in time to see the gaping wound close and slowly heal, leaving just a small leaf-shaped scar where the tree stabbed into me.

The queen steps back and Rune jumps to my side, offering support as my legs start to wobble a little. I keep my eyes locked with the dryad's, waiting to see what she'll say or do next. Having offered my heart for her inspection, I feel pretty confident she'll let me live.

Instead of addressing me, she and the other dryads turn away in unison, reforming their half-circle around the dead tree. For a long time, everything is completely still, the only sounds are leaves shifting in the slight breeze. Rune and I stay silent as well, paying our respects for the life lost. I glance to the side and see the fallen wolf is back on its feet, gingerly walking to rejoin its pack.

I return my eyes to the stump that died today, that I killed with errant, dark magic, even if it was an accident. A tear falls down my cheek, and I vow to hold onto this pain so I'll remember the cost of power gone astray.

Once the dryads conclude their silent ceremony, all but the queen return to the trees from which they emerged. Meanwhile, her highness returns to me and bows her head.

When she stands erect again, I see a new growth coming from her center. A thin branch stretches toward me, like a sapling sprouting in front of my eyes. It's just a foot long, a mix of green and brown, with smooth bark.

The dryad queen wraps the thin twigs of her fingers around the new branch, and with a swift pull, rips it from her body. It's a little startling, like watching someone reset a dislocated shoulder, and I try not to cringe too visibly.

She looks at the branch for a second, inspecting it carefully, and then hands it to me.

"You are forgiven," the dryad says, then turns and walks back to her tree.

I watch until she's gone, retreated back inside the

stump, before finally looking down at the gift she gave me. It's not much to take in, but it feels special, important, even alive.

"Do you know why she gave me this?" I ask Rune.

The fae smiles at me, then looks back at the row of ancient trees.

"If I had to guess," he says with a smile, "I'd say that's your wand."

CHAPTER FOURTEEN

The death of the dryad weighs heavily on me as we hike back to the main road. Even though I now carry the casing for my wand, it feels like a gift and a condemnation in one. I am blessed and cursed by this magic in equal measure it would seem.

We are quiet on our hike, as Rune takes my hand, allowing his warm, calming energy to flow through me.

It works, though I still feel an inexplicable ache in my heart, in the place where the dryad queen pierced through my soul, and I wonder if that will ever go away. Part of me hopes it doesn't, as I don't want to ever forget the price of my power.

With my free hand, I rub at the scar that remains, tracing the lines of the leaf design.

Of all the things I've seen and experienced since the three princes walked into my bar, this has been the most surreal.

When we reach the end of the forest that connects to the main road, Rune casts his charms to once again hide us in the back of a pickup, and I fall asleep with my head in his lap as we head to Budapest.

I don't wake until we arrive in the city. It's midday, the sun high in the sky, casting warm rays of light that take the bite out of the winter cold.

By the time we reach the cemetery and make our way into the tomb, I am desperate to see my baby.

My gaze lands on her small form the moment my eyes adjust to the dimly lit underground space. She's on a blanket on the floor with Darius, who's singing her a song in a language I've never heard. His voice is soft and soothing, and I melt a little at the sight.

Not wanting to interrupt, though I know the vampire knows we're here, I stand and wait, watching with a small smile on my face.

When the song ends, he looks up, his dark eyes shining, his smile when he sees me luminous, and I rush over to him and Rain, throwing myself into his arms. Rain coos and seems to smile when she sees me, but it could just be gas.

Either way, I'll take it.

Success? he whispers into my mind. I tilt my head to look into his eyes and nod.

Darius kisses me, taking his time to explore the texture of my lips, his tongue flicking into my mouth, warming the center of my body instantly, then he moves to nuzzle my neck. "You are glowing, my love," he says.

I nod. "Rune helped me control my powers while in the forest, but I've been bursting since we left."

"Allow me to remedy that," he says.

I moan into him at the promise of such delights, but get distracted by the baby next to us.

He winks. "I was about to put her down for a nap."

"Where is Zev?" Rune asks as he putters around the room tidying things that aren't dirty.

"Out getting food. We ran out this morning and haven't seen Erzsébet since you left."

Rune raises an eyebrow at that. "If you both are okay here, I will go find her and let her know we have been successful in our quest. We need to make your wand as soon as possible."

"Be safe," I say, reluctant to let any of these men out of sight with so much uncertainty in our lives right now.

He crosses the room and kisses my cheek, then kisses Rain's head. "I will be very safe," he says. "Stay here until I get back."

He leaves, getting sucked up into the world in a way that feels like a sci-fi movie. Beam me up, Scottie.

Shaking my head, I return my attention to Darius as he gently lays Rain in the crib and covers her with a blanket. She falls asleep instantly, with the innocence of a well-protected child. I wish, not for the first time, that I could document her strange start to life with a baby book. It would certainly be the most unique one any child has had, I'm sure of that.

Darius is ready and waiting to take my blood as I move back to him. Wordlessly he pulls me close, slipping his arms around my waist, pressing his strong, muscular body against mine. I tilt my head and with gentle fingers he brushes the hair off my neck and leans forward, his breath warm against my skin.

When his teeth plunge into my vein, I'm once again set on fire with the mixture of pleasure and pain it brings. I close my eyes and grip his body, my fingers digging into his back as I press closer against him.

He drinks in my blood, the glow in my skin fading back to normal. By the time he finishes, both of us are desperate for each other.

We could go to the back room, he says into my mind.

Before I can respond, Zev returns, carrying two grocery bags. The werewolf instantly zones in on us, his nostrils flaring and body immediately reacting to the sexual charge in the room.

"I would ask how you are, but I think I already know," the werewolf says, his green eyes devouring me in one look, his voice husky and filled with his own need.

He sets the groceries on the table and slowly walks over to us. Darius still has his arms around me, and Zev positions himself behind me, so that I'm sandwiched between the two men.

My heart rate ramps up as the electricity between the three of us nearly overwhelms me.

Zev places his hands above Darius's, wrapping his arms around me just below my breasts, brushing against them as he does.

He brings his lips to my ear and whispers. "I am so glad you are back safely. To be apart from my mate for so long is… unpleasant."

As it always does, the word mate makes me swoony and I lean into him, allowing the two men to tighten their hold on me. I have no idea what this might lead to, but I enjoy the feeling of them both against me. And they clearly do as well, if the hardness in their pants is any indication.

Darius kisses me as Zev nuzzles my neck, exploring the sensitive skin with teeth and lips and tongue. His hands push up, caressing my breasts, his fingers brushing against my hard nipples through my clothes.

I'm lost in the sensations of both of them. They are in my skin, my blood, my heart and soul. They are so much a part of me, I don't know where I end and they begin.

After some time, which could be minutes or hours, as time has lost all meaning, Zev turns me to face him. "It's my turn," he says gruffly, as he claims my lips with a barely contained and nearly bruising passion. Darius pulls my ass against him and begins to slide his hands down the front of my pants.

He teases me at first, while Zev nibbles my lip and cups my face as he unleashes his desires into me. Darius lets his hands explore without giving me what I really need.

When the vampire's fingers finally slide into me, I moan into Zev's mouth, nearly exploding then and there, but he doesn't give me the satisfaction quite yet, instead he pulls out until he's barely touching me, then rubs at the most sensitive spot before plunging back in.

Zev has moved his hands to my breasts, and as he kisses me, he slides his hands under my shirt and bra, cupping my breasts, his thumbs rubbing over my nipples--now without any clothing interfering.

I'm delirious with the pleasure, stunned that I get to enjoy them both.

I'm about to fly off the edge of the cliff, overwhelmed by the feeling of having both men play my body like an instrument, one they are very skilled at finding the right notes on.

As the climax inside me builds, Zev moves his mouth to my shoulder, the same one that already has a small mark where he bit me before. He bears down with his teeth, claiming that spot again, as Darius increases his rhythm between my legs, and I close my eyes and let it all roll over me. My mind explodes in fireworks as the waves crash into me and my body is rocked to the core. My legs are jelly but both men keep me on my feet as they coax my climax out longer and longer, as more and more waves hit me, until I spill into their arms, a limp noodle so blissed out I can hardly think.

Without words, because none of us have any, Zev lifts me into his arms and takes me to the makeshift bed Darius made. He lays me down and spoons me while Darius stays to watch Rain--through some unspoken agreement between the two.

I pull the werewolf's arms more tightly around me, enjoying the feel of him pressed against me, and fall into a dreamless nap where I am safe and warm.

I wake sometime later to the sound of arguing and a baby crying. Zev is no longer by my side, and I'm so groggy I can't tell how long I've been out.

When I walk into the main room I see Erzsébet there with the three Sexies. Rune is comforting Rain, who needs a diaper change by the smell wafting from her, Zev has food laid out and is eating a sandwich, and Darius is yelling at the witch queen.

"It's not safe. She's not going. Final word."

Erzsébet narrows her eyes at the vampire, then turns to Zev, who shrugs casually, less heated than Darius. "Her safety is most important," he says between bites. "I agree with the vampire."

Rune finishes changing the diaper and cradles her. "I agree," he says. "Going back to the Grand Hall poses too many risks we can't account for. Bernie's enemies already know she's been there, so the council surely has it surveilled."

Erzsébet frowns. "Your commitment to this

woman is impressive, but it is misguided. The longer she is without a wand, the less safe she is."

Tired of being talked about, I walk forward. "What's going on?" I ask. I move instinctually to hold my baby, then stop, putting my hands behind my back. The episode from the forest has me more afraid of my powers than ever.

"You must return to the Grand Hall to complete your wand," Erzsébet says.

"Can't you just take the materials and do it then bring it back?" I ask, though as soon as I say the words I know that's not going to be enough. Like acquiring the pieces, I have to take part in the crafting. It's an instinctive knowledge that hits me, and Erzsébet notices when it does and nods.

"You understand, then," she says.

I sigh. "Yeah. I do."

I look at Darius, the angriest of the three. "It won't work if I'm not there."

"Then make it here," he says through gritted teeth.

Erzsébet shakes her head. "We must go to the crystal cave within the Grand Hall for her to choose her tip, then we must forge it over the ancient fires. Only then will it be strong enough to contain her magic."

"It's going to be okay," I say, trying to assure myself as much as I am the Sexies. "At least one of you should stay here to protect Rain. Maybe two of you, just in case. She's the real target."

Erzsébet nods. "That is wise. Which one of you would like to accompany Bernadette?"

All three step forward.

"It is still full daylight," Erzsébet says. "So perhaps the vampire should not travel during this time."

"I'm the best able to fight off my own kind should it come to that," Darius says, "and I have a mental bond with Bernie that can help protect her. I suggest we should wait until dark. Bernie needs to eat before she goes at any rate."

Zev growls. "I am her mate. It should be I who accompanies her."

"And I know the most about wand making," Rune says.

I look at all three of them, torn about who to bring. I need them all, but I'm determined at least two of them should stay with my baby.

"I wish I could pick all of you, but I think Darius is right. So far only vampires have found us, and he's our best defense against them. Plus he can communicate with you two telepathically if needed".

Erzsébet nods. "Very well. Eat and rest. I will retrieve you at sunset. Be ready."

She leaves quickly, without any other niceties, and Zev hands me a sandwich I didn't see him make. "Eat. You haven't been eating enough."

I haven't been doing a lot of things enough. Showering and brushing my teeth come to mind. But sweet Jesus I am starving.

So I sit and eat and think about all the things going on right now. "I don't suppose you bought a phone charger at the store today did you?" I ask Zev.

He shakes his head.

"Damn. I need to call AJ. I'm worried about her, and Morgan's. Need to make sure it hasn't burned down. Again."

"It didn't burn down last time," Rune says. "It was just singed a bit."

I chuckle at that. "Right. Either way, she's probably just as worried as I am."

"I'm sure she knows you're dealing with a lot and will be in touch when you can," Rune says.

I laugh. "You don't know AJ."

Sandwich finished, I grab a water bottle and guzzle it, then head to the makeshift area we are using as a bathroom. Makeshift area is my fancy way of saying "bucket in the corner." It's not elegant and I try not to think too much about it. At least it magically empties itself.

I handle my business and find some clean clothes waiting for me, courtesy of Zev. Grateful--especially for clean underwear--I change into some trendy jeans with ripped knees, a long-sleeved top with giant lips on the chest, and a very comfortable gray cardigan.

Feeling as refreshed as I'm going to get, I join the guys and wait for Erzsébet to return.

While we wait, I ask Darius about the song he was singing to Rain.

"It is an ancient song we used to sing on the longest night of the year, when my people had the most freedom to wander. It is a song of hope and cheer. My mother used to sing it to me, once upon a time."

We continue talking about our lives before we met, their lives, of course, being much longer and more dramatically filled with interesting things than mine.

I tell them about my time at Juilliard and how my love of piano developed. I tell them about the man who fathered Rain, who broke my heart. About my friends there who didn't stay in touch once I got pregnant and left. About the crazy shit AJ and I got up to as children.

When Erzsébet returns, Darius and I are ready to go. I say goodbye to my baby, who's freshly fed and swaddled, then I kiss Zev and Rune before heading into the night with a vampire and queen witch and glowing skin that paints a bullseye on my back.

THE GRAND HALL looks as it did in my last dream. Crumbled and broken, though the dead bodies have been removed, thank goodness. Andor finds us as soon as we arrive, his face a mask of worry and anger.

"Where have you been?"

I look around. "Me?" I ask, confused by the aggressive tone in his voice.

"I've been worried sick since the attack." He takes my hand in his, his eyes wide and sincere. "I know you do not want to be my lover. But I hope at least we can be friends. I have spent my life waiting for you, waiting to protect you and help empower you."

"Um... thanks," I say, unsure how to respond to his intense claim on me. It doesn't feel good, but it's their way and I can't judge them for it. I just can't play along either.

Erzsébet purses her lips. "Step aside, Andor. We are here to make Bernadette's wand."

His eyes widen in shock. "You got all the ingredients? Already?"

Feeling a bit cocky with my success, I nod. "It wasn't that hard." It totally was, but he doesn't need to know that. For some reason I feel inclined to make it very clear how much I do not need him.

I wonder if he can trade for a different witch to bond with. Maybe file for designated lover divorce.

Erzsébet clears her throat and leads us through the tragically demolished hall and through a corridor that takes us to the crystal cave, according to her very curt guided tour.

Andor follows, of course, but at least I have Darius by my side. He doesn't seem to like the guy very much, which I don't hold against him. He's already sharing me with his two best friends. A random guy isn't going to be able to get a foothold in our group.

When we enter the cave, a hush falls over our small group as the magnificent beauty of it all settles into us.

Lining the walls and ceiling are crystals of all shapes, sizes, and colors, glistening and glittering with an internal light that illuminates the entire cave. In the center is a large fire pit with a glowing blue flame burning within. A giant black cauldron hangs over the blaze, suspended by nothing but magic.

Witch fire.

Erzsébet stands next to the fire. "Bernadette, take out your dragon scale and wand casing and come here."

Darius follows me, pushing Andor aside when he tries to scoot in, and stands at my back like a bouncer while I follow the witch's instructions.

"I understand you were gifted a piece of the dryad queen, yes?" Rune must have filled her in when he fetched her earlier. "That's very special indeed. She's been alive for millions of years, and I don't know of another wand made from her being."

Shit. No pressure.

"Place the branch and the dragon scale into the cauldron," Erzsébet says.

I do as instructed, and a light flares up then dies down. Heat engulfs me and I resist the urge to wipe away the sweat dripping down my face. Erzsébet moves closer to me and produces a sharp blade, then slices a chunk of my hair off.

"Hey, that's going to grow back all uneven."

She ignores me, handing me the clump of hair. "Put this in."

I do.

Another flare of light.

Another burst of heat.

"Finally, you must bleed into the cauldron while reciting this spell." She clears her throat before continuing.

"A test és a vér, a csont és az iszap annyira isteni tartja a varázslatomat."

That's a lot of Hungarian to learn in one sitting, and I ask her to repeat the words twice before I attempt them myself. I take her knife and slice into my arm, holding it over the cauldron. Then I do my best attempt at speaking the spell.

For a moment nothing happens, and I worry I've messed up, but then the contents of the pot begin to sizzle and purple smoke pours out. As the sizzling gets louder, I hold my breath, waiting.

I'm so on edge that when the entire cauldron explodes into pieces, sending shards of cast iron everywhere, I scream in alarm.

Darius is lightning fast, pulling me away and shielding me with his body, though he needn't have bothered as Erzsébet had already cast some kind of containment spell to keep everyone safe.

When the pieces fall to the ground and the fires return to normal, I pull away from my vampire and look around the room at what remains. "Does this mean I've ruined my wand?" I ask, heartbroken. That would be just my luck. There's no way the dryad queen will give me another body part, and that's assuming I can get another dragon scale without getting burned to death.

Tears burn my eyes and Darius takes my hand, speaking directly into my mind.

We will find another way.

I shake my head, swiping a tear. *There is no other way.*

When I look to Erzsébet, I'm surprised to see a calm smile on her face. If my wand is destroyed, she's taking it very well, which makes me think not all is lost. She raises her own wand and speaks a word that sends all the pieces into place. With the floor cleared, I now see what sits at the center of the fire.

A beautiful wand engulfed in blue flames, the base slightly thicker than the top, the green and brown coloring of the wood now slightly darker. My jaw drops. It seems to glow and beckons me to it.

"Go on," Erzsébet says. "Only you can wield it."

I take a tentative step forward, afraid to stick my hand into the flames but also compelled to do so. I bend down to pick it up, the heat constant but never burning me. Immediately I feel magic connect to the wand as golden light glows around us both.

The wood is carved in an intricate design that looks elven to me, and I smile, pleased at the beauty of it.

Be of pure soul.

The voice in my mind isn't Darius's and with a start I realize that it was the dryad queen's voice, as the mark on my chest begins to ache.

I smile, turning to Darius and Erzsébet. And Andor, I suppose, who's standing behind Darius looking sad.

"It's incredible!" I say. "Now what?"

Erzsébet smiles a truly happy smile and it brings out the beauty in her stately features. "Now, you must allow a crystal to choose you. The wand itself contains the magic, but the crystal tip allows you to control it."

I look around the cave. "How do I know which one is choosing me?" I ask.

Erzsébet gives a slight shake of her head. "You have to find one that speaks to you. I won't be able to hear it, so the decision rests squarely on your shoulders."

I turn back to the walls of shimmering stones, now panicking that I don't speak crystal well enough to make the right choice.

I try to follow the witch's instructions, listening to each gem I pass, but none of them are in a chatty mood. I make another round, trying to start the conversation, but get nothing in return. It goes on forever. I throw out Hungarian words, speak in funny voices, try to communicate telepathically, and it's all for naught.

Hours later, I slump to the ground in exhaustion. "I'm not vibing with any of them," I say dejectedly.

Erzsébet scans the room, then walks over to a ruby and plucks it from the wall like she's picking berries from a bush. "Try this. Rubies are especially useful for protection."

I like the sound of that.

"Put it on the tip of your wand and say *kötvény*."

I do as she says, and as soon as I speak the word, the stone embeds itself into my wand forming a beautifully smooth tip.

"I love it," I say, studying every detail.

"Now try a spell," Erzsébet says.

"Um. I don't know any off the top of my head."

She frowns. "We must remedy that. Now's as good a time as any for you to learn the food spell you seemed excited about. Say *étel*."

I swish my wand and repeat the word.

Instantly the ruby explodes in my face. Fortunately, Erzsébet has her wand at the ready and deflects the careening shards so they don't blind me. The base of the wand, thank heavens, is still good as new.

"That was clearly not the correct crystal," she says, moving on to pick another. "Try a diamond. They are very powerful."

She hands me the largest, most perfect looking diamond I've ever seen and I gasp. This is worth a fortune. Holy shit.

Unable to process the fact that I'm holding more wealth in my hand than probably exists in my entire hometown, I place it on the top and speak the spell to bond them.

The resulting wand is so stunning I'm rendered speechless. I nervously prepare to try a spell, praying it works.

It too explodes in my face.

I just destroyed two priceless gems, but I don't have the energy to dwell on that because I'm starting to doubt my powers will ever be controlled.

Undeterred, Erzsébet picks another gemstone. And another. And another. Each with the same result as the last.

After several more hours of painfully awful attempts to make the tip of my wand, nothing works. We are surrounded by bits and pieces of the stones and I'm no closer to having a functioning wand than I was when we arrived.

I rub my eyes and yawn, and Darius comes to me, putting an arm around my shoulder. Andor's face turns dark at the contact, but quickly smooths out to neutral when he catches me looking at him.

Erzsébet paces the cave. "I'm sorry, child. It's clear an element of your wand is at odds with the others. I'd venture it's the tip, but we've tried every type of stone."

For someone who was already feeling pretty sad, her words take me to a whole new plain of sorrow. "You're saying there's something wrong with the scale? Or the branch?"

She shakes her head, eyes still scanning the room in search of answers. "That would never be my guess, but I've also never seen a quality wand reject this many gems. I'll need time with my spellbook in order to…"

Erzsébet freezes as a green hue fills the room. It doesn't come from the crystals lining the walls, but rather the walls themselves.

"Someone's in the garden," the witch says.

"What?" Andor says with disbelief. "That's impossible, my queen. Apart from yourself and Bernadette, no one knows of the underwater passage."

"Timót knows," Erzsébet answers, eyes boring down on Andor. "Weren't you with him as he prepared to leave for the caves?"

Andor appears stunned by the queen's statement, pushed back on his heels. He shakes his head. "No, I only helped him prepare. I had nothing to do with his travels."

Erzsébet turns to me, reading my face for information before asking her question. "Have you shown or told anyone of the entrance?"

"Not unless someone's reading my mind," I answer honestly. "And that happens way more than I'd like, so I can't make any promises."

Darius is already standing at the exit to the crystal cave, waiting for the rest of us to follow. "No sense in letting intruders make the first move," he says. "Lead us to the garden."

Erzsébet follows the vampire's command, moving quickly to the exit and into the corridor. I head after them with Andor close on my heels. I hear him muttering under his breath, but can't make out the Hungarian. I'm sure I wouldn't understand even if he was slowly speaking directly at me.

We reach the garden door and the witch queen puts her hand against the stone before reaching for her key. "I feel magic... but nothing dark."

She lifts her wand and aims it at the door while her other hand retrieves the key. "Darius, stand in front of Bernadette. I'll blind the cave when the door opens."

I move behind the vampire, putting my hands on his sides and peering around his right arm. He reaches back and rests a hand firmly on my side, offering what little comfort he can provide in this nerve-wracking moment.

With a quick flourish, Erzsébet opens the stone door and yells, "*fényes vak!*"

I'm impressed and jealous as I watch the brightest burst of light leap from the tip of her wand. Whatever crystal she's got has no problem doing shit without imploding. The light envelopes the garden cave, as every plant inside disappears in the hot, white glow.

"Jesus Christ, bub, turn that shit down!"

It takes all of a half second for me to recognize the voice. Against my better instincts, I rush into the room, blinded by the light as I do so.

"AJ?!"

"B?!" my best friend's voice cries back. "Where the hell are you? I feel like I'm back in high school getting the shine down from the cops."

With me in the room, Erzsébet has no choice but to retract the blaring light and let everyone be seen. It takes a moment for our eyes to adjust, but I finally see AJ standing at the edge of the stream with Zev by her side. He's dripping wet from the swim, but it looks like my water nymph gal just shook the droplets off.

We sprint to each other and hug like sisters who have been separated for years instead of days. I look over her shoulder at Zev, who's doing an excellent job at containing his jealousy after not getting the first hug.

"What the hell are you doing here?" I ask when we finally pull apart.

"Well, some bitch who's name rhymes with Mernie won't answer her damn phone, so I had to buy a goddamn plane ticket to... where are we, Hungary? Turkey? I confuse the two every damn time..."

"But A," I cut in, trying to get her bouncing brain to settle in one place. "Why did you come? Did something happen?"

She takes a deep breath, suddenly serious now that she has to explain herself. "I've been talking with that ghost, the one you stuck in the bar with me. Thanks for that, by the way. Nothing like doing bar prep while a freaking ghost sings old pirate songs--"

"A!"

"Right, sorry. Anyway, he's been around a long

time, knows a lot about Morgan's, your family, the witches, everything."

AJ takes a beat to look at the other faces in the room, then back at me, a sadness taking over her eyes. "The ghost thinks your grandpa is full of shit."

"What? What do you mean?"

"The letter, coming to Budapest, all of it," she says. "He says it's a trap."

CHAPTER FIFTEEN

Too many of AJ's words clash in my brain, keeping the sentences from leading to any sort of comprehension. As I wait for the pieces to fall into place, Erzsébet walks over and steps between me and my friend.

"Very pushy," AJ says in response to Erzsébet's arrival. "You must be the witch wolfy was talking about."

"I'm sure I am," the queen responds in a soft tone that belies the look on her face. "May I ask how you got here?"

"I'm Bernie's best friend, and I'm also a water nymph so don't try any shit."

Erzsébet looks a little confused, and rightly so because AJ's answer doesn't make a lot of sense. Zev walks over to join our little pow wow, taking my hand in his while putting his other hand on AJ's shoulder.

"I brought us through the channel, remembering the way after Bernie showed me," he says, then gestures to AJ. "She arrived this morning and I caught her scent after you all left the tomb. Our seance back in Massachusetts brought forth a spirit who apparently continues to offer valuable information."

"Sidebar," AJ says to me with a smile, "the ghost is totally hot." I'm not sure if she's joking or not, since I'm pretty sure the ghost is invisible.

"What did the ghost say?" I ask. My brain's finally caught up enough that I know gramps has been pulled back into this and I need some clarification.

"His name is Leo Ransom," she says, "and he said the letter arrived *after* all the shit went down." AJ has an excited look on her face as she dives into her mysterious story. "No one brought it, it just arrived, like floated down into the basement and went inside that keepsake box."

"What?" I fire back skeptically. "How can a letter just fly itself into a box?"

AJ raises an eyebrow, not all that impressed with my dubious tone. "I don't know, Bernie, maybe it has something to do with ALL THE MAGIC."

She punctuates the yelling with a cute little smile,

which is a classic AJ move. It drives me nuts but it's also pretty endearing.

"So what does that mean?" I ask. "What does it mean about my grandpa?"

AJ shrugs. "Beats me. It did seem a little weird that he left a letter saying he knew he was going to die, but then he hid it away for half a year, and then was just like, 'go to Budapest, bitch'."

Spelled out like that, it does feel a little insane that our first response was to follow the letter blindly, hopping on a plane to head straight to Budapest. That said, I've since met a dragon, been heart-stabbed by a tree, and had the best sex of my life. If this is a trap, it's very slow to spring.

"Who did the letter advise you to meet?" Erzsébet asks me, a quizzical look on her face.

"My father, I told you that--"

"But what was the name given, child? What name did the letter use?"

I have to think for a second, but I'm sure I remember correctly after reading that letter at least fifty times before accidently burning it to ash. "Timothy Trendle."

Erzsébet continues staring at me, though her mind has clearly gone to a far off place. Her brain seems to be sorting through puzzle pieces, just as

269

mine had a few moments before. The difference, of course, is that I was trying to make sense of a single sentence, and I'm sure Erzsébet is sifting through the entire history of magic.

"Interesting," she says, slowly turning away and pacing between the deep green ferns. "Unless done in secret and with a magic envoy, your father and grandfather never met. Lauren and Timót kept their relationship secret, as they were advised to do, and then he returned to Hungary before you were born."

I never gave it much thought growing up, but neither Tilly nor Ed ever really spoke of my father. Mom did all the storytelling, and even that was sparse. He was an all-but-forgotten figure.

"But what does that prove?" I ask, not yet seeing the point. "I've never met him either, but I can still find out his name and come looking for him."

She stops her pacing and nods, then looks back at me. "If you were to introduce me, how would you do it?"

"Huh?"

"Tell AJ my name."

For the love of all that's holy, why do magical beings love speaking in so many goddamn riddles?

"Fine," I say, knowing that the only way to get

through is to play along. "This is... Erzsébet. It sounds much better when she says it. You happy?"

I look back at the queen, who is, indeed, looking rather happy.

"And why don't you translate my name into English? Why not call me Elizabeth?"

I'm not entirely sure where this is headed, but my interest has definitely turned a corner.

"Because that's not the name you told me," I answer. "You're not American, feels like it would be weird to change it."

"I agree," Erzsébet says. "And yet that's what your grandfather appears to have done with his letter. He took the name Timót Tarijan, which your father was given at birth and used all his life, and offered you a translation. Why?"

She's clearly five steps ahead of me and I harbor no illusions of catching up, so I'm just going to see if I can get the answer. "I don't know, why?"

Her smile fades and her eyes narrow. "I don't know, either. I consider it very fortunate that you came here. I ensured your safe passage to the Grand Hall once you arrived in Budapest, but I knew nothing of this letter. Someone else motivated your voyage, and it's of the utmost importance we find out who... and more importantly, why."

Super. All that wordplay and we've got more questions than we started with, plus my fated Budapest trip now feels like a bad decision.

Darius flashes over to my side, taking the hand not held by Zev. It's not a possessive or jealous move, just his attempt to comfort. When AJ sees that I've got a Sexy on either side, each holding a hand, she crosses her arms and flashes a knowing smile. My cheeks immediately turn fire-engine red.

"Who do you suspect?" Darius asks Erzsébet. "Surely you have suspicions."

"Suspicions, yes, but I don't know where to cast them," she answers. "Until we find Timót or the one responsible for his death, I have no information worth acting on."

"So you don't think that was my father in the cave?" I ask. Since seeing that charred corpse, I've had a nagging doubt about who it was. For whatever reason, I feel like the experience would have been more visceral if it was actually him. Does Erzsébet share in my disbelief?

"I can't say, Bernadette," she says in an apologetic tone. "But with a dead dragon, a stolen dragonling, and this…"

She reaches into her pocket and pulls out the pendant that I took off the body, the one she quickly snatched away from me. I forgot about that feisty maneuver and now I'm back to not fully trusting the witch and wanting that necklace back.

"These pendants go to the *Érintett*--those who, like your father, are able to glean some magic from the witches in their stead," Erzsébet says while looking at the pendant.

"So the body *could* have been my father's?" I ask impatiently, cutting off the witch's thought even though I know there's more to it. I'm also just giving AJ a few seconds to catch up because she looks unbelievably confused.

Erzsébet shakes her head. "It's still possible, but the *Érintett* pendants are made of white gold. This piece could never endure dragon fire, much less the heat needed to kill a dragon."

I look at the pendant in her hand. Aside from a smudge here or there, it's still in pristine condition. Meanwhile, the body next to the dragon was all but turned to ash. In retrospect, the whole thing seemed pretty damn staged. Sort of like someone wanted me to take that pendant and leap to the conclusion my dad was dead.

"Enough," Erzsébet says, hastily pocketing the white gold charm and looking at everyone in the room. "We have much to do and, I suspect, little time to do it. And we've added another non-witch member to our ranks, which makes things more difficult."

It's not a jab, per se, but the look on AJ's face shows she's definitely taking offense to the witch's words.

"Bernadette, you'll need to work on your wand in solitude," Erzsébet continues. "I'll give you a book on power binding and cursed elements. Read it carefully."

I'm not going to argue, but I definitely don't love that I've been given homework while the entire magic world is trying to find and kill me. Especially when I bet the queen of the witches could probably give a pretty quick synopsis of my reading assignment.

"Andor," she says, turning to look back at the little man who's still standing by the door. Once again I'd forgotten he was with us, and with how much he wants to be noticed by me, I'm sure he's aware that I keep losing sight of him. "Any luck locating that other spellbook? The one that's gone missing?"

Erzsébet really slows down and emphasizes each of her words, laying on the subtext pretty thick. I'm not sure what they're talking about, but they've obviously had this conversation before.

In response, Andor gets a bit fidgety. He might be

thinking about his answer, or just nervous about giving it.

"No, my queen, nothing yet," he says quietly. "I've asked nearly every witch who would have had access, and no one recalls seeing it around. With how few in our ranks have the power to possess and read those spells, I'm at a loss for who could have taken it."

Erzsébet keeps her eyes on Andor while he makes no attempt to meet her gaze.

"What's gone missing?" I ask. I don't really care if this is a private conversation between the two of them. My daughter is in the most danger and I come in a close second, so I feel like I've got a right to know anything and everything at this point.

After another few seconds of beating down Andor with her glare, Erzsébet turns back to me. "An old book, one known to contain dark spells. It went missing two days after your father left."

Another interesting tidbit that seems ultra-important and yet just leads us to one more dead end. What the hell was my father up to and where did he go? And who sent the letter to get me here?

Just as Erzsébet opens her mouth to give further instructions, AJ raises her hand. It's a strange, school-girl gesture, and she's got an impatient, angry look on her face while she waits to be acknowledged.

"Do you have something you need to say?" Erzsébet asks, a thin veil of politeness covering her testy words.

"Yes, I do, thank you... *Elizabeth.*" AJ would never hesitate to mouth off to a stranger, and it seems being in a magical garden in the presence of the mightiest witch has changed absolutely nothing. "Just to clarify... B, did you see a freaking dragon?"

We all stare at AJ silently for a moment. I'm the first to burst out laughing, followed immediately by Zev and Darius. I'm guessing they've missed having AJ around almost as much as I have. Hopefully someday we'll have a little extra time to get her caught up on everything that's happened.

Erzsébet simply turns and walks to the exit, calling over her shoulder as she goes. "Bernadette, the spellbook will be waiting in the tomb. Andor, guide them back." She pauses after giving him the instruction, like she's waiting to see his reaction. It seems like she doesn't trust him, yet she's still giving him responsibilities. It's hard to keep up with the witch's mind games.

"Take extra caution," Erzsébet says to all of us. "I expect we'll be visited by vampires again before too long."

AJ's eyes go wide. "*Again?*"

I take her hand and we all follow to the door.

"Yeah, again,' I say. "I also talked to a tree. Lots to catch you up on, but not until I figure out how to make my stupid wand work."

We reach the exit and Andor takes the lead. He still looks a bit rattled, and I'm starting to wonder exactly what's affecting his mood. The missing book sounds like it might have Andor more preoccupied than the hunks who are always by my side, keeping him from the prize he thought he'd won.

"Who's the small guy?" AJ asks as we walk down the corridor and start to head through the Grand Hall. There's no way Andor didn't hear her, but he doesn't bother looking back. I don't answer, instead just shush AJ with a finger to my lips and give her an *I'll tell you later* look.

THE WALK to the tomb is thankfully uneventful, even a little entertaining as AJ, who's never seen the outside of Massachusetts, gawks at old buildings and signs in Hungarian. She seems genuinely perplexed that people don't speak English in this foreign country. God love her.

I actually have to clamp my hand over her mouth when we arrive at the graveside portal into the tomb because she won't shut up about her fear of getting buried alive. When she watches Zev disappear through the hole in the ground, Darius has to stop her from running away and physically holds her over the opening until she's sucked into the tomb. When I follow and land next to her in the spacious room, she immediately slugs me in the arm.

Thankfully, before we end up in an all-out brawl, Rune walks over with my sweet little girl, and AJ rushes over to hold her.

And when Rune casually--seemingly without noticing--glances his fingers against her hand as he hands her Rain, I wink at him. His calming power takes instant effect on my shaken best friend.

"Oh my God, look how big you are!" AJ says, even though Rain has at most gained a third of a pound since they last saw each other. "Did you miss your auntie? Fart, barf, or do nothing if the answer is yes." She doesn't cast her gaze away from the child as she tilts her head in acknowledgement of Rune. "Oh, hi elf."

Rune gives a playful wave, then looks to me as AJ wanders the tomb without paying much attention to her surroundings, totally distracted by the baby. It's very sweet to see them together again, and it gives me a moment to collect my thoughts and discuss things with the guys.

"Wand still doesn't work," I say to Rune, answering the question I'm sure he would have asked. "Either the dryad gave me shitty wood, the dragon let me take a shitty scale, or I need to track down a crystal tip that the world's most powerful witch has never heard of."

Rune nods solemnly, then heads over to a small table and grabs a book I don't remember seeing before we left. "This arrived moments before you did," the fae says, reminding me that Erzsébet said she'd send a book about wands.

"Oh good." I accept it from his outstretched hand, enjoying the brief but calming sensation as our fingers touch. "Any chance you already read it and have all the answers?"

My question is mostly in jest, but also loaded with hope that Rune will have some sort of guidance to offer. Now that I'm away from Erzsébet and Andor, in this empty space with a chance to sit with my thoughts, I realize how close I am to my breaking point. The dragon scared me, the dryad queen scarred me, but neither of those things rocked me the way this failure has. Killing the ancient tree, exploding crystal after crystal, feeling lost in a language I can't speak but need to cast spells--it's all too much.

I feel the impossible weight of what I'm carrying slam into me like a physical force, knocking me to my knees, breaking the floodgates of my heart wide open.

I'm torn apart by every decision I don't know how to make. Every problem I don't know how to solve.

A sob forces itself out of me, clearing the way for the storm of emotions that has been building to pour out.

Tears flood my eyes, blinding me as I bury my face in my hands, my shoulders shaking as I unleash the torrent of pain I wanted so badly to ignore and bury.

But pain never stays buried long. It grows from neglect into something fierce and wild that demands attention. Ignoring your pain only feeds it.

The time of reckoning has come as I give an honest accounting of the unfair burden I've been given.

And I feel so alone. Without my grandparents, who were always there for me. Tilly who always knew the right thing to say at the right time. Ed who worked harder than anyone I ever met and would give you the shirt off his back if you needed it.

I feel...

So.

Utterly.

Alone.

And then... I feel them. Three sets of hands reaching to comfort me. To soothe me.

Three strong, solid bodies forming a tight circle around me.

Zev to my right, Darius sitting before me, and Rune behind me, his peaceful calm flowing over me, though it's not enough this time to ease the hurt that's consuming my raw and beaten heart.

"I don't know what to do," I say between sobs. "I don't have any control. No wand works for me, and there's no time for me to figure this out."

"We'll make time," Darius says softly, his cool fingers brushing my hair out of my eyes as he speaks. "We are here to fight this battle as long as it takes."

I sniff and wipe at my eyes. "Yeah, well, a lot of your old friends are going to come fight too," I say. "And I don't think they'll be all that eager to let me learn more magic."

Zev puts his head on my shoulder, offering companionship instead of words. It's a sweet gesture, but I know it's because he has nothing to say. There's no solution.

"I murdered a magical being that had been alive

for millions of years," I say, the tears returning with force. "*Millions* of years, and then I showed up. You're all in danger because of me, and I'm only making things worse. Everyone who comes near me gets hurt. I should just give Rain to one of you to hide, paint a target on my back, then sit and wait for the council to come for me."

"Or maybe I'll just break your neck so you can't say dumb shit anymore."

AJ's returned to listen to the conversation while still rocking the baby, and though her words sting, I had missed the bite of them, of her. The hard truths that the Sexies don't always have the heart to share with me.

Darius takes my hands in his, ignoring AJ as he leans forward so our faces are inches apart. I hesitate a moment before looking up, unsure if I'm ready to look anyone in the eyes without breaking down again.

When I finally do, I see tears in his dark eyes. Darius has shown his heart and passion over the last few weeks, but I don't think I've seen him this emotional. I grip his hands tighter, trying to give us both a little extra strength.

As he maintains eye contact, I feel our connection pulsing in my veins. It doesn't so much comfort or calm me, but instead reinforces what has been growing between us through our shared blood exchange, that we feel each other's pain; he's not just trying to make me feel better, but also show that we're going through these trials together.

"When Cara died," he begins, his voice so soft it's barely audible, "my world came to an end. It wasn't just losing a dear friend, but losing the faith I had in a greater cause. I stopped believing in goodness, and stopped believing in myself. Nothing gave me hope, not my friends, not my family, least of all my life. After all, I was an immortal beast and the heir to a throne occupied by the monster who killed someone I cared deeply for."

Though I'm not looking at Zev or Rune, I know they're hanging on every word, just as I am. Perhaps even more so, as the vampire is describing what ultimately ended their friendship.

"I gave into my bloodlust and took thousands of lives," Darius says, anger starting to color his voice. "Without a reason to care, I had no reason not to kill. I spent centuries embodying my worst self, and I would have gone on that way... if not for your grandmother." I squeeze his hands tighter at the mention of Tilly, and Darius gets a little brightness back in his dark eyes.

"She fought with such bravery in the face of

endless rage. Love compelled her to risk her own life, to help others, to bring light into the darkness. Whether or not she knew then, it was all to create you."

For the first time since he started speaking, Darius looks away from me. His mouth hangs open, waiting for the words to come, but struggling to get them out. I feel his internal strife inside me and I will him to power through.

"I intended to kill Matilda Morgan the night we met."

His words hit me like a shotgun blast to the chest. A generation before I arrived, my blood-bonded soulmate wanted, and maybe tried, to kill my beloved grandmother.

"Perhaps I would have," he continues as I refocus on his words, ignoring the burning in my soul for the moment, "but not for looking into her eyes and understanding that she wasn't afraid to die." Darius meets my gaze once again. "She feared more for my wayward soul than she did her own life. I hadn't felt that since my days with Cara, and Zev and Rune. I hadn't felt cared for, and that made all the difference."

I'm compelled to reach up and wipe his eye, to touch his face, to show that I don't fault him for what happened, but rather appreciate him even more for what didn't happen. He pulls my hand away from his cheek, kissing my fingers gently, and then continues.

"Since you came into my life, every day between this one and the moment I met your grandmother has been a validation. Your light is the antidote to my darkness. I would relive every moment of anguish from my past for a moment in your eyes, seeing the love you have for the goodness in others."

Darius stands gracefully, going from seated to upright in a way that only someone with crazy strong thighs could manage. He holds his hand in front of me to help me stand as well.

"You've already changed lives, Bernie," he says, a look of pure reverence on his face. "Before you were even born, you managed to change hearts. The three of us have found our way because of you, and, by the same token, you shall find your wand."

I take his hand and stand, immediately clutching his face and bringing him toward me, kissing him passionately because I might die if I don't.

But then I pause, struck by something.

I look into his black eyes, my own eyes as wide as saucers, forced open by a major epiphany.

"You didn't find your way because of me," I whisper.

Darius says nothing, too confused to respond. Everyone is silent, waiting for me to explain myself.

"You found your way... because of this."

I reach into my pocket slowly, my hand trembling as I do, and grasp the star that's been with me throughout all these adventures, subtly helping me control my magic. Is it really this simple?

I take a second to wet my lips and remember the word I repeated countless times back in the crystal cave. I close my eyes and press the tip of my wand against the star. It's far too big to serve as the tip, but I feel in my heart this is the right choice.

"*Kötvény,*" I say, speaking the word with confidence for the first time.

There's no explosion. Nothing backfires. No one in the room yelps in pain.

Rather, I feel the star fracture in my hand. It's quick and painless, like I've broken a cracker. When I open my eyes to check out my handiwork, a small chunk of the star has broken off, and is now fused to the end of the dragon scale wrapped in dryad skin. The star is cut to perfection, revealing a luminescent shine, like it truly did just get plucked from the sky and placed on my wand.

I exhale a breath I'd been holding, relief coursing

through me. So far so good. But I'm not in the clear quite yet.

"You've done it," AJ says, stepping forward before I stop her with a raised hand.

"I made it this far before," I say. "This next part is the real test. If I kill us all, I'm super sorry."

I take another breath, then envision the food I've had in my mind since everything went to shit earlier this evening.

"*Étel.*"

A sparkle of light swirls out from the tip of my wand, dancing a few feet in front of me before disappearing. Now, in its place, sits a plate with two enormous, glorious lobster rolls.

I look around, still in shock, checking to make sure nothing blew up without us realizing it. But everything looks in order. And my spell actually worked.

Tears burn my eyes, but this time for an entirely different reason. My throat clogs with emotion when I speak. "I did it," I whisper, staring at my wand in surprise.

I had no doubt, Darius says to my mind.

Zev skips the words and instead pulls me into a passionate kiss, ending it with a quick nip of my lip.

Rune just smiles, and I see the pride and joy in his eyes.

AJ, well AJ responds in typical AJ fashion.

"Oh, I know you brought enough to share with the class," she says, a huge smile on her face.

I pick up one of the buttery rolls and sink my teeth in. Holy hell. It's just as good as the ones Nanny and I used to get on our summer trips to the beach.

"I'll trade you the other roll for my baby." I can feel the wand steadying my magic, containing the pressure, and I know for the first time since this all started that I'm in control. I may only know one spell, but it's a start. And I miss holding my baby more than anything.

AJ's quick to take me up on the offer, practically throwing Rain into my arms as she rushes for the food. I hug my baby girl tightly, feeling like I'm not about to accidentally kill her for the first time since these powers took up residence in my body.

"You're safe with mama now, sweetie pie," I say as her cute little eyes slowly open. "I'll protect you from the bad guys."

I'm nuzzling her nose with mine when there's a popping sound and a very annoyed voice interrupts our celebration.

"Where is he?"

Erzsébet's voice shatters the mood and scares the shit out of me. She stands below the entrance to the tomb, though none of us saw her come in.

"Did Andor not remain with you?" she asks, deep lines of concern running across her forehead as she looks around the tomb.

"No," I say. "Darius was the last to come through the ground, I assumed he went back to find you."

The witch shakes her head. We've been through a lot in the last couple days, but this is definitely the most upset I've seen Erzsébet.

"Where should he be?" I ask. I'm really not sure if everyone sleeps back in the Grand Hall, if there's a curfew, how any of it works. Also, Andor's powerless compared to, like, everyone. What's the problem?

"He should be helping me locate an important book full of dark magic," she answers. "Instead, I think he's helping someone else steal it."

CHAPTER SIXTEEN

I swallow the last of my lobster roll awkwardly, licking my lips of crumbs while I think of a response. "Um... what?"

Way to wow them with your articulateness, Bernie.

Erzsébet sighs, and with a wave of her wand and a spoken word, creates a luxuriously overstuffed loveseat made of indigo velvet that she sinks into. "I've had my suspicions about him for some time now. I've been subtly testing him over the last few days, seeing what choices--"

"Wait, hold up," AJ says, stepping forward, hand on hip, sass on face--typical AJ. "You're just gonna Mary Poppins some shit for yourself but my bestie is getting it on werewolf style with her men on the floor? She's the mother of the Last damn Witch, and these guys are all princes. You're really going to keep them in a shitty, unfurnished grave?"

I press my lips together to keep from laughing out loud. Leave it to AJ to ignore the big problem and focus on what really matters. Comfort. Nothing lightens the mood like AJ. Also, how the hell does she know I've crossed the threshold in my relationship with the guys? Well, two of them, at any rate. Does her nymphness give her sex spy powers? My cheeks burn with embarrassment at that thought.

Erzsébet narrows her eyes at AJ, staring at my friend for several long moments.

"You dare speak to a queen that way?" she says in an icy tone.

AJ just shrugs, taking a big bite of lobster roll and speaking through a mouthful. "I don't discriminate," she says. "I talk to everyone like this."

I worry for a moment that Erzsébet is about to turn this uppity lass into a frog or something, but then the super serious queen of the witches laughs. She *laughs.* To say I'm stunned would be an understatement. I don't think I've seen her laugh--or even really smile much--since we've been here.

"Fair enough," Erzsébet says. She waves her wand again, speaking several words under her breath, and the air sparkles with electricity before the space transforms itself.

I gasp, but I think it's more of a collective gasp. Everyone in the room who isn't Erzsébet is stunned.

Where once were the remnants of an ancient tomb dotted with a few chairs, a table and a makeshift crib for my child, is now a room fit for royalty.

The loveseat Erzsébet reclines on now has a matching couch and two chairs, with a complementary ottoman with a full-service tea tray. Side tables have appeared in a rich mahogany wood.

The ground is covered in overlapping rugs featuring Hungarian designs in bright colors. And the walls each have a few accent art pieces that are bold, full of emotions, and exquisitely rendered.

One in particular looks like a sunrise and sunset overlaid with each other… with a single leaf of undetermined color in the center. It evokes every emotion, every season, every fleeting and infinitely important passage of time that has affected humanity. I blink.

And then I see it.

The gleaming white grand piano in the corner. Rune, knowing me too well, takes Rain as I nearly trip over my own feet to get to it, walking as if in a trance. I sit at the stool and reverently open the fallboard exposing the black and white pattern that has been a staple in my life since I can remember. I run my fingers lightly over the keys, like a lover memorizing their partner's skin. "How did you know?"

Erzsébet walks over and puts her hands on my shoulders. "I've watched you, child. Many a moment from your life has played out on the crystal viewer in the garden."

She sits down next to me on the bench. "Play something," she says. "I've seen, but never heard you play."

I don't have to be asked twice. Without any self-consciousness, I strum my fingers over the ivories, setting their songs free.

The melody fills the cavern, bouncing off the walls and echoing in the underground space. I pour myself into the tips of my finger, transferring my soul to the piano itself, trusting it will translate my core being into music.

I am not disappointed.

I'm so transfixed by the depth and beauty of the song that the world around me disappears, just as it always has. When I play, it is just me and the music.

When I finish, I'm surprised to note my skin is glowing. I frown and reach for my wand. When my hand grips it, my skin returns to color.

KARPOV KINRADE & EVAN GAUSTAD

Erzsébet's eyes are shining, and if I didn't know better, I'd almost say she's about to cry.

"That was more than I could have ever imagined," she says, turning away from me to inconspicuously wipe her eyes.

"Why did I start glowing when I played?" I ask. "I thought my wand would fix that."

Erzsébet sniffs, then turns back to me, her face once again composed. "When you play, you channel your deepest magic. You can't help it. It's a part of you." Before I can ask another question, like how to stop it from happening if I'm playing in public, with humans, she continues speaking. "It is why I put the piano here, to help you learn control of your powers. You have used your music as a kind of wand--a channel--your whole life, even before your magic was returned to you. Some of it has always been inside you. You cannot strip a witch of all her magic entirely without killing her."

She frowns, her eyes unfocused as she appears lost in a memory from the past, and I wonder if she's thinking of her dead daughter. My heart constricts and my gaze lands on my own child. A chill pierces through me, throbbing at the scar over my heart, as I imagine what it would feel like to lose her. And I know with everything in me that I must become as strong and as powerful as possible.

My child might die if I don't.

Erzsébet clears her throat and refocuses on me, her light grey eyes now sharp and clear. "You need to master your powers, Bernadette," she says. "Which means mastering yourself. Your discipline with music will be of benefit. If not for that, I fear you would not get far enough in your training quickly enough to be of much use in the coming days and weeks."

The way she says 'coming days and weeks' makes goosebumps form on the back of my neck. I mean, I already know the three kingdoms are after me and my kid... but I get the distinct impression she means something else entirely.

Erzsébet presses her lips together and begins pacing. Rain coos at the fae who's holding her as he rocks her gently, AJ by his side like a sexy sentinel. Darius is standing still as a statue, watching us both with unreadable eyes, and Zev has taken over the couch and looks like a restless wolf as his eyes follow Erzsébet's movement.

Everyone's waiting for the witch to say more.

"Besides those coming from the other realms," she says, "I fear we have dissenters here in our homeland to contend with."

Awesome.

"Are you saying there are witches coming for my baby as well?" As I ask the question, I start to feel a little rage building up. "Even though she's the one who can save them all?"

"If you recall, I mentioned diminishing numbers within the Kő when you first arrived at the Grand Hall. For several years, the men who show the greatest talents for magic, those most likely to become *Érintett*, have been disappearing without word. I have long held my suspicions, but never had proof. Given recent events, I believe..."

"My father's behind it," I say, giving voice to a small suspicion that's been slowly growing in the depths of my mind.

She looks up in surprise. "What do you know?"

This will be hard to explain, because I don't really *know* anything. I just have questions and doubts. "Pieces haven't added up," I say. "That letter to my grandfather that AJ's ghost crush says was a lie. Men with magic going missing. The burned corpse with my father's medallion in perfect condition. I... knew something was off in the dragon's lair but now... now I'm sure. Plus... it makes sense, given human nature. It seems inevitable that men who serve the ambitions of more powerful witches would look for a way to gain the upper hand eventually."

Erzsébet nods. "Your instincts are strong, Bernadette, as I've always suspected they would be. Your mother was powerful in her own right, if misguided, and your grandmother was one of the strongest witches I've ever known. Even your father had more power than most men. In hindsight, that seems to be part of the problem."

"What did he do?" I ask. I've only been able to piece together the basic shape of what's happening. Erzsébet clearly knows more details.

"I can't speak to specific crimes, but power and status have always been on your father's mind. He petitioned fervently to be the Kő chosen for your mother. To be the one to sire the mother of the Last Witch. He knew it would give him prestige and authority within our order, and he worked hard to earn it. It was a privilege many wanted, but none so much as Timót."

I cringe. It's so gross to imagine all these men arguing over who gets to sleep with--and impregnate--my mother.

Erzsébet continues. "He also championed Andor to be your chosen, which seemed strange but nothing of too great concern. It has made me more aware of

Andor's movements these last few months. I suspect it was him that placed your grandfather's letter."

"Why? Why him and not my father?"

"Timót would not have wanted to bring any extra attention," Erzsébet says with a shrug. Then, with a slight sneer, she adds, "plus, translating your father's name into English seems like the type of stupid thing Andor would do. All while thinking he was being very clever."

The witch's distaste for my former Chosen lingers on her face a moment longer, then her look is once again reflective.

"I should have paid Andor more mind when plans changed. When your grandmother refused to send you here when it was time, and instead, you went to New York and chose your own path."

Her words stir in me a memory of when I first told Nanny about my acceptance into Juilliard. She still had the occasional lucid moments back then. I don't really think she knew what Juilliard was, but she still seemed so happy about the news. "Good," she'd said, taking my hands in hers. "Carve your own path. No one owns you, Bernadette Morgan." Her tone had been fierce, her eyes focused, and I remember being surprised she'd used my full name. She never did that except when I was in trouble, or when she wanted me to really remember her words. At the time I chalked it up to her deteriorating mind.

Now it seems she had a very real point to make, and it was about this order and their plans for my uterus.

Gross.

"Nanny always wanted you to go," AJ says, surprising us all.

I turn to her. "What?"

She shrugs. "Nanny. Even after she started going nuts, she still talked about how Bernie was going to leave to do big things with her big dreams."

There are tears in AJ's eyes as she walks over to me and sits on the bench to my right, her fingers plunking discordant keys as she talks. "I'm not as self-less as her. I wanted you with me. Life in Rowley was miserable without you. But I know you didn't belong, and so did she. You were always meant for bigger things."

Erzsébet cuts in, ruining whatever moment AJ and I were about to have. "I don't know what Timót is planning. But if he does have a grand scheme, he's been working on it for decades. And now it would appear he has a book of dark magic, a dragon, and perhaps a small following of angry, power-hungry men."

"What an ass-wipe," AJ says. "But what can he do? He's got shit on our Bern here, right?"

Erzsébet shrugs. "Hard to say until we know the extent of his plans."

I stand and walk to the couch to sit next to Zev, who pulls me against him. "I'm losing track of how many enemies we have," I say. "And now the order that's supposed to protect us is also against us?"

Erzsébet's eyes narrow, her face fierce. "Your father is not the order, as much as he might like to imagine himself being. And we witches have far more power than them. We will not let you fall into their hands. But you need to train. Starting now."

She waves her wand and chants some words under her breath, and against three of the walls shelves appear, filled with books and ancient scrolls. It's more than I could read in several lifetimes, let alone memorize in a few days.

I instantly feel way too overwhelmed. I pull away from Zev to stand and study the books, taking one out and flipping through the pages. Frowning, I put it back and do the same with another and another. "These are all in Hungarian," I say, feeling frustration tighten my gut. "How am I supposed to learn enough to be of any help when I can't even speak the language?"

I'm expecting some kind of pep talk or even scolding from Erzsébet, but it's Darius who speaks first. "In a way, you do know the language," he says, walking over to me.

I set the book down as he approaches and takes my hand in his. "Our blood exchange binds us, almost as one."

I nod. That's definitely true, but I have no idea how it solves our problem.

"I am fluent in Hungarian," he says, then turns to Erzsébet. "If I'm not mistaken, there's a spell that might allow us to share more than just our emotional and physical connection. It would allow us to share our knowledge. Experiences. Memories," he adds softly.

My pulse quickens at the many layered implications in his offer. "So I would become fluent in Hungarian as well?" I ask.

He nods. "Eventually. I can't simply transfer the information, but as you study, the words and knowledge would flow into you like music, quickly and organically."

Erzsébet purses her lips. "A spell does exist, Darius. I'm glad to see you remember your studies. Unfortunately, it would likely mean her dreams would become consumed by you and eventually drive her mad."

Well that's not a great side effect. Darius might not remember all the details from his studies.

"That's not true," Zev says, standing and walking to us. "Bernie is my wolf's... and my... mate. That bond strengthens her mind."

I glance at Rune, who is standing with Rain, watching us with such kind, loving eyes. And I feel a twinge of sadness that he and I haven't had as much time together as I'd like. Especially in this moment, when his brand of magic feels so necessary.

He seems to be on the same page as he stares into my eyes and nods thoughtfully. "There's an ancient tonic fae drink before they pass to the other side. It enables the mind to stay strong even as the pain of death encroaches. If Bernie were to drink it before the spell was cast..." Rune trails off, mercifully doing all the complicated fae math in his head instead of saying it out loud. "I think Zev is right," he surmises. "She would not fall into Darius's mind the way another might. She would be well protected."

"This is not a spell I ever invoke on a young witch," Erzsébet says. "But clearly Bernadette has chosen a much different path than most witches." Erzsébet pauses, considering. "That might be for the best. I'm willing to try it if Bernadette is," she says, looking at me. "But it must be your choice. This could be very dangerous."

I look to Darius, then Zev, then Rune. Each of them nod, giving me the only confirmation I need. "Let's do it. There's no way I'm going to learn all this without the help."

AJ pops up from the piano, closing the fallboard so hard I flinch. "Hold up. You're about to download hundreds or thousands of years of memories and knowledge into my bestie. That seems like a thing we should chat a bit more about first, don't you think?" She turns to me, her eyes full of worry. "Will you even still be you? What if he turns you into his mini-me?"

Darius scowls. "My mini-what?"

I chuckle and just shake my head. "I think I'll be okay, AJ. I don't know why I feel so certain, but I do. And I need this if we're going to save Rain."

AJ looks over at her godchild, her face softening instantly, then her gaze snaps back to Erzsébet. "Fine, but is there any way of backing real Bernie up? Just in case?"

Erzsébet looks confused and I can't help but laugh. "A, they can't upload me into the cloud. You have to trust me. I'll be fine."

THREE HOURS LATER, I'm about to eat my words and hope I don't vomit them back up.

Rune has made his potion. Zev and I had a quickie in the other room to solidify our mate bond. His idea, not mine, but I didn't hate it. I don't think it was at all necessary for the spell, but I'm not complaining. Meanwhile, Erzsébet left and returned with a bunch of crystals that she laid out on the ground to form a pentagram.

"You and Darius will stand in the center and exchange blood as I recite the spell," Erzsébet says.

I nod. "Got it."

Rune hands me the potion. It's steaming and smells like feet. He looks at me apologetically. "I'm sorry I can't make it taste better."

I shrug, figuring I've had worse.

I shoot it fast and as it burns down my throat I fight against vomiting up everything I've ever eaten and some internal organs as well.

I gag and struggle to breathe. I definitely have not had worse.

But I feel the power thrumming through me as I take Darius's hand and step into the center.

His dark eyes are luminous as he stares at me.

"Are you sure about this? What is done cannot be undone."

"I'm sure," I whisper, knowing this is going to bond us in a way that is frankly terrifying. There won't be any part of each other we can hide from the other after this.

With sweaty hands I grip his, my body shaking as Erzsébet begins to speak in Hungarian. This is a long, complicated spell, and it reinforces what I'm about to do. There's no way I could learn something like that right now. Not when I struggle with basic nouns.

"We must drink at the same time," he says, cutting open his own neck with a small knife, letting the blood pool.

Darius leans in and I feel the familiar tingle of anticipation as his teeth brush along my pulsing vein, sinking into my flesh.

I lean into him, letting my tongue flick at the blood trickling bright red against his pale skin. And then I move my mouth over the wound, sucking more deeply as he takes in my blood.

Before I close my eyes, I notice golden light swirling around us, creating a cocoon. And once I close them, I feel the magic pulsing like a drum beat inside me as his hands tighten on my back. Erzsébet's words fade, though I know she still speaks, but now all I hear is Darius.

He sings into every pore of my body, every molecule of my existence.

I ride the wave of these feelings, and can sense myself falling into him.

Then darkness rises, and a panic grips me as I realize I'm

falling

falling

falling

falling.

I can't stop.

I'm losing myself to him and the panic threatens to overwhelm me entirely.

Before I reach the bottom, I hear a growl and feel the claim of my wolf mate on my heart, pulling me back into myself.

And I feel the calming magic of Rune protecting my mind. Protecting me.

I let the wolf and the fae hold me as the vampire takes me in and gives me all he is, and I see into the mind and heart of a being with darkness and light at war within himself. With memories too buried to unearth. With crushing heartache and aching beauty.

And I hold all three of them to me, filling them each with my light, my love, my soul.

It might have been a moment or an eternity, but when I come back to myself, to my body, to the pentagram and the reality around me, everything is as it was.

The furniture is still there. AJ sits watching, biting her nails, which she hasn't done since grade school. My child sleeps peacefully in Rune's arms. Everything is as it was.

Except it's not.

I'm not.

And one look at Darius proves he is not either.

He pulls me against his chest, his grip desperate, his eyes gleaming. "Bernie. God, Bernie. I love you."

After some time I pull away and smile. "I love you too. Now let's get to work."

I SPEND the next several days pouring over books and blowing a lot of shit up with my wand. Darius and I are closer than we have ever been, as my mind shifts to contain more and more. My knowledge expands in a way I could never have imagined, and I relish the power I feel at how quickly I'm learning and memorizing a language I only first heard a few days ago.

While I focus on training, the Sexies take turns serving as lookout above the tomb. They seem more nervous with each passing hour, waiting for the inevitable attack. I try to stay optimistic, thinking that every day without a vampire assault might mean we're closer to being in the clear. No one else shares that point of view.

My progress is impressive, but Erzsébet is never satisfied. She's chosen to stay in the cave with us, keeping me on task every waking second of the day. When I'm not eating or sleeping, I'm working.

She pushes me hard, and on more than one occasion Darius or Zev or Rune has stepped in to protect me, but I usher them away each time, knowing I have to be pushed, even if it feels like it's going to kill me, even when I feel like my head will explode. If I don't go the extra mile, I won't be ready, and I know time is running out.

It's the sixth day of my training, just after sunset, that time officially runs out.

We are in another training session--really just one long ongoing session that I sometimes get a break from to eat or nap--and I'm trying to use magic to grow a seed into a tree.

"It is easy to destroy," Erzsébet says. "It is so much harder to create."

I've finally made progress as something green and alive pushes through the dirt, when Erzsébet freezes, her face alarmed.

"They are here," she says, her eyes wide.

The three Sexies all stand at full attention, and I feel waves of worry hit me.

AJ looks around confused. "Who's here?"

Darius looks at me with worry on his face as Erzsébet answers. "Everyone."

CHAPTER SEVENTEEN

No sooner have the words left Erzsébet's mouth than Darius flashes out of the tomb. Rune and Zev instinctually step to my sides, prepared to fend off whatever might harm me. AJ steps closer, wanting to be part of the circle of protection. I clutch my wand, ready to fling a few spells at whoever tries to mess with us. I may not have memorized--or even opened--all the books Erzsébet brought me, but I got the guys and AJ to help me find the most useful spells for combat, healing and protection.

"We need to get to the Grand Hall," Erzsébet says, though she shows no signs of moving.

"It's not safe for us to travel."

I know he's fast, but it still surprises me to hear Darius' voice back in the tomb.

"How do you know?" I ask as I turn to look at him. "What did you see in the five seconds you were gone?"

"I know where to look," he answers briskly. "Vampires have the city surrounded."

I want to believe he's exaggerating, but that's not really the vampire's style. If he says that Budapest is surrounded, it kinda means we're in deep shit. Plus, after our bond, I can feel everything. And right now, I feel his worry.

"Wolves?" Zev asks.

Darius looks between Zev and Rune. "I imagine the wolves and fae are walking the streets, looking for signs and smells."

Rune turns to look at Erzsébet, my child still cradled in his arms. "Where are we safer, here or the hall?"

The witch queen looks at me as she answers. It's clear that the only real "we" that matters when it comes to safety is Rain and me.

"There's more magic at our disposal in the Grand Hall, but we can expect more visitors there as well." She looks around the room, assessing our current home base. "While we're harder to find here, we're trapped."

"See, Bernie?" AJ says, making some obvious

point that's not yet obvious to me. "This is why I said I didn't want to go into the tomb. Bad shit happens."

"Can't you just, you know, magic us over there?" I ask Erzsébet.

"I can move books and chairs and loaves of bread," she says, waving her wand around and making those very things disappear, as though to prove her point. "But a living being can't be pulled apart and reassembled that way. Many have tried, just as many have died."

I guess that'll just count as part of my lesson for the day, and it's one I'm certainly glad I learned before murdering myself trying to save time on travel.

I glance back at the Sexies, who are having a hushed discussion. Their group asides usually involve these three taking on enormous personal risk in an attempt to keep me safe. Darius is trying way too hard to shield his thoughts and emotions from me, so I waste no time butting in.

"What?" I shout across the space, bringing the secret conversation to a halt. "What's this little pow-wow about?"

Zev checks in with the other two before walking over to me, losing the game of *who gets to argue with Bernie*. They chose well, as his sexy voice can usually make me cave.

"I'm going to walk through town and then north along the river," he says, telling me the plan instead of asking. "That'll give me a sense of who's been sent and where they're looking."

"While he walks," Darius jumps in, keeping the thread going before I have a chance to tell my mate he's not going anywhere. I'm automatically opposed to any division within the group, to the point I'm hardly listening to the words as Darius continues. "I'll travel the back streets between here and the entrance to the Grand Hall, finding the most clandestine route. Zev and I can aid each other if needed, and he might also distract a few watching eyes away from the streets as I walk."

"No," I say the moment Darius finishes his sentence. "If we break into smaller--hey!"

But my mate has already been sucked into the world, out of our tomb before I can even finish my thought. I'm shocked by him leaving, and I can't quite tell if it's because I feel legitimately betrayed or because I'm so used to them doing as I ask.

Darius follows right behind him, our mixed blood stinging in my veins as I watch him go. Rune comes to me, bringing me into his arms, remaining as my one true pillar of support. And then he outs himself as an accomplice.

"The last word we shared on the matter was to not let you have a say in it," he says with a sheepish smile.

"Why the hell not?" I spit back at him. "We're stronger together, you know I'm right. Separating is the stupid choice in like every horror movie ever-- when the group breaks up, they're picked off one by one."

"And yet the dragon scale and the dryad arm came when you set out with just one of us by your side," Rune answers smugly. He's not acting smug, but the swiftness with which he pokes a hole in my argument feels very self-satisfied.

"This is different," I murmur back, not really sure if that's true.

"It is, and it isn't," the fae says. "We are stronger together. I'm stronger when you're by my side, undoubtedly. But I gain strength from doing something that could help you, even if we're separated. The same is true for Zev and Darius right now. They know their success will help you and Rain, and that compels them forward. It strengthens them."

His argument feels too much like a set up for when the three of them leave me to face their families...and that hurt is too close to the surface to touch on right now. Instead, I focus on the present, and

Rune is right. They are focused and driven. They are furious but contained. Calm. They will do anything to keep us safe. And they will make anyone who hurts me pay.

Damn right we will, Darius mentally says. This is the first time our mental connection has reached this far, and I get some small solace from that.

I smile at Rune. The fae always knows how to make a case that plays to my logical side and touches my heart. I lean into him more, wrapping my arms around his back and enjoying the comfort. Who knows how many more minutes or seconds of this peace I'll have before we're all running for our lives. Or saying goodbye for who knows how long.

"You've managed to attract three smart, sweet men, Bernadette." Erzsébet now faces me, finished with the business of sending books and furniture back from where they came. "And they're right, this is our best hope for getting to the hall without being noticed. Inside, we can regroup and decide where to go."

"Do the tunnels lead anywhere other than the river and the dragon caves?" I ask.

"Oh yes," Erzsébet says. "If we know where we need to be, the channels beneath the hall can take us almost anywhere. We can head to the vampire realm

KARPOV KINRADE & EVAN GAUSTAD

and send a bolt of fire right up the king's asshole, if we please."

It's the very last thing I expected the queen to say, and I assume I misheard until AJ chimes in. "Yeah, boss bitch. Bern, this queen is wicked better than your mom."

Erzsébet fights back a smile and I'm sure she enjoyed the compliment. Then the serious expression returns to her face. "Enough of this, you need to learn a spell in the next few moments so you can cast it without killing anyone."

I hope her plan is for me to somehow grow a shitty radish, because I feel like that's about where my skills max out.

"What's the spell? What does it do?" I'm terrified of the answer, and get even more freaked out as Erzsébet raises her wand and points it at her own chin.

"*Arc a mások.*"

My gaze is on the tip of her wand as she mutters the spell, but my focus immediately shifts to her face as it turns into a swirling ball of flesh and light. I'm horrified and fascinated watching her face glow and melt and move. After just a few seconds, it finally settles back into place, and the sight is even more disturbing than what just transpired.

She's Zev.

"Holy shit," AJ and I say in unison. I turn to Rune, my eyes the size of apples, to see if he witnessed the crazy face theft I just saw. I'm immediately annoyed at how unimpressed he looks.

"What?" he says, gauging my reaction. "Did you think she was going to do something else?"

I spin back to the witch, in no mood to lose a magical IQ test. "Does that spell make us all look like Zev? Are there different, non-Zev-face spells?"

"Bernadette, have you ever thought that you ask too many questions and could stand to have more patience waiting for answers?"

This is the wrong time to be scolding me, especially while wearing the face of my wolf mate, but when AJ laughs I know I've already lost this fight.

"Yessah mum, she's definitely been told she has that problem." AJ always sounds extra Massholey when it's at my expense.

"Please continue," I say in my most patient voice, eager for everyone to get their goddamn heads back in the game and off of my case.

"The words always stay the same," Erzsébet explains. "What changes is your intent and the image in your mind."

It's so strange to hear these words coming from

Zev's mouth yet carried by the witch's voice. I try to shrug off the weirdness of it all and focus on what I need to do to learn the spell.

"Is there a way I can practice?" I ask, thinking of all the tiny plants I murdered earlier in the day.

"*Visszatérési,*" Erzsébet says with the wand pointed back at her face, thankfully returning to her normal self. "You must first practice on yourself, but I'm confident you'll master this one quickly."

"*Arc a mások* and *Visszatérési,*" I say, repeating the spell and counter-spell. I'm mostly interested in my ability to get my own face back so I don't get stuck looking like some rando for the rest of my life. "Alright, here I go. Does it hurt?"

"Hm," Erzsébet says thoughtfully. "It's been so long since I experienced pain the way a new witch does. Probably. I imagine it does hurt."

Fun.

I point my wand toward my chin, absolutely terrified of myself but trying to maintain confidence and a clear vision.

"*Arc a mások,*" I mutter breathily, struggling to push the words out because I'm so afraid of what they'll do.

First I feel warmth from the wand in my hand, which is always a byproduct of a spell. The heat quickly hits my chin and begins to spread over the rest of my face. Just as I start to think it's not that painful, the sensation changes from burning to gripping, like someone with a giant hand has palmed my face and is squeezing with all their might. It definitely hurts and it's ridiculous that Erzsébet had to think about it.

It only lasts another second or two and then stops abruptly. I feel entirely normal, and start to wonder if anything changed at all, but the look on AJ's face confirms that something's different.

"Welp," she says, fighting back the urge to either laugh or vomit. "You didn't nail it."

"No, she did not," Rune confirms, looking somewhat sickened.

"What? What's wrong, what do I look like?"

Erzsébet approaches, an eyebrow raised as she thinks of how to fix my problem. "Who did you envision when you incanted?"

"A guy," I answer plainly. "Just a generic guy. I sort of imagined a man I walked past when we first got here, but I was going for a very general look."

Now Erzsébet cracks a smile. "That explains it," she says before conjuring a reflection in front of me. The face that stares back is only a partial face. The nose is missing and my mouth is an empty, toothless hole. The eyes are also missing pupils and I've only got bangs, no hair on the rest of my head. I'm like an unfinished mannequin.

"Jesus! I'm gonna have nightmares about me," I say right before Erzsébet dissolves the reflection.

"You can't do this with a general picture in your mind," the witch explains. "It needs to be a face you know, perhaps not intimately, but well enough that you can picture the details."

That makes sense. Could have used the full lesson before I disfigured myself, but maybe she knew this was the best way to learn.

"*Visszatérési,*" I say with the wand to my chin, feeling a less intense but still noticeable pressure as my face returns to being my face. "Okay, let me try again." I lift the wand, steeling myself for the abuse I'm about to endure, but then pause. "I guess it still needs to be someone who won't draw attention, right? I shouldn't, like, turn us all into Darius."

Erzsébet nods. "We want to blend in with the crowd as best we can. A powerful being might still sniff us out, but this gives us a fighting chance of making it to the hall unnoticed."

With that, she says the incantation with her wand pointed to her own mug, and I watch as her bright, churning face slowly morphs into the mask of a younger woman, someone I don't recognize at all. The new face smiles, then Erzsébet's voice speaks. "This is a barista at my favorite cafe downtown."

The image of a powerful, centuries-old witch stepping out for a cappuccino makes me really happy for some reason. Maybe someday she'll stop by Morgan's and we'll whip her up one of Rune's fancy drinks.

I refocus on the matter at hand, pointing my wand at my face and thinking of who I should impersonate. Who won't draw eyes? Or, perhaps more importantly, who do I want to be if eyes are drawn?

"Arc a mások," I say for a second time, now much more prepared for the sensation about to overtake me. It definitely still hurts, but much less so since I know what's coming. If I keep at this for a few thousand years, I too will probably forget that it's painful.

When the spell completes and the shifting stops, I look around the room, waiting for reactions.

"Fascinating choice," Rune says thoughtfully.

AJ walks over to inspect my handiwork. "Yeah, you look like a guy this time. Less of an abomination. Oh wait, you look like--"

"Andor," Erzsébet cuts in. She seems thoughtful, weighing the pros and cons of my decision. "This could go either way, Bernadette. Depending on who we see, that face could either hasten our problems or buy us precious minutes."

I'm mostly glad the spell worked and I have a believable face, but also thinking those same thoughts. "He can't be too well known by vampires and the other attackers. But if there are defected members of the Kő anywhere, this might be the face I need."

Erzsébet doesn't answer, but I see approval in her eyes as she looks at both Rune and AJ, who's still holding a sleeping Rain. "Now it's time to shift the others."

AJ shakes her head and raises a hand. "I'm good, I'm just a girl from Mass walking the streets of Budapest, no one knows--"

"They know, AJ," Erzsébet says in her disappointed mother voice. "You've been with Bernadette through all of her recent trials, and the connection between you two is more than skin deep. You'll have a magnetic pull for our adversaries if you walk out looking like yourself."

For perhaps the first time in her life, AJ doesn't argue. Maybe, like me, she's wondering what the witch means by our connection being more than skin deep. Is there another crazy secret being kept and we're actually sisters? I can't dismiss anything, but I suspect it's more likely there's a power within our friendship. A bond so strong it has its own kind of magic.

AJ turns to me, a look of love in her eyes that fades quickly as she gazes into the face of a Hungarian man she's never met. "Okay, who are you going to turn me into?"

I smile as I lift my wand. "You'll see," I say. "Also, this hurts like balls the first time."

"What--"

"*Arc a mások,*" I say, cutting her off before she can do anything. Her face ignites with brightness and then rearranges itself, finally coming to rest as a familiar face that no Hungarian will recognize. "Can you do the mirror thing for her?" I ask the disguised witch queen.

She quickly does so and I watch AJ, who no longer looks like AJ, stare back at herself with a big smile.

"Oh hell yeah."

She looks at the reflection, seeing Michael, my ex-boyfriend who was secretly gay and, more secretly, a shifter.

"This is awesome," AJ says at her reflection. "I'm a freaking unicorn."

"Let's move along," Erzsébet says. "We'll want to leave the moment Zev and Darius return."

I walk over to Rune, forming a clear image of Joe, the regular at Morgan's who was another casualty of all this witch business. It's an emotional choice, but a face that will blend here and will be easy for me and AJ to spot in case we all get separated. Rune doesn't care to look in a mirror, trusting that his face has changed and otherwise not worrying about it.

We decide Erzsébet will take Rain, since she'll be the best prepared to cast a protective spell and also has the face of a young woman who would make sense to be carrying a child. I hug my baby tightly, fighting off the fear of what might happen to her if plans go south tonight. I don't kiss her the way I normally would because it feels strange with a face that's not mine, but I mutter a thousand I love yous as I strap her into the harness.

After a few more minutes of standing in awkward silence, both me and AJ compulsively touching our strange, male faces, Zev and Darius return. Erzsébet steps forward immediately to show them Rain and explain the spells we cast. It's good she does, otherwise I might have rushed over to kiss one of them and that would have gone horribly wrong.

"The main streets are teeming with fae," Zev says

after it's been sorted out who he's talking to. He averts his eyes every time he looks my way, which is understandable. I wouldn't like it if my lover suddenly looked like someone I was inclined to kill. "The disguises will help, but we need to try and keep our distance from those standing watch."

"I walked two routes," Darius says, looking at me but clearly not liking what he sees. "I suggest we start traveling together at first, but break into smaller clusters if need be."

We agree to move together following Darius' lead, and Erzsébet and I each cast spells to transform the beautiful faces of the werewolf and the vampire. I turn Darius into my high school music teacher, who's face I'll never forget since I spent a billion hours in his classroom. Erzsébet morphs Zev into an older man who she says used to sit in the square above the Grand Hall and feed the pigeons.

Wands in hand, faces obscured, and a route selected, it's time for us to move from the safety of the tomb into the uncertainty of the city streets. One by one we get sucked up and spat back out above ground. The sun has set and the darkness makes me fully realize how frightful this next step is. A vampire could swoop in unseen and kill any of us before we knew what was happening. I'm practically paralyzed with fear as we start to walk out of the cemetery.

Rune, his gorgeous face turned into the less handsome but still appealing mug of Joe, walks by my side and puts a hand on my shoulder. The new face has done nothing to take away from his calming powers.

"Push that fear away, Bernie," he says, his soothing voice unchanged. "We all feel it in these moments, but it can only hold you back."

"Maybe I need to be scared in order to stay alert," I say back, my argumentative instincts taking over.

"True awareness comes from confidence," he responds. "Not from fear. You're an incredibly powerful witch, surrounded by those who love you and want to protect you. Put your belief in that, not in your fears."

It's a good pep talk, as I've come to expect from Rune. As we step through the cemetery entrance and head into the crowded streets, buzzing with nightlife, I grip my wand a little more tightly under my sleeve. Let's do this.

The first few blocks are the scariest, and my eyes dart from face to face, trying to figure out who's a harmless Hungarian or hapless tourist, and who's a paranormal fighter here to kill my child. Everyone looks exactly the same.

We naturally split into two pods, me walking with Erzsébet, my baby, and Rune while Zev, Darius and AJ stroll together about ten feet behind us. This makes us a little less conspicuous, I hope, and also lets us move more quickly through the crowds.

About halfway to the Grand Hall I start feeling less threatened. The disguises are working and the streets are too busy for us to stand out. I'm not sure how we'll get into the Grand Hall once we get to the square, but so far this travel plan has worked.

And then we round a corner, and I come face to face with the one person I didn't expect, and certainly didn't want to see.

Me.

But not me.

Andor.

We're feet apart, staring into each other's eyes. I know exactly who he is, but he's got no idea what's going on. He'd been walking with his head down, wearing a cloak, clearly trying to get somewhere unnoticed. But now unnoticed isn't an option.

Before I know what I'm doing, my wand is raised and a flash of light shoots from the tip, hitting him in the chest and knocking him down. We're close enough to each other that passersby likely didn't see the wand, but they definitely see the man fall to the ground.

I've got no strategy beyond staring at the person I magically tasered, but Erzsébet is instantly kneeling by him and chanting some sort of quiet spell. After she does so, Andor stands next to her, still as a statue, eyes glazed over.

"He'll be in a trance until we're at the Grand Hall," she says to me in a hushed whisper. "But the magic blast from your wand almost certainly..."

Her eyes finish her thought instead of her words, as she looks over my shoulder. The rest of us follow her gaze and see a group of men walking in our direction. They're dressed like Darius was the first night he walked into my bar, and their menacing looks and skin tone give them away pretty fast. Regular people won't immediately know who or what they are, but these vampires definitely don't blend in.

They're half a block away from us and moving at a brisk pace. I turn back to Erzsébet, hoping she's got an awesome plan that will diffuse the situation quickly.

She looks back at me, a frantic energy in her eyes. "Run."

CHAPTER EIGHTEEN

"Run? From vampires?" My voice is incredulous, but I, like everyone else, am already following the command, my legs pumping hard as I try to escape a flock... or is it herd?...of vampires trying to eat me.

Which begs the question, what do you call a group of vampires?

Setting that thought puzzle aside, I pull my wand out of my sleeve, aim at our pursuers and mutter *tűz*, the Hungarian word for fire, grateful that my connection to Darius allowed me to learn so much so fast, even if it still doesn't feel like nearly enough. Behind me, several vampires burst into flames. My stomach turns on itself at the sounds of their screams, and I don't feel any sense of victory.

Erzsébet flicks her own wand and whispers a spell, casting a kind of net around us that glows white against the night sky.

"This should mask your location, for a time at any rate," Erzsébet says, holding my child out to me. "Take her. I will throw them off your trail. Use the river to get to the garden."

Oh shit.

With fumbling hands I strap Rain onto my chest and tuck her blanket around her just as something hits me from behind, knocking the wind out of my lungs and sending my legs lunging out from under me.

Panic clutches my chest, making it hard to breathe for a moment until I realize what's happening.

Shock is replaced by relief when Darius catches me into his arms. "I've got you," he whispers. It's weird AF coming from the face of my high school band teacher, but comforting all the same. *We're going to the river,* I think to Zev, making sure he knows where to go in case he can't see us to follow. I don't bother sending a thought to Darius, as our minds are already linked.

I twine my hands around his neck and hold on

tight as he carries me at super speed, zig-zagging and changing direction now that we're cloaked.

Before she's out of sight, I watch Erzsébet charge in the opposite direction, letting herself be seen long enough to catch the eye of a vampire. And either she or Rune casts an illusion that makes it look like we're with her.

My eyes search for the others, frantic to make sure everyone is safe. Zev has shifted to wolf form, dropping his magical disguise entirely, and he's giving AJ a ride so she can keep up. I don't see Rune or Andor, which panics me for a moment, but Darius calmly assures me mentally that the fae is fine. He can take care of himself--and the traitorous order member.

Erzsébet seems to glide on wind, making excellent time as she lures the enemies away, and I make a mental note to get that spell from her when this is over.

The net of power around us is still visible as we make haste, but it seems less vibrant. Like it's fading.

Hurry, I whisper into Darius's mind. *What will they do if they catch us?*

They won't catch you, Darius says, answering my question by not answering it.

Hopefully Erzsébet's spell will last long enough to

get us where we need to be so we won't have to
find out.

I want to help more, to whip out my wand and
blast them with more fire, but that would negate the
effects of Erzsébet's cloaking spell--giving away our
location, and we can't win in a faceoff with them, not
out here. Maybe not even with the magic of the Grand
Hall, but at least we'll have a slight advantage there.

As we get more space between us and the attackers, I wonder if I can guide us to the right spot in the
Danube River. I can visualize the area where Zev and
I emerged after visiting the dragon cave, but I'm shit
with directions and not sure I can guide us there
easily. Suddenly I know the answer, and I know it's
my connection to Darius providing the knowledge. I
have a map in my head of Hungary, and I can zoom
in to see different areas in more detail. I also instinctively know where we are in relation to the map.

This is a wicked cool gift.

*Zev, I'm going to need AJ as soon as we get to the
water.*

This wolf mate telepathy could not be more
useful. I look over my shoulder as Zev increases his
pace and Darius slows enough to let him catch up
to us.

We are going so fast, weaving through alleys as Darius follows the map towards the river that runs through the center of the city. The river that should give us a back door to the Grand Hall, since getting to the courtyard portal would 1: take us longer since it's on the other side of the river and 2: for sure be surrounded by fae or wolves or the undead, or if we're super lucky, all three.

The river has the advantage of spanning the length of Budapest--a much larger target to try and defend. The vampires can't have every inch of the banks guarded, even if they know about it being a portal, which hopefully they don't.

Let's hope I'm right.

I choose a part of the river that's close but also most likely to be free of any witnesses--or vampires.

Darius never tires as he carries me and Rain through streets, then woods, until we reach the water's edge. He sets me down gently and snow crunches under my feet. A tree heavy with icicles and gleaming a brilliant white in the darkness gives a winter wonderland vibe to the moment. The ebb and flow of the tide creates a gentle soundtrack to our adventures, but I know the water is going to be freezing.

Which won't be a problem for Darius, but the rest of us might die from it.

Zev and AJ catch up, and I see the cloaking web around us cracking and fading and know we only have a few more minutes before we will be visible to the enemy again, though it seems Erzsébet has done a good job of sending them on a wild goose chase. I just hope she's okay. But first thing's first.

"AJ, I need you to use your water nymph powers to, I don't know, put us in a bubble once we dive into this river," I say, wasting no time as she climbs off my wolf mate's back.

"No prob, B, but that looks colder than a witch's titty. Why are we diving into a river anyways?"

"It will take us where we need to go," I say. "Where's Rune?" I'm not leaving without the fae. And Andor, I guess.

An illusion flickers before me and Rune and Andor appear. Andor continues to act under the spell Erzsébet cast, his eyes glazed over. He offers no resistance.

I sigh in relief at seeing the fae, though I need a moment to process him having Joe's face. "Everyone ready? We dive in on three." I hold Rain close to me and say a silent prayer to whatever gods or goddesses are in charge of keeping people from freezing to death. Then I count. "One. Two. Three."

I expect the cold, but I am not prepared for how *cold* the cold is. Zev wraps himself around Rain and me, letting his werewolf heat warm us both as AJ does her thing. She puts her arms around Zev and me, so we're all swimming downward in a big, clumsy hug. As far as speed is concerned, it doesn't feel like the ideal formation.

However, a moment later, the water is sloughed off of us, and though the temperature hasn't increased, we are dry and drifting down into the depths of the Danube, swimming but not. It's a strange kind of flying swimming as we are cushioned by air bubbles. Turns out AJ knows her shit.

I lead us deeper and deeper until I see the small cave that leads us out of the river.

Though we could talk if we wanted, we are all silent, and the muted sounds and heaviness of being underwater surround us.

We have to go into the dark entrance one by one, and I'm sure the others feel as claustrophobic as I do squeezing into the pitch-black tunnel. When I feel the break in the passage, where we could go to the Grand Hall or the dragon caves, I stay to the right.

Seconds after I move through the opening, I'm

swimming up toward the water's surface inside the Grand Hall garden. I climb onto dry land, amazed that I'm not hypothermic, or even wet.

I do a quick headcount once the others have joined me, starting with my baby, who's stirring a bit but otherwise seems okay. Her early childhood is either going to make her the coolest person ever or scar her for life. Probably both.

It dawns on me that we all have our normal faces back. AJ's a girl again, and the vampire, fae and werewolf are once again their sexy selves. I'm guessing the threshold of the Grand Hall undoes enchantments. If I had a magical underground stronghold built to protect an endangered species, I wouldn't want anyone sneaking in disguised.

Darius is at my side in a moment, our beings tethered together like magnets. Zev, who stayed in wolf form, shifts back to human, and AJs eyes bug at his sexy nakedness. I ignore her and instead look for Rune, who appears last with a bleary-eyed Andor in tow, looking like he's starting to regain his wits.

Good, because I have questions.

Darius, always in my head, instantly restrains Andor, and Rune, who doesn't need to be in my head to know what I'm thinking, uses his fae plant magic to will some vines to grow from the garden and tie Andor to a tree.

"Thanks, boys," I say, as I hand Rain to the fae and walk over to Andor.

His milky brown eyes widen in alarm as I approach. "Bernadette, it is not what you imagine."

I cock my head. "Really? What do you know about my imagination?" I ask.

"I have done nothing with bad intentions. I am only trying to help you."

"You're lying," I hiss, rage boiling in my veins like lava.

"I only wanted to help your father protect you. Together, we could be very powerful," he says, his expression pathetically hopeful.

I hold out my wand and let lightning dance on the end of it. "I'm already powerful," I tell him, my voice much colder than the white-hot anger in my gut. "Tell me what you and my father are planning. Is he still alive?"

Andor pinches his lips closed, as if that might help him avoid saying anything incriminating.

I look deep into his eyes and feel a new kind of power welling up in me. Once it reaches my throat I throw it at the man before me, wrapped in the force of my words. "Tell me!"

Something cracks in him, I see it in the flicker of his eyes as his soul is dimmed, and then, he begins to begrudgingly speak.

"Your father is the strongest of us all. He promised to make me your Chosen and that together we would create the Last Witch and rule." His face contorts and he bites his tongue to keep from saying more.

Darius steps up to me, a frown on his face. "You are compelling him," he says softly.

"But... that's not one of my powers."

"It is the vampire's powers," Erzsébet says, now standing at the edge of the stream, completely dry and the picture of elderly stealth. "And now, it appears, it is one of yours. No witch has ever survived a vampire mating ritual of this nature for so long with her sanity intact, so we really don't know what to expect from you."

"Am I... am I becoming a vampire?" I don't know how to feel about that. Not bad exactly, but at the same time I have a child to raise, and I'd like to be able to do that in the sun.

Erzsébet shakes her head. "No, you are becoming something more. What that is will be determined by time."

So many questions, but Andor struggling against

the vines reminds me we are in the middle of something more important than the subtleties of my magic as it relates to my mate bonds.

I do glance at Zev though, wondering what surprises my connection to him might have in store.

The wolf nods. *Our dance has only begun,* he says to my mind, and I shiver at the promise there.

Erzsébet walks over to Andor, stopping a few feet in front of him. "You have betrayed our order, you have betrayed my sisters. What is Timót planning with the book of dark spells?"

His eyes fill with tears, but I have no sympathy left. "I do not know. I swear it. He said we needed them to protect Bernadette and the baby. That even though I was not the father, I could still serve Bernadette and be her prince, if only I brought him the book."

Zev growls and I can tell he's ready to rip Andor's guts open. Darius is still, expressionless, and looks ten times scarier than if he was all ragey. And Rune is holding my child, but if he wasn't…

"What did my father want with a dragonling?" I ask, trying to use that compulsion trick again, but I don't feel the power in the same way anymore. "It was him who took it, yes?"

Andor looks away, unable to make eye contact with me. "He did not tell me about the dragonling."

Erzsébet laughs, but it is not one that reaches her eyes or sounds in any way joyful. "You are a tool, Andor, and Timót has been using you. You are useless."

She waves a wand over his head and speaks the word *alvás*. Andor instantly falls asleep.

"We must head to the Grand Hall where the base of our power is stronger, and gather the other witches to raise our defenses. I bought us some time, but it won't take them long to find us. Come."

We follow her, but I glance back at Andor limply hanging from the tree, the vines still wrapped around his torso and legs. "Are we just going to leave him there?" I ask.

"He would probably prefer that to what I will do if I see him again," Darius hisses, his face hardening in anger.

Zev grunts in agreement, and I don't argue further. I'm pretty pissed at him as well. And at the choices made that put him in this position. It might have started as a plan for protecting their kind, but this whole order needs a serious facelift to bring it into the modern era of women getting to make their own decisions about their bodies.

I reach Rune and take Rain from him as she begins to fuss. "She needs a feeding," I say. He nods but looks worried.

"This isn't a great time for that," he says.

I shrug. "Tell that to the crying baby."

I tuck her into my chest and let her suckle for the first time in a long time as we keep walking. I'm relieved that my supply is still strong enough to feed her, but mostly pleased at how skilled I've become at nursing on the go. Here's hoping I'm getting some awesome upper arm definition from it. That doesn't feel like too much to ask given how heavy she starts to feel after a while of doing this.

When we enter the Grand Hall, at first I think it's empty. It's dark and seemingly vacant, but my skin crawls at the sense of someone...or something present. I instinctively slip Rain back into her harness, freeing up both my hands, wand in one. "They're here!" I whisper, fear clutching my throat.

But my warning comes too late.

Dozens of vampires step out of the shadows, surrounding us. Then an equal number of fae step out, and finally the wolves slink toward the center of the room.

It's a real party.

Pandemonium breaks out as Erzsébet begins

341

fighting them with blasts of magic. I follow suit, using my wand to cast fireballs as I search for a path to freedom and safety.

Rain begins to cry and I try to cover her face as I continue fighting hostile creatures from all the realms. Zev is back in wolf form, attacking everything in sight. Rune is creating illusion after illusion to keep them away from me and Rain, creating a small break in the onslaught.

Holding my child tight to my chest, I run for it, flinging fire around me until I'm surrounded by a wall of flames I didn't even know I could make.

This buys me enough time to get out of the main room, and just as I turn a corner into a darkened tunnel I've never been in before, a hand grabs my arm.

I scream and pull away, raising my wand. But the person on the other end of the hand steps out of the shadows, mutters a spell and blows purple dust into my face.

I cough and choke, and when I try to speak my vocal cords don't work.

I've lost my voice.

I can't cast spells.

I try to scream but nothing comes out. I try to

pull away, clutching my child, fear crawling into me like a thousand spiders.

"Be still," the man says. "I have not come to harm you. I'm trying to help you."

I narrow my eyes and point to my throat, hoping I'm making very clear how I feel about his *help*, and his iron grip on my arm which is definitely going to leave a bruise.

"Your voice will come back in a few minutes. I didn't want to draw attention and this was the fastest way."

His words make a kind of sense, but I'm not in the mood to listen.

"Bernadette, I know you don't know me, but I promise I only want the best for you." He pauses as if considering what to say next, and I try once again to yank away from him, nearly dislocating my shoulder in the process. Damn he's strong. Too strong.

But as I look more closely at him, my chest tightens. The cheeks. The shape of the eyes. I gasp, though no sound comes out, and he nods, smiling.

"You see the resemblance, do you not?"

Without the power of speech, I simply nod.

I'm finally meeting my father.

CHAPTER NINETEEN

I'm powerless to scream, cry, or question.

I can't do any of the things I thought I might do if I ever met my father. All I can do is stare.

And feel afraid.

For the second time in as many months, I'm meeting a parent I long thought was dead, and everything about the encounter feels treacherous. There are vampires and wolves and fae all battling to find and sacrifice my child, almost definitely with the intention of killing me in the process, and yet I'm just as frightened staring back into the face of my dear old dad.

His hazel eyes look gentle. They don't have the same anxiety that Andor couldn't help but display. Despite the alarm bells clanging in my head, Timót looks calm and collected. He's clean shaven, his curly black hair peeking out from under his hood. He doesn't look as evil as I want him to.

"You fear me," he says, hitting the nail on the head. "And you should. You should fear everyone, dear daughter. That's what comes with being so important to so many."

Fighting continues in the room behind us, as all of the attackers and my sweet princes clash mere feet away. I want to reach into their minds, to ask them for help, but I can't distract them. Not when so few are up against so many.

One thought from me could get them killed.

Timót follows my gaze, watching as bodies fly through the room. "It didn't have to come to this," he says softly, then looks down at Rain. "I'm sorry your ancestors put you in this position, little one."

He looks fondly at the child, not with the love of a grandparent, but the admiration of someone who knows Rain's importance. It's a bit chilling since he should care about the baby regardless of this cursed prophecy. I'd tell him as much if I could speak.

"Wait here," he says as he moves back toward the main room. The last thing I want to do is follow his command, but I'm in a tough spot. The passageway behind me is pitch black and I've got no idea where the hell it might take me. Meanwhile, I'm not going to rush back into harm's way with my baby strapped to my chest. That feels like the quickest way to get everyone killed.

Timót pauses in the entryway to the main room, taking a small pouch from his pocket and emptying a fine powder into his hand. He gives one last look back at me, then throws the dust into the air in front of him. It forms a cloud as it settles between him and the hall, and then he strides right through it.

Walking boldly into a room full of vampires seems like a very stupid move, but the effect of the powder immediately explains his boldness. As the particles settle on his hair, skin and clothes, Timót becomes invisible.

It's a nifty trick, and I can't help but wonder if he brought enough to share. I remind myself that he's not on my side, that he's betrayed the witches, stolen from Erzsébet, put all of us in harm's way. Not to mention he tried to auction me off to his lackey. At the same time, the enemy of my enemy is my friend. He's got to be better than the vampires currently attacking all the people I love most in the world.

I'm worried sick about AJ, caught in the middle of this with no real magic to protect herself unless she's underwater. I'm nervous for Erzsébet, who's powerful as shit but also old as dirt, and probably getting really tired of fighting vampires all the time.

I'm worried for Rune.

For Zev.

For Darius.

The second I imagine my vampire lover, it's as though I inhabit his body. I don't see what he sees, but I feel his movements, I sense the danger around him. It's too much to bear, and I shake my head to regain my own thoughts. Now, noting my own sensations again, the constriction of my throat feels better.

"*Tüz útmutató,*" I whisper, proving that my voice is back and summoning a small ball of flame that rests at the end of my wand. I turn back to the dark corridor and send the fire out in front of me, illuminating the narrow space which seemingly goes on forever. I don't see any doorways or connecting halls, so my choices are stay put, walk into battle, or head for the darkness. Something tells me I'll be choosing darkness.

"B!"

I spin around, breaking my concentration and losing my fireball, but happy nonetheless as I see AJ standing at the end of the tunnel in front of me. She's got a gash above her cheek and burn marks on her arms and clothes, but she's alive.

She runs over and hugs me and Rain, and I squeeze her back while keeping my eyes over her shoulder, hoping no vampires are about to follow her into this room.

"Is everyone okay?" I ask, thrilled to pieces that I can speak again.

She nods, then shrugs. "Erzsébet's riding on Zev and shooting fire all over the freaking place. It actually looks pretty badass. I was with Rune and he's been casting illusions left and right so no one could see us, except for one wolf," she points to the gash on her cheek. "Rune saw you come in here and he told me to follow. " She pauses. "I'm not sure where Darius is."

My heart knots up at her words, and I reopen my mind without hesitation, hoping I can connect with him enough to at least know where he is. I feel him in battle, moving with unimaginable speed through cold air, and I breathe out my worst fears. He's alive.

And no longer in the Grand Hall.

He's too far away for my comfort, but I hope he's at least safe. Being apart is almost physically painful, which doesn't bode well for our future.

"My father's here," I say to AJ, my mind leaving Darius and coming back to join my body. AJ spins in a circle, looking every which way.

"Where? In this tunnel?" She pushes her sleeves up and starts to walk past me. "I'll bust his goddamn lip."

I grab her arm to keep her from going further into the darkness. "He pulled me into this room, then turned himself invisible and went out into the main hall."

"Uh-huh, sticking with the absentee father act," she says. "So what, are you waiting for him? Are we killing him? What's happening?"

I look back down the dark passage, feeling more and more like that's our only option. If AJ could stumble over and find me, it's only a matter of time before a vampire or werewolf does the same.

"I think we need to go this way," I say as I take AJ's hand. "We just have to trust everyone will be alright, but I want to get Rain as far away from the vampires and my father as I can."

I can tell AJ's nervous but on board. I conjure my little torch again and we start to slowly head down the hallway. It feels like the floor slopes down, taking us deeper into the heart of the earth. Even with my fire lighting the way, it still feels oppressively dark in this confined space.

We've moved a few hundred paces or so when I hear more than just our footsteps. The sound is soft at first but grows louder as it nears, and I wheel around, wand raised and ready to bring fire and pain to whoever's in pursuit.

I've got a harming spell on my lips as the figure nears, but right before I speak it the words catch in my throat. Thank God they do, otherwise I might have killed my sweet fae prince.

Rune looks frightened and winded, and I rush into his arms. The normal calm is missing from his touch, which is alarming as anything else, but understandable given what he's been through.

When I pull out of his embrace, I nearly scream. Timót stands next to Rune, having just shed his invisibility charm.

I step back and start to raise my wand, but Rune reaches down and stops me.

"No," he says in a hoarse whisper.

"Rune, you know he's not on--"

The fae cuts me off by raising a finger to his lips. "He's guiding us out. Please."

I've never heard desperation like this in Rune's voice. I look to my father, anger coursing through me for so many different reasons, but still feeling like I might need his help in order to survive. I glance at AJ, who looks just as lost as I feel, but the fact that she's not screaming at my dad to get bent must count for something.

I take one last look back up the corridor, wishing with all my might that I would see Zev and Erzsébet's charging down the hall, coming to our rescue. All I see is darkness.

I grip my wand tightly, ready to use it in the most violent ways, and then step aside to let Timót lead the way.

"You're sure about this?" I ask Rune as my father steps past. The fae gives a quick nod, then gently touches my arm. I'm worried he saw something out there that has him so disturbed, because his normal powers just don't seem to be there. What could have happened? I shudder at the thought and turn to follow Timót, taking AJ's hand in mine so I can keep her close.

The path widens as it goes deeper. We walk on and on, and it's starting to feel like we're miles below ground.

Finally, the hallway leads into a large, open space. It's a perfectly circular room with a soft orange hue. I let my guiding fire go out and can still see from the natural brightness in the space.

In the middle of the room is an enormous star, with hundreds of points extending from its sapphire center. The blue glows and pulses, flooding light into each of the points that seem to direct to small doorways along the rounded walls.

Erzsébet mentioned that the tunnels beneath the Grand Hall could take a person anywhere. Seeing this star, I know instantly that this is the room of portals.

I look at Rune, whose eyes are dancing between the doorways that might take us to any number of places. Timót is counting the points on the star, seemingly trying to pinpoint a certain direction. AJ has her eyes on me, probably hoping I've got some idea about what's going to happen next.

Sorry, girl. I'm wicked lost.

"Here," Timót says, walking to the center of the star, then turning and moving along one of the points until he reaches the wall. "This will get us to safety."

"And where is safety?" I ask. I followed blindly enough to this point, but I need more answers before I walk behind this traitor through another dark doorway.

"A different realm," he answers. "Where we can't be followed. And where I can tell you everything you need to know."

My eyes move to Rune. He's never led me astray in the past, and I'm trusting him to help me stay alive now. He meets my gaze, grits his teeth, and nods. It's clear he's not 100% comfortable with the choice, but I understand there are no perfect answers at this point.

I walk to the center of the room and then pace the point of the star, just as my father did. AJ follows me, with Rune bringing up the rear. The sapphire glows beneath all of our feet, but most brightly under mine. This room knows my powers. Hopefully it won't let my steps be misguided.

"Ajtó tól halál."

The spell Timót mutters sounds incredibly dark, both in the way he says it and the words he uses. I'm not familiar with the specific incantation, but I definitely recognize the Hungarian word for *death*.

"What realm are we--"

Timót grabs my hands.

I feel a strong shove in my back.

And before I can ask, we're all falling in a portal.

Darkness ripples around me, and I have the same sensation of dropping that I did when traveling into the tomb. This one lasts much longer and feels much more tumultuous. I clutch Rain close to my chest as she cries at the top of her lungs, finally rattled from her blissful sleep. Beyond Rain I can also hear AJ's screams, which tear at my heart, but at least let me know she's still alive. I keep one hand tightly clasped on Rain while the other holds my wand. If I'm going to survive--if anyone is going to survive--I must keep these two things safe.

And then stillness.

I'm on my knees, planted on the ground. My fingers reach down and touch smooth stone below me. I open my eyes and see a gray, rocky landscape. The sky above is an ominous shade of ash, like a volcano erupted not too long ago. The rocks around us are the color of charcoal, and I can't see a single living plant in any direction.

If I were to draw a picture of a safe place, this would not be it.

This whole place is the color of death.

Timót stands before me, a curious look on his face. He reaches a hand down to help me up, then shakes his head when he sees me raise my wand.

"As I said, you're right to fear me. And I know you don't trust me, and likely never will." So many of his words sound like they were pulled from the exact playbook my mother used the first night we met. It's the worst kind of eerie.

"But," he goes on, "I swear on all the stars that I'm trying to keep you alive. You and Rain. Fight me as you might, I'll still make you the princess of the new *Érintett*."

With a baby strapped to me and him having the high ground, I decide now is not the moment to start a duel with my father. I reach for his hand and let him pull me to my feet. I'm sure he's expecting questions, but I'm not ready to give him the satisfaction of speaking more, so I turn to find Rune.

And that's when my last shred of hope floats away.

Where there should have been my trustworthy fae, another now stands.

Andor.

I knew something felt wrong, and I should have listened to those feelings. The calming touch, the sound of his voice, none of it was right. I listened to my eyes when I should have trusted my instincts.

"I needed a familiar face to help move you along," Timót says. "And I wanted to bring your future prince along for the journey."

My stomach churns as I look at Andor--pathetic, meek, and hopeful. He's been lied to his whole life about how relationships work, and it's made him a pretty disgusting person.

"There's a useful spell that allows you to change the face of--

"Yeah, I know the spell," I say, loathing every word I have to speak to this so-called father. Whatever he says about wanting to protect me, and however much he believes it, I'm going with my instincts now. He's a piece of shit.

"Impressive," he says in response to my magic knowledge. "You're learning quickly. I'm excited for the day when you'll rule, use your powers for good, and finally understand the purity of my intentions."

"You know Bernie can destroy you, right?" AJ asks. I appreciate the support, but she's talking smack I'm not sure I can back up. If this guy can pull one over on the queen witch, he's got some tricks up his sleeves.

As if on cue, he pulls a slender wand from the arm of his robe and aims it at AJ. Since hearing that the witch line was limited to just females, I've wondered exactly what powers the *Érintett* possessed. For some reason, I figured wands were a bridge too far for the men; looking at the slender staff in Timót's hand, jet black and shimmering, it's clear I was wrong.

"I most certainly do know that. I, in turn, could also destroy her, so I'm hoping we can reach a truce until our plan unfolds."

"What plan?" I hiss. "Are you just hoping to siphon power off a baby witch like the rest of them?"

Timót looks at me but leaves his wand pointed at

my friend. Andor slowly inches toward me and the hairs on my neck perk right up. "We don't want the child sacrificed, Bernadette," my father answers. "That's a foolish interpretation of the prophecy, meant to mislead the other races. No, we want to keep the mother and child together."

That would sound like good news coming from a man who exuded less evil. The way he pairs me and Rain, I can't help but picture the two of us chained together while a bunch of powerless warlocks feed off our magic.

"But there are many steps in the plan before anything comes to pass," Timót says, now returning his focus to AJ. "And the first step is to remove unnecessary obstacles. *Lélel nak a szikla!*"

I turn, a scream ripping from my throat as AJ falls in a heap on the ground. Before I can think about what I just witnessed, I'm raising my arm, wand aimed at Timót, ready to unleash every bit of anger and power I have onto his worthless soul.

But my arm doesn't move.

My hand is frozen by my side.

My wand drops from my fingers, clattering on the stones below.

A few feet away, Andor stands with his own

wand, a band of light stretched between it and my right elbow.

"Excellent work, young prince," my father says. "Your secret practice has done you well."

Andor beams at the compliment, though he keeps an apprehensive look. He's wronged me and he knows I don't like it.

I look back to AJ, slumped on the ground like a puppet whose master has gone to bed. I squeeze my eyes shut, willing it not to be so but feeling the deepest despair engulf my heart.

"Why!!!" I scream, feeling power surge through me in a way I haven't felt since my wand first touched my palm. "Did you kill her?"

Timót looks at the body, then down at his wand. "I don't know, honestly. I've never tried that spell before. I don't believe she's dead, but we have to leave her all the same."

The fire raging in my soul burns even hotter, and whereas I used to fear these moments, I'm now inviting the powers to flood through me and strike this man down.

"I'll explain in due time, Bernadette," my father says, his wand now trained on me as though he expects some type of reaction. "There's a movement in the magic world, led by myself and others who have long been forgotten. What you see now as betrayal is the exact opposite. I'm leading men who want to expose the wrongs of the vampires, of the fae, of the wolves. And yes, of the witches. They're not so innocent as Erzsébet would have you believe."

Darius, I speak into my mind, trying the only thing I can think of.

No response.

Zev, my prince, I say, hoping the mate bond travels between realms.

Silence.

Tears rush from my eyes, falling onto the head of my poor child. I wanted to save her from danger and I've made things infinitely worse.

"Bernadette--"

Hearing my name on Andor's lips is the final straw. That he feels any power over me is something I'll die before I accept, and a combination of magical compulsion and angry free will turn my face toward him.

The last thing I see are the whites of his eyes as I scream scorching light. Flames flood out of me, knocking him to the ground and searing his flesh. I watch as he writhes for a few moments and then stops moving completely, his body already blackened, almost as grotesque as the corpse from the dragon cave.

I look back to Timót, who keeps a steely gaze on me, though he's lost a bit of his luster.

With a clear mind and the utmost control, I summon my wand into my hand, aiming it at my father. Killing my mother hurt my heart a little. Seeing my dad die won't be nearly as sad.

"Before you do anything rash," he says, his wand still targeting me, "you should know that we're not alone."

"That's fine," I spit back. "I'm happy to kill everyone else you brought here."

He cracks a pitying smile and shakes his head. "I know you feel that way, but these others… they're not so easy to kill. *Lobogás*!"

He points his wand straight up as he yells the incantation, sending a bolt of deep red light into the sky. Seconds after his action, before I can think to react, we're surrounded.

I blink.

Then blink again.

They approach in the sky, coming from all directions.

We're surrounded by dragons.

Dozens of them. They all have that iridescent

glow coming off their scales, but they present different shades of blue, orange, green and purple. Giant wings create flurries of wind with each flap as the creatures hover in a circle above us.

None of them is as big as the mother dragon we found dead, so I assume these are all younger dragons. *He's been stealing baby dragons from their mothers.*

Young as they may be, they are still huge, easily big enough and probably powerful enough to roast me and my baby like marshmallows.

My wand feels impotent in my hand, and I feel real terror well up in me.

Timót walks over to me slowly, wand still drawn to show he's not taking any chances.

"You'd be wise to calm down if you want to live." He holds my gaze for a long moment, trying to convey some sort of message, trying to make me see something.

"*Bizalom,*" he whispers. It's the Hungarian word for trust, and him saying it makes me want to scream.

He approaches me cautiously, but with too much confidence for my liking. "Together, we can rise to greatness. We can conquer all other nations and rule, taking for ourselves the eternal youth of the vampires, the strength of the werewolves and the magic of the fae. We will be undefeatable."

I frown. "Does what I want matter in any of these worlds domination plans?"

"I assumed you would want no part of this," he says smugly. "Which is why I've brokered a deal with someone near and dear to you. I get eternal life and the baby... and he gets you."

My heart skips a beat, as my gut twists on itself at the implication of his words.

I feel him before I see him.

I turn slowly, desperate to be wrong, certain I'm not.

I squeeze my eyes shut, pushing away the tears, before I open them and face the man who has betrayed me. Who has made a deal with the devil to save me... by paying far too high a cost. A cost I will never be able to forgive.

And the truth of that crushes my soul.

I open my eyes, schooling my face into neutral at the beautiful man before me. "Hello Darius."

THE END

WANT to know how this trilogy ends? Grab A Werewolf, A Vampire, and A Fae Go Home on Amazon. Also be sure to sign up for our newsletter. You'll also get **TWO FREE BOOKS** plus a weekly inspirational newsletter. Just let us know where to send your FREE books>> http://thenightfirm.com/karpov-kinrade-newsletter/

ABOUT KARPOV KINRADE

Karpov Kinrade is the pen name for the husband and wife writing duo of USA TODAY bestselling, award-winning authors Lux Karpov-Kinrade and Dmytry Karpov-Kinrade.

Together, they live in Ukiah, California and write fantasy and science fiction novels and screenplays, make music and direct movies.

Look for more from Karpov Kinrade in *The Night Firm, Vampire Girl, The Last Witch, Dungeon Queen, The Witch's Heart, Of Dreams and Dragons, Nightfall Academy* and *Paranormal Spy Academy.* If you're looking for their suspense and romance titles, you'll now find those under Alex Lux.

They live with their three teens who share a genius for all things creative, and seven cats who think they rule the world (spoiler, they do.)

Want their books and music before anyone else and also enjoy weekly interactive flash fiction? Join them on Patreon at Patreon.com/karpovkinrade

Find them online at KarpovKinrade.com

On Facebook /KarpovKinrade

On Twitter @KarpovKinrade

And subscribe to their newsletter at ReadKK.com for special deals and up-to-date notice of new launches.

~ ~ ~ ~ ~

If you enjoyed this book, consider supporting the author by leaving a review wherever you purchased this book. Thank you.

A reverse harem paranormal romance with humor and good liquor. (with Evan Gaustad)

The Last Witch

A Werewolf, A Vampire, and A Fae Walk Into A Bar (The Last Witch, 1)

A Werewolf, A Vampire, and A Fae Go To Budapest (The Last Witch, 2)

A Werewolf, A Vampire, and a Fae Go Home (The Last Witch, 3)

A reverse harem Greek Mythology adventure with a badass heroine and some serious kickass action. (with Liv Chatham)

Dungeon Queen

Warrior Queen

A standalone reverse harem paranormal romance with mystery, suspense and plenty of twists. (with Heather Hildenbrand)

The Witch's Heart

The Night Firm

A reverse harem fantasy romance with mystery, suspense and depth.

I Am the Wild

I Am the Storm

I Am the Night

A standalone dark paranormal romance with mystery

Wanted

In the Vampire Girl Universe

A fantasy romance with mystery and intrigue.

Vampire Girl

Vampire Girl 2: Midnight Star

Vampire Girl 3: Silver Flame

Vampire Girl 4: Moonlight Prince

Vampire Girl 5: First Hunter

Vampire Girl 6: Unseen Lord

Vampire Girl 7: Fallen Star

Vampire Girl: Copper Snare

Vampire Girl: Crimson Cocktail

Vampire Girl: Christmas Cognac

Of Dreams and Dragons

Standalone fantasy romance novellas

The Winter Witch (with Heather Hildenbrand)

The Spring Witch (with Heather Hildenbrand)

Forever Bound

Get the soundtrack for I AM THE WILD, OF DREAMS AND DRAGONS and MOONSTONE ACADEMY wherever music can be found.

Nightfall Academy

Court of Nightfall

Weeper of Blood

House of Ravens

Night of Nyx

Song of Kai

Daughter of Strife

Paranormal Spy Academy (complete academy sci fi thriller romance)

Forbidden Mind

Forbidden Fire

Forbidden Life

Our ALEX LUX BOOKS!

The Seduced Saga (paranormal romance with suspense)

Seduced by Innocence

Seduced by Pain

Seduced by Power

Seduced by Lies

Seduced by Darkness

The Call Me Cat Trilogy (romantic suspense)

Call Me Cat

Leave Me Love

Tell Me True

(Standalone romcon with crossover characters)

Hitched

Whipped

Kiss Me in Paris (A standalone romance)

Our Children's Fantasy collection under Kimberly Kinrade

ABOUT EVAN GAUSTAD

Evan grew up in Northern California before moving to Los Angeles in 2001. He worked as an actor and a writer in LA until 2015, and now splits his time between writing and running the drama department at the School of Performing Arts and Cultural Education in Ukiah, CA.

Follow him on Amazon.

ALSO BY EVAN GAUSTAD

A series about that time the world didn't end even though it was supposed to.

by Evan Gaustad and Clint Gage

It's Not the End of the World (Sisyphus Series, Book 1)

Countdown Phoenix (Sisyphus Series, Book 2)

A reverse harem paranormal romance with humor and good liquor. (with Karpov Kinrade)

The Last Witch

A Werewolf, A Vampire, and A Fae Walk Into A Bar (The Last Witch, 1)

A Werewolf, A Vampire, and A Fae Go To Budapest (The Last Witch, 2)

A Werewolf, A Vampire, and a Fae Go Home (The Last Witch, 3)

Made in United States
North Haven, CT
29 January 2023